ALL THEY WANT FOR CHRISTMAS IS . . .

Jane

1. A relationship that runs deeper than the foam on my cappuccino.
2. A shot at writing about Tom Hanks while he's still alive instead of slaving away over celeb obituaries at the *New York Herald*.
3. A chance to develop "compassion" in my articles and not be "overly critical of my subjects," as per my boss, Marty. As if! I am *so* not critical, Mr. Short-Sighted Idiot with the Sexy Blue Eyes. You just wait and see.
4. A wish that my sister, Ricki, and my best friend, Emma, would break away from those self-centered jerks they're dating and find the real deal. If the real deal exists, and I've got my doubts.
5. A second chance to live the life I misplaced somewhere . . .

Ricki

1. To make Nate happy.
2. To run my Christmas shop in Nag's Head, North Carolina, and listen to the surf over a cup of coffee with my best friend, Ben.
3. To figure out why Nate isn't happy, what I'm doing to make him unhappy, and then make him happy.
4. To spend Christmas in New York City with Jane and Emma, and Nate, if he isn't still mad at me for getting mad at him for spending so much time with his why-isn't-she-your-ex wife.
5. To figure out why—if I've got the guy and the job and maybe even the ring—I'm so unhappy . . .

Emma

1. The pregnancy test is pink . . . the pregnancy test is pink . . . Okay, I will not freak out. I am calm. Controlled. After all, Randy and I want to have a baby—just not my ex-boyfriend Jonathan's baby. What was I thinking, having ex-sex with that cheating cad? I'm calm, I'm calm. Of course, this is the end of my career at the bank. I'll be demoted. Run out of town. Abandoned by Randy. Living on the street in a box under a sagging wreath. Oh. My. God . . . I'm sorry, what was the question again?

Christmas. It's a time for going into debt, neuroses-gone-wild, dates from hell, seriously spiked eggnog, and maybe even a miracle or two. And for three women on the verge of what seems like certain holiday disaster, it just may be the season to toast the best times of their lives . . .

Books by Carly Alexander

GHOSTS OF BOYFRIENDS PAST

THE EGGNOG CHRONICLES

Published by Kensington Publishing Corporation

THE EGGNOG CHRONICLES

CARLY ALEXANDER

KENSINGTON BOOKS
http://www.kensingtonbooks.com

KENSINGTON BOOKS are published by

Kensington Publishing Corp.
850 Third Avenue
New York, NY 10022

ISBN 0-7582-0643-7

First Kensington Trade Paperback Printing: October 2004
10 9 8 7 6 5 4 3 2 1

Printed in the United States of America

THE EGGNOG CHRONICLES

Hooks, Premises, and Killer Endings

December, 2003

Jane

1

"People have died for millions of years and been put to rest without my shining obituaries," I told my boss over the phone. "I think you'll survive one day without me."

"Of course, of course, Jane," Marty responded in that hushed New York accent that reminded me of a younger, less hyper Woody Allen. "But first and foremost, I wanted to make sure you're okay. Ms. Jane Conner on a sick day! You, who never call in sick and rarely take vacation. Well, are you okay?"

"Fine." I pressed the hot teacup against my forehead, over my temple, against the throbbing cheek that wasn't plastered to the phone. My eyes burned like pearl onions and the network of pain inside my head was so tangled and intense, I just wanted escape. "I'd be perfect if I could have everything above the neck surgically removed."

"Oh, dear." Confusion and concern mixed in Marty's voice. "Well, that's not good at all, is it? We've got to get you into shape."

"I'm working on it." The teacup was scalding my cheek, but somehow that felt good. "I've got an appointment with an ear, nose and throat guy to zap this thing once and for all."

"Good. Very good." Sometimes Marty Baker spoke so softly I

imagined he'd trained for the priesthood. It's amazing that a man as kind as Marty had risen to a position of power in the editorial pit of snakes, but I counted myself lucky to have him as a boss. Besides his mild manner he was cute in a nebbishy sort of way. He'd be a possibility if I didn't have steady studly Carter. "Good to see a specialist," he went on. "Well, okay, then. You rest up. The only questionable item is the Yoshiko Abe interview."

I switched the phone to my left ear and pressed the hot mug to my aching cheek as I remembered the Japanese violin prodigy I was slated to meet this afternoon. "Oh, right. Can you reschedule?" I wanted to sit with an adolescent musician like I wanted a hole in the head. On second thought, the hole in the head might assist in sinus drainage.

"She and her mother are flying to San Francisco tomorrow for the Klein competition, then back to Japan, so it's just got to be done today. But not to worry. I can put someone else on it. Genevieve will do it."

Genevieve? My nemesis.

"Not her," I objected, trying to avoid the image of Genevieve Smythe resting her pert little size six Pradas on my desk and laughing at my notes. "Can you give it to someone else?"

"Oren is on loan to Arts until after Chanukah, and Lincoln is on vacation. It's got to be Genevieve."

"I'll do it." I hated myself for saying it, hated that I'd spend the afternoon cajoling another pent-up prodigy instead of pampering myself in bath gels, but it seemed to be the only way to make the image of the diabolical, power-mongering Genevieve disappear from my scope. "Make the interview for three at Oscar's and I'll do it."

"Are you sure?" Marty sounded concerned. "It's not fair to you, really. If you're not feeling well—"

"Just reschedule it, okay?" I said, losing patience with Marty's idealistic concerns about fairness in the workplace. Did he really believe in that myth?

"Okay, okay. Oscar's at three. And you feel better, okay? Let me know in the morning if you need more time to recover. We'll talk tomorrow, then."

Tomorrow. Closing my eyes, I imagined that by tomorrow I would feel better. Tomorrow I'd be able to breathe through my nose, wonder of wonders. In a few days I would wake up and not have to spend the first hour of my day hacking and snorting into a tissue. I would be freaking out from cigarette cravings and wanting to have sex with my boyfriend again. Order would be restored, damn it.

I hung up from Marty and went back to my number two priority after getting healthy—my novel. I tucked a strand of jet-black hair behind one ear and hitched my nightgown up so that I could sit in lotus position on the sofa with my laptop balanced on the triangle of legs. Since I had the day free—sort of—I had planned to crank on the novel, a work in progress that I had started writing in the middle, mostly owing to the fact that I understood the gravity of a killer first line and therefore had not yet been able to come up with one.

The first line.

Ignoring the pain in my face, I sucked the salt from the end of a pretzel stick and wondered what that elusive opening sentence might be.

Every book needs a great first line to hook the reader with subtle promises of texture and intrigue, engaging emotional involvement, poignant insights, pithy observations, and yeah, some of that romance crap, too.

"Sure, romance sells," my agent friend Raphaela had told me. "But follow your muses. Do something different. God knows, we'd all like to read something fresh."

"Fresh," I said now over a mouthful of pretzel. "Right." So I'd have to trash the story of my ill-fated marriage and the subsequent steady stream of loveless relationships. Not that I really cared. In the city that never sleeps, romance—especially bad romance—was so ten minutes ago.

I gnawed on the pretzel, savoring. Numm . . . burnt black on one side, fat crystals, crispy but not crumbly. With my sinuses clogged I could only half taste it, which made it less effective as a placebo: I still wanted a cigarette. Was it a mistake to quit smoking while I was trying to break into a new field of writing?

I had a good thirty pages under my belt, which my friend Emma Dee was reading for me. Thirty pages of smoking sex and cutting dialogue. As soon as I sold this book, which, of course, I had to write (a mere technicality!) I could quit my job at the *Herald* and stay home every day. I leaned back against the upholstery and focused on the pretzel taste, slightly diminished since my sinuses were blocked, but I wasn't going to let a sinus infection ruin my cushy morning at home. This was the life of a freelancer. Big sigh! Sleep in. Work in my nightie. Ignore the phone. I hadn't felt so free since my mother died nearly four years ago.

Which might sound like a terrible thing to say, but there you have it: having watched her suffer on a respirator during the last few months of her life, I'd been relieved. As the oldest child, and the only one in town at the time, responsibility for Alice's care had fallen on my shoulders during the short span from diagnosis to death—May to October. A smoker all her life, she wasn't surprised to hear lung cancer, though I think she'd hoped for a fighting chance of survival in the beginning. But two months after the diagnosis, she was told to get her affairs in order, and less than a month after that my mother, a former Poet Laureate at Columbia University, could barely rasp out a simple haiku. That summer had ticked off so quickly: the doctor's visits, the daily pilgrimages to the apartment I'd grown up in on the Upper West Side, the negotiations with health care workers and the addition of oxygen tanks and a fat hospital bed that faced the sliding glass windows. With my younger sister Ricki up in Providence starting summer semester of grad school, I'd been thrust into the caretaker role, the loyal, local daughter who could do nothing more than be present to observe the process with a sense of alienation and helplessness.

If death is truly the final journey of a lifetime, shouldn't we have some say in planning the itinerary? I could accept losing my mother, but to see her slip gradually into breathlessness was an image that caused me pain for years.

I shuddered, then noticed the blank monitor mocking me. Quickly I typed:

Just because I haven't nailed down a plot doesn't mean that I won't.

Yes, the words still flowed for me, along with post-nasal drip. I was blowing my nose as the phone rang again. I snatched it and barked out a hello.

"Jane, it's me. What are you doing home?" It was Ricki, her voice backlit by strains of "Hark the Herald Angels Sing" and the jingle bells that chimed whenever the door of her shop opened.

"You sound like a Hallmark commercial," I told her as I balled up the tissue and tossed it into the pile on the coffee table.

"My life *is* a Hallmark commercial," she said merrily. After grad school Ricki had followed her heart and (in my opinion) a beef jerky of a man to the Outer Banks of North Carolina, where she'd opened up a shop that featured warm and fuzzy Christmas paraphernalia.

When I had visited her last August I'd felt a mixture of amazement and horror at my sister's skill in creating a Christmasland that featured holiday crafts and decorations, a myriad of exquisitely decorated trees, and an overwhelming potpourri of scented items. I was impressed by the functional items such as napkins and chair covers and potholders—all decorated with miniature Santas or angels or holly sprigs. With the smell of spiced cider and the chime of the bells, the shop transported sweaty tourists from the beach to a wonderland of Christmas nostalgia. "This shop is like a scene from *It's a Wonderful Life,*" I'd accused my sister, and Ricki had swooned over the connection, adding: "I love that movie! I sell the DVD in 'Film Forest,' that section behind 'Santa's Workshop.'"

That was my sister, the Christmas junkie. I wasn't sure how her studies at Brown University had led her to this sentimental retail folly, but at least she seemed to enjoy what she was doing.

"I called the office and they told me you were sick," Ricki said. "What's up?"

"Another sinus infection. And this after I gave up smoking."

"Janey! You're smoke-free? Congrats! Was it going to be my Christmas present?"

"Don't get too excited. Right now I'd kill for a cigarette, though a butt just might kill me."

"Poor baby! Are you taking care of yourself?"

"I'm on it. This time, I'm not messing around with the GP. I'm going straight to a specialist. Got an appointment with an ENT in—" I checked the clock—"soon. I'd better get out of here."

"Are we still on for the 'Singles in the City Christmas' dinner? I was just about to book my flight to New York but I wanted to make sure you're not planning to fly off for an interview in Belize or Paris or Prague."

"I write celebrity obits now," I said with the dull tone of a woman announcing the death of her career. Granted, in the beginning I'd been intrigued by the formula—encapsulating a life in three hundred words or less, but lately I'd become bored with it. *Dead Reporter Walking.* "My days of exotic assignments are over, at least for the time being." Not that I'd ever landed an international assignment, but it was useless to remind Ricki that my promotion to the Death Squad was a far cry from a Pulitzer nomination. The day I was hired by the *Herald,* Ricki called various Manhattan liquor stores until she located one that would deliver a bottle of champagne. She was my one-woman cheering squad; the quixotic optimist to my goth fatalist.

"So we're on for Christmas?" she asked. "I'm planning to come early this year. We can ride the Ferris wheel at Toys R Us and wait in line at FAO Schwarz. Ice-skating at Rockefeller Center. Lunch at Tavern on the Green. Dessert at Serendipity. I love New York at Christmastime!"

I pictured myself chain-smoking out in the cold while Ricki sought Christmas inside the Fifth Avenue department stores. I would need an entire carton to keep up with my sister the tourist. "I was thinking more along the lines of a stiff vodka at Firebird," I said, "but the answer is yes, book your flights. We'll do the holiday thing here."

"Oh, goody. Goody gumdrops."

"Ricki, I think the Christmas music is affecting your brain function. And what about Nate? Tell me he's not going to sulk for months because you're spending Christmas with me."

"Nate's going up to Providence to be with his kids. He'll be fine," she said. "You go, see your ear, nose, and throat guy. Feel better."

"Later," I honked, my head thick with congestion and pain. And already it was time to close my laptop and get dressed and seek help from the sinus guru. Hard to believe it was December already, but I was relieved that Ricki was coming for Christmas. She would make me drink spiced cider, watch a few Christmas videos, and mist over about that little girl who thinks she's found Prancer. Nothing wrong with having a good Christmas cry with your little sister at Christmas. Hey, what are holidays for?

2

The plot of my novel—or the lack thereof—haunted me in the shower, on the subway, and on the street as a hansom cab eased through traffic in a chorus of horse clops and jingle bells. I was still sifting through the air for ideas as I stepped into the waiting room of Dr. Parson's office, a chrome and glass affair with a Park Avenue address that made me marvel at the fact that my insurance would cover a tony specialist with these digs. I was a writer in need of a story, a person in need of a way out of her own life. Not that I hated writing obits for the *Herald*. It was just that, pardon the pun, it was a dead-end job in a stifling cracker box environment, and writing a breakout novel seemed like the perfect route to the superhighway of financial and creative freedom.

A well-moisturized woman in the waiting room leaned over her crossword puzzle while an elderly gentleman tried to nap in the corner. Not too crowded. Hopefully, I'd be in and out faster than you can say "sinusitis."

I skirted around a fanciful tree, fake evergreen branches iced with silver snow and dotted with lavender ornaments and lights, and leaned my elbow beside a menorah to sign in at the cutout leading to the receptionist's brightly lit office. "Nice tree," I told the receptionist, adding, "though I'm surprised you don't give equal time to Kwanzaa. Maybe an ear of corn or a unity cup?"

A vacant smile froze on her face. "You are so right," she said in the blank tone of a person who didn't have a clue. "And you are?"

"Jane Conner."

She handed me a clipboard with forms and asked for my insurance card. I wondered if I could center my novel on doctors—exploit this behind-the-scenes medical drama. But as I filled in the perfunctory information, I overheard the nurses and clerks talking about where to order lunch, complaining that one deli always got the order wrong, while another was pricey.

Hardly inspiring.

I was stuck leafing through the magazines fanned out on the glass end tables. A nice selection, though with my headful of pain I wasn't up for tightening my abs, eating heart-smart or checking off lovemaking dos and don'ts. Sarah Jessica Parker smiled slyly at me from the cover of *Vogue*'s "Age Issue" (like that's a winning topic!) and Jennifer Aniston's dream marriage was yet again the featured phenomenon in another magazine. I flipped to the contents pages, scanning for celebrity names who might be missing from our files. Part of my job at the *Herald* was to make sure we had an obit prepared in advance, a profile that we could tinker with over the years, doing the final update upon death.

"I can't believe you do those things before the person dies," my friend Emma had said back when I first started filling in on the Death Squad. "Isn't that like reading the last chapter of a thriller before you buy it?"

"You'd be surprised at how much of the paper is written in advance," I told her. "Don't you remember last fall when that local paper ran an editorial about the Yankees losing the playoffs when the team actually won? The news staff tries to cover all possible outcomes, but in that case some bozo ran the wrong piece."

"Still, it seems weird," Emma had said. "A little morbid."

Emma works in banking, and I guess the mentality there is

that you do not count your deposits until the money comes in. Fair enough. I think I managed to diffuse her indignation by selling myself as a biographer: a writer who works hard to capture the essence of a person's soul and the sweet nut of his or her greatest accomplishment. There's truly an art to writing an obit; I'd realized my lack of craft when my mother died and the rest of the family had expected me to compose the customary death notice for the paper. I remember striking all the creaky adjectives in the form—"beloved" and "loving" and "dear" and "adoring." None of those words described my mother, and yet when they fell out of the announcement it read like a synopsis from TV guide. I struggled with that sucker right up till the print deadline. Then there was the formal obit, the one that was supposed to indicate something of her personality by mentioning book clubs and bridge clubs, her professorship at Columbia, her raspy smoker's voice at poetry readings. I would have failed miserably without the words from Mom's older brother, who said: "She was a tough broad who knew what she wanted and didn't hesitate to let you know, a real New Yorker." If I were asked to write my mother's obit all over again today, I'd still quote Uncle John.

I reached into the neat fan of magazines to pick up the smiling face of Tom Hanks and wondered what he was up to these days. He seemed like the ultimate Mr. Nice Guy: spending time with his kids, giving supportive quotes about wife, Rita, appearing at charity events, stepping out of the limelight to produce films so that someone else could win the Oscar for Best Actor. Never met him, and in the office Genevieve had started the file on him so I didn't really have the authority to chase him. But the article said he was filming a movie in New York and was planning to spend the holidays here.

Hmm.

If I were a supportive mush-ball, I'd pass this information on to my colleague. But I'm not, and Genevieve has a habit of stepping on the toes of my Manolo Blahniks as she minces toward the boss.

I would see if Mr. Hanks would do lunch. That had to be the greatest perk of the job: the response that rippled through agents and assistants and development people the moment I mentioned that I worked for the *New York Herald*. Some obituary writers used the phone and the Web and explained their mission in dulcet tones, but I liked to meet my subjects over lunch with a cocktail and a laugh. Last year one of my lunch dates, an anchor for a major network, had dubbed me the "Angel of Death" after a whimsical exchange at a high profile restaurant that made a few columns here in New York.

Was I flattered? Absolutely. Although I certainly didn't grow up wanting to write obits, the *Herald* is known for its editorial send-offs of the dead. Überfans of obits across the country read the *Herald* in search of clues as to how life cycles play out—similar to the reasons people read biographies. Obit buffs also appreciate the way our profiles reveal a defining line of the deceased: the fingerprint that made the person unique, the trait that identified their soul. So for me to be dubbed one of the best of the best—even if the field was a graveyard, so to speak—was truly an honor.

My boss, however, wasn't too pleased at my publicity flash. "I worry that we're getting off-track a bit," Marty had said in the hushed tones of a funeral director. "Yes, we cover celebrities, however, the *Herald* has never been a publication that seeks glamour. We need to pursue a well-rounded segment of the population: politicians, humanitarians, Pulitzer Prize winners. The Cuban immigrant who changed the face of child care in this country. The anthropologist who devoted his life to finding Bigfoot. The middle-class man who soldered an invention in his garage . . ."

Blah-blah, blah-blah, blah-blah.

Marty and I had covered this ground before.

"I'm one step ahead of you," I had assured Marty, telling him about how I was meeting with the winner of a bake-off in Minnesota as well as with one of the scientists leading the way in brain-stem cell research. And that bake-off winner wanted money for a twenty-minute phone interview.

"Jane Conner?" the woman in white jacket called. I tucked away my career stress and followed her into an office where lacquered chests holding various pointed metal devices of torture surrounded a padded chair with a headrest. I looked over at the toxic warning on the red wastebasket and let my heavy head roll back against the chair, reminding myself to ask the doctor why I kept getting these insipid infections.

"Ms. Conner?" Dr. Parson cordially shook my hand. His dark eyes and hair were a striking contrast to his lab coat, which seemed cut extra small to make him appear taller. "I don't believe we've met before. How did you hear about me?"

Translation: *Bring on the accolades.*

"I work at the *Herald,*" I said, peering through the black hair that feathered over my eyes, "and everyone there says you're the master of sinuses."

That brought an intense stare, but no smile. He strapped on a headband with a silver disk in the center, and I couldn't help but think of Bugs Bunny impersonating Elmer Fudd's physician. "And what seems to be the problem?" Did he say "pwob-wem" or was that my imagination?

"Chronic sinus infections. This is the third time since September, and I've had it."

He slapped on latex gloves, staring at me as if I were suspect. "What makes you think it's sinusitis?"

"Major headaches and ribbons of green snot." I grinned. "Charming, I know, but it's your specialty, right?"

"Are you in pain?"

"Only from the neck up. I figure if you can lop my head off, I'll be just fine."

He didn't laugh. Just probed my ears without asking. "Tip your head back."

I did, and he shoved his white light into my nostrils and stared angrily into my orifices. "Whoa." I pressed back into the chair. "Major boogie action, and we just met."

Talk about in your face. I felt relieved when Dr. Humorless moved away to make a note on my card. But then, without warning, he doubled back and blasted my left nostril with a spray— the ENT equivalent of bathroom cleanser.

"Will that help?" I asked.

"It will numb you a bit, while I take a look inside."

"Don't tell me," I said. "You actually shrink down like the Magic Schoolbus and take a ride inside."

"This will only take a minute, but you're probably tender."

Tender didn't begin to describe the sensation I felt as he reeled thin, plastic tubing with a white light on the end up into my nostril. I squirmed, sure that the little white probe was taking candid shots of my brain, recording all those choice labels I was forming for Dr. Parson. Humorless sadist. *Looney Tunes* Napoleon. And those were the clean versions. Then he redirected the probe and it dug down, down, down, clear to the toes of my Jimmy Choo boots.

"You have a sinus infection," he said, reeling the line out of my body, taking tears and mucus with it.

Wincing, I pressed one hand to my face and grabbed a tissue with the other. "Glad you concur with my diagnosis," I managed, trying to be a big girl about this and ignore the urge to slap his hands away. This required great restraint, as his hands were already on my neck, squeezing and kneading, choking. I have always believed that my neck was the way into my silk boxers. A well-placed kiss or a gentle fingertip could work wonders there— at least, it could before Dr. Parson tromped through.

"Did you know you have a lump on your thyroid?" he asked, as if I'd reshaped my thyroid just to piss him off.

"Did you know you have a hair growing out of your nose?" I countered.

That did it. He squinted at me, pressing the back of his hand to his nose.

"Kidding!" I said quickly. "I'm kidding."

He backed away, folded his arms and leaned back against the counter, a safer distance for us both. "That nodule on your neck needs to be investigated," he said coolly. "I can send you for sonography, but honestly, that's often inconclusive and usually leads to a needle biopsy, which I would recommend you start with. I'll do it for you today, if you like."

I reached out to the counter for a tissue, then pressed it to my nose. "What about my sinuses?"

"I'll write you a prescription for that. An antibiotic and a nose spray will take care of it."

"But you think my neck is swollen from the sinuses?" I was having trouble piecing all this together. "Did the infection spread to my throat? Maybe that's why I keep getting these things."

He shook his head. "The two are totally unrelated. You can take a few days to think about it, but don't let the thyroid go unchecked." He pinched my throat again. "That's the thyroid, right here. You can call me next week and let me know."

At that moment, the last thing I wanted was to spend half a day trying to track down a physician, especially when that doctor was the grim Dr. Parson. "Just do it now," I said, hoping this wasn't just a way to jack up the insurance bill to pay for this Park Avenue office.

As he prepared for the procedure, I felt a sting of apprehension. "Do you use general anaesthesia for this?" Why did my voice sound like I was auditioning for Alvin and the Chipmunks? "Or just a needle to numb it?" I thought of the novacaine shot I'd gotten from the dentist and wondered if I'd be able to swallow after a shot to the neck.

Dr. Parson pursed his lips into an even deeper frown, and I wanted to tell him that if he kept that up he'd need Botox before the day was out. "Actually, if I gave you something to numb the area, it would be more painful than the needle I'm going to use. It's called an F. N. A.—a fine needle aspiration. You'll see that it's very thin."

And very long, I thought, wincing at the lethal-looking syringe on the counter. If Keanu Reeves had a weapon like that in *The Matrix,* there would be no sequels. One wave of the syringe and the machines would fall to their knees.

But I could take it. Women were so much better at tolerating . . . well, everything, and I figured if I could survive chronic sinus pain, a little jab to the neck would be minimal.

In fact, the needle biopsy was okay—not nearly as unsettling as the image of Dr. Parson coming at me in protective goggles, gloves and reflective headband.

"I'll have the results in three to five days," he said, removing his gloves with a "thwack."

Honestly, I was just desperate to get those antibiotics into my swollen nasal cavities. Dr. Parson had prescribed an antibiotic I hadn't tried before; a drug "directed toward the sinuses," he promised. I hurried through the checkout and copay, shrugged on my elegant Ralph Lauren cashmere coat and dashed into the elevator. I needed my pharmaceutical fix! The cure!

3

"I shouldn't be here," I said an hour later as I scanned the menu at Duke's, my favorite neighborhood bar, café, and overall hangout spot. "Aren't sick people supposed to stay in bed and drink chicken soup?"

"You need to do whatever feeds the soul." Emma closed her menu and tore off a piece of Irish soda bread. "Gotta have lunch, right? It'll be short, though. I'm due back at telemarketing hell by one."

Once I'd returned to my apartment and gotten those wonder drugs into my system, I'd paused in the kitchen and stared into the fridge. Leftover Chinese, or Lean Cuisine? I needed cultural nutrition, which mere food couldn't provide. So I called Emma, who was glad to escape from work for a quick lunch.

I lowered my menu to watch Noah, the waiter, pass by with a tray of drinks for a table in the back room. "I'd kill for one of Duke's bloody marys right now."

"So have one. You don't need to go back to work."

"I've got an interview . . . which never stopped me before," I said. "But it's not a good idea with the antibiotics."

"Oh, right!" Emma nodded sagely, her maternal streak emerging. Emma Dombrowski was one of the most motherly people I know, and now that she and her boyfriend had broken up it looked like she might not get the baby she wanted. Wasn't that just the way life kicked you in the teeth? Teenagers in high school were having these babies they didn't want while Emma, who had bought a two-bedroom condo with a nursery in mind, was left empty-armed and unfulfilled.

"Right now you need to focus on feeling better," Emma went on as she pressed a dab of butter onto the bread. "I'm glad you finally saw a specialist. Did he mention a saline flush? Peggy at work had one. Said it was painful, but seemed to do the trick."

"He didn't seem too worried about my sinuses," I said. "He just wanted to stick a needle in my neck."

"What?" Emma's blue eyes opened wide over her mouthful of bread.

"He said it's probably nothing. Apparently I have a lumpy thyroid. I'm just looking forward to feeling better. I'm feeling fragile, but I've got this interview that can't wait. Then, I'd planned to do some of my own writing, but I'll see how I feel."

Emma nodded. "How's the book going?"

"It's going well," I lied, figuring that if I pretended the book was rolling along, maybe my karma would fall into line. "I just wish I had more time to work on it. I'm always stuck in the office until seven or later, then I don't have the energy to get creative all over again. So . . . if you've read those pages, what do you think?"

"I think . . ." Emma squinted, as if trying to remember. "I think it would help if I could read the beginning. I think it's really great, what you've done, that you've done so much, but—"

"Go on and say it," I interrupted. "You hate it."

"No, not really." She toyed with the lights on the garland. "The thing is, I just don't understand these people. I can't tell what makes them tick; whether or not I'm supposed to like them."

"You don't have to like them. The question is, do they interest you?"

"Well . . . I have some trouble with the guy who's cheating on his wife, and the woman is so obsessed with her weight. The way she drinks down the boullion then weighs herself, then takes those diuretics . . ." She shook her head. "I didn't buy it."

"Have you ever heard of bulimia?" I asked, feeling a little put out.

Emma pressed her hands together in a gesture of prayer. "Don't be mad, Jane. I know they're real problems, but I just didn't believe it in the story. I mean, the issues are so far from your life. Maybe they're not the best choice for you?"

"Write what you know," I said. It was the mantra of every workshop for beginning writers. "You hit that one."

"And I wasn't sure if it was going to develop into a romance or a mystery or . . . what."

I nodded. "You're right. You're absolutely right." I'd slugged my way through without an outline or a plan. "I need to approach this with better organization." At work it was easy to churn out pages of text, much of which was edited down to fit in the precise columns that wrapped around photos and squeezed between ads. But when it came to writing The Novel, the lack of clear guidelines and the pressure to be brilliant was overwhelming. Who would've thought that creative freedom could be so daunting?

"It's clear that you're talented," Emma said earnestly. "I really admire that."

"You don't have to shovel it, Emma. I was writing without an outline. Pretty stupid of me."

"But I can tell you worked hard on it. And you know what? We all work too hard. I think that's a problem for New Yorkers. You know, when I call the bank offices in Chicago, everyone lams out of there at five. People might be on the phone with you at four forty-five, but within minutes they wrap things up and head home. Meanwhile, we're an hour ahead, so already it's pushing six and I'm entrenched in work. What's wrong with us?"

"We're workaholics," I said, wishing I could apply the same diligence to my novel.

Emma rubbed the porcelain-white skin on the back of her hand. "Leave at five in Chicago and the boss calls it effective time management. Leave at five in New York and you're off the fast track. What's that about?"

As we griped about work Duke came over and took our orders—two salads, which he promised to get out quickly so Emma could get back to work. "Jane, you are the last person I'd ever expect to have a dry lunch," Duke said wryly.

"Antibiotics," Emma explained, nodding at me.

"That explains it," Duke said as he went off for our diet Cokes.

"I'll drink to that," I called after him, raising my water glass. First, let me say that I have never slept with Duke, mostly because he never made those moves and subsequently he has become something like a brother to me. There was some speculation a while back that he might be gay, since he was still single and had never dated anyone I knew, but Emma talked me out of that one . . . or at least, she talked me into respecting Duke's privacy and forgetting about the question altogether.

He brought our drinks, gracefully balanced on a round tray. "Lemon on the side, ladies. Let me know if you want a whiskey chaser for that." Duke has an innate sense of cool, which is probably why he can get away with hair down over his shoulders at his age—early thirties, I think—though he's never told me.

"Thanks, Duke," I said as he disappeared into the back room.

Emma pushed the bread basket away. "God, I have to stop eating compulsively, but I'm so stressed. I hate my job now. Really, really hate it. I hate telemarketing." Part of Emma's executive training program at the bank was a rotation into nearly every department and property owned by the corporation. Telemarketing was just one of the many adventures in banking Emma would suffer to earn an executive title and an office with a window.

"Don't we all? I think most of the nation would join you there, the president included."

"But I don't hate the people who do it," Emma said. "I mean, to them it's a job, and for some of them it provides food and shelter and medical coverage for their kids."

I slugged back some ice water. "Your point being?"

Emma lifted her auburn red hair—hair Clairol would kill for—from her collar, then dropped it onto the back of her navy suit jacket. "I don't wish these people ill. I just don't want to go back to that damned office after lunch. The sleaze factor is so high."

"Poor Emma Dee." Emma's girlfriends had started calling her that in middle school, when we decided that her last name, "Dombrowski," needed fixing. These days, it was one of the first things Emma checked out when she met a guy—his last name. For Emma, a new last name would be one of the bonuses of marriage. "So I guess telemarketing is not the place to find that Christmas lover?"

Emma shuddered. "Not unless you want him to call you out of the shower to sell you credit card protection you already have." She shook her head. "I wish this rotation would end."

"When do you finish with the telemackerels?" I asked.

"Not soon enough. I'm there until March first."

"Oh, poor Emma. It's going to be a blue Christmas for you."

"It won't!" Her eyes flashed with defiance. "This is going to be a wonderful Christmas—the Christmas of my liberation. Jonathan managed to ruin the last few holidays for me and I'm determined to make this the best Christmas ever."

"Jonathan? Brrr." I shuddered. "Did someone open a window, or did his ghost just pass through me?"

"You know, I thought I'd miss him, but I don't. Not at all. It's kind of scary."

"He was more work than he was worth, and you should be glad he's gone."

"I am." Emma fingered the fake garland lit with tiny lights that was draped along the room divider beside our table. "But it's hard at Christmas, you know? Hard not to have someone."

"You mean a man to validate you?" I made a mock gasp. "Emma Dee, I gasp on your behalf."

"Don't go all Femi-Nazi on me. I'm talking about a man to exchange gifts with. Someone to share the brandy and snuggle beside the Christmas tree." Her fingers framed the tiny white bulbs so delicately, I had to stop in my tracks and really listen to what she was saying. It was the ultimate American dream, really—

spending a happy holiday with someone you love. It was fodder
for Christmas carols and cards, coffee commercials in which
Johnny makes it home from war in time for Christmas morning
or the man gives his mate a diamond necklace under the
Christmas tree, print ads with his-and-hers cell phones spilling
out of Santa's voluminous bag.

"Oh, what am I saying? You've got Carter."

I nearly choked on a lettuce leaf. "Carter is *not* a boyfriend."

"Then what would you call him?"

"A boy, but not a friend. Carter is a way to relieve stress. You
have a high math aptitude, right? Here are the equations: Great
sex = great time. Commitment = annoyance overload."

"And you don't love him," Emma said thoughtfully. "I had
that with Jonathan, and I'm so glad he's out of my mainframe.
But we deserve more, Jane. That's my Christmas wish for us.
Someone to love. A man for all time."

"Humbug. We may want a man like that, but December
twenty-sixth always rolls around with a few extra pounds, a handful of department store returns, and a truckload of regrets. For
me, those regrets usually involve some loser who thinks I understand him because I'm the first girl who's dropped her bloomers
since his wife divorced him."

"Aha! So you *have* been disappointed," Emma said.

"Not anymore," I said with a coolness I didn't feel. "That's my
new policy. Keep your expectations low and you'll never be disappointed."

"Ah, but low expectations breed lackluster results."

I tilted my head. "Where the hell did you learn that?"

"I don't know," she said, her eyes filling with panic. "Maybe
telemarketing school! Oh, God, I have to get out of that place.
The sales patter is seeping into my brain."

"But you love your job—at least most of it—and you're so well
suited for banking." Unlike me, Emma has always enjoyed working with numbers. She clings to the solid sense in calculations;
the surety and reliability that one plus one will always equal two
(unless you are me, balancing my checkbook, and then every-

thing seems to equal a zero balance). "Stick it out until the next rotation, kiddo. They wouldn't have put you in the training program if they didn't realize how smart you are."

"Do you think?" Emma asked as Duke delivered our salads smoothly and disappeared again. "I'm such a wreck. Sorry! It's still killing me, Jonathan and the weather girl. Talk about public humiliation. I became the ditched one—the dumpee—and all you have to do is tune into Weather Watcher on channel six to see why."

"Oh, Emma, don't go there. It's not about him." We'd been over her ex's exploits way too many times. "It's seasonal blues." I stabbed a grape tomato. "What's that line? I think it's Shakespeare. 'Now is the winter of our discontent.'"

Emma turned away, her bottom lip quivering in an unexpected show of emotion. "Yeah, but I usually don't feel that way until after Christmas."

"You know, I've read that the post-Christmas blues are really a product of lack of sunshine. Our spirits are up for the holiday, and then suddenly it's over and we're cornered in darkness, stuck in the darkest phase of the year. In Australia, people don't suffer post-Christmas depressions. Instead, they're bummed out in July. Weird, huh?"

Emma swallowed and wiped one tear away with a pinky finger. "Let's move to Australia. I hear they have like, eight men for every woman in the outback."

"Oh, Emma," I sighed, batting at fake berries on the garland with one hand. I was torn between trying to make my friend feel better and defending the right of my feminist sisters to find happiness without a man as arm candy—even if that candy was just a Christmas accessory. "You'll find someone. Maybe not for this Christmas or the next, but if you're setting your sights on companionship, I'm sure you'll accomplish your goal. You're a wicked taskmaster when you focus on something."

That tweaked a smile from her. "I *am* relentless when I establish a goal. It's one area of my job review where I always excel."

"I, however, waiver and wobble. I'm dying for a smoke."

"Good. That means you must be feeling better."

I tried to inhale through my nose and shrugged. "Not just yet. But it's good to know those antibiotics are doing their little sock 'em, rock 'em thing." I knew that antibiotics take a good twenty-four hours to take effect, but having launched my campaign to cheer Emma up, I was on a roll. "Oh, I forgot to tell you, Ricki called. She's booking her flights."

Swallowing, Emma nodded. "Excellent. It's so nice of you guys to let me in on your dinner."

"Don't thank me. You're doing most of the cooking."

"I make a mean crown roast."

"I *am* impressed. I'll supply the wine."

"And eggnog. Don't forget the eggnog with a touch of brandy."

Honestly, I have never understood how that oddball drink became lumped in with Christmas foods, but then, there's also bread pudding and fruit cake. Sometimes, I just go with the flow and add nutmeg. You can't let Christmas traditions overrun your life—especially when those traditions include hooking a man on your candy cane.

4

That afternoon, as I sat across the table from yet another shiny-faced prodigy, I longed for a pretzel stick or a lollipop or a flaming sword to take away the yearning for a cigarette, the yearning for a reason to escape this meeting and hang outside the door of Oscar's while collecting my thoughts.

Instead, I sat in a booth facing my lovely Japanese subject, Yoshiko Abe, and her mother, both of whom had bowed when I introduced myself. Sitting across from them might have been a mistake, as it was the position of confrontation. In deference, Yoshiko and Mrs. Abe kept their eyes averted from mine. I'd done interviews like this countless times, and I wasn't looking forward to an hour of trying to extract personal information from a woman and child who for cultural reasons could not allow me to make a connection.

"Would you like to order?" I offered.

Yoshiko lifted the menu politely, her long fingers elegant against the laminated card. "Oh, I don't know." She turned to her mother and said something in Japanese. The mom answered back in Japanese, pointing to various items on the menu.

Trying to appear attentive, I waited for the answer.

Most foreign musicians pose a challenge, especially the young ones. There is the language barrier, of course, though most of my musicians speak English and I am fluent in French. These brilliant children also tend to focus exclusively on their craft with a level of discipline unmatched in the United States. Consequently, prodigies like Yoshiko often have no lives beyond their musical aspirations.

"My mother," Yoshiko said, "she would like to try the prime rib very much, but she worries that she had a very large lunch."

Was that a yes or a no? I wiggled my toes in my boots, wishing her mother would make up her mind. "The prime rib is delicious," I said. "And how about you? Something to eat?"

"Oh, I don't know." Shyly, Yoshiko lowered her head to the menu once again.

I felt annoyed by their passive aggression and in no mood for a dance of semantics. Then I recalled that the Japanese language does not include a polite word for "no."

"How about if I order some appetizers that we can share?" I suggested. "The sampler platter?"

Yoshiko translated and Mom nodded. "Yes," the girl said, "that would be very nice."

With that taken care of, I told Yoshiko that I had been researching her accomplishments. I knew that she had begun studying violin at the age of two, had performed her first concerto when she was just five, and had been touring since she'd turned eight. Last year, at the age of fifteen, she was the youngest violinist to win the Irving M. Klein String Competition. I asked how that accomplishment had changed her life, and Yoshiko shrugged.

"Not much different," she said. "Same old, same old."

"What do you do when you're not playing the violin?" I asked. "Do you have any hobbies? Ways to relieve stress?"

"I travel on tour," she said, skittering over my question. "From the concert to the hotel. I plug in my laptop, then must do homework and e-mail it to my teachers."

Nose to the grindstone, I thought with a smile. "And how about fun? What do you do for fun?"

"I have my violin," she said, her eyes bright. "A del Gesus. It's fantastic."

If I was going to dig through to her favorite TV show or a secret passion for pistachios, I was going to need a new angle. "What's your favorite snack?"

She squinted. "Potato chips?"

"Your favorite outfit?"

"Sweats?" Again, a question, as if she were unsure of her answer.

"You like comfortable clothes?" I asked. "Sweat pants and loose jackets?"

She frowned. "Oh, those are fine, but I like the big woolens. You know? Sweats, with reindeer knitted in?" Her fingers flew through the air like prancing reindeer.

"Sweaters." I tried to smile encouragingly, but my face was still stiff with sinus pain. "Do you have a favorite movie or TV show?"

She frowned, touching her little pin. "I like TV but I don't have time to watch. But I do love Brad Pitt. Do you know him?"

"I know who he is," I said. Our appetizers arrived. As Yoshiko and her mother sampled the spicy wings and fried mozzarella sticks, I decided to stop the interview for now. It was tepid at best, which, considering my physical health and Yoshiko's lack of life experience, was not a surprise. Oh, I could write up some history, throw in some facts, even describe the way she had brought tears to my eyes in her performance of a Stravinsky concerto. But there was more to life than single achievements, and it was the *Herald's* mandate to provide a thorough picture of the celebrities we profiled; to cover the subject's grand achievement, and yet to paint a fuller portrait with his or her passions and fears, idiosyncracies, and personal sense of style.

A crush on Brad Pitt was just not a lasting facet of Yoshiko's personality, but when I thought of her world, I realized how much of it was spent in concert halls and hotel rooms and airports. In a way, it was not a life at all, but a relentless stream of rehearsals and performances.

As Yoshiko and her mother nibbled on appetizers, I chomped on celery sticks and tried to gather a clue from her clothes.

Yoshiko wore a snappy little black blazer—looked like a Liz Clai-
borne to me—over a chiffon-print shirt with velvet trim at the
waist. Her jeans looked well worn, as did her chunky Steve Madden
boots. Nothing remarkable about this teenager, though I did admire the little pin on the lapel of her jacket. It reminded me of a
model of an atom.

"That's a very nice pin," I said.

Yoshiko smiled, touching the pin. "Thank you very much. I
made it."

"You did?" It wasn't a real hook, but it was a nice detail that
might prove to be an inroad to her personality. "You make your
own jewelry?" I leaned forward to admire the pin, a spiral of silver wires looping around three polished stones, two green and
one purple. "How interesting. Do you use wire cutters?"

Her eyes lit up, and she put a hand over her mouth in a coy
gesture that was almost comical. "I use blow torch," she admitted.

Beside her, mother rolled her eyes and shot a disapproving
comment in Japanese.

I shot Yoshiko a smile. "Do you have any other jewelry cre-
ations?"

She nodded. "I have many now. It started when my uncle
brought in the torch to work on a pipe, and I played with bending a piece of metal. After that, it sort of happened. I keep the
torch in my room at home. My mother is worried that I will harm
my fingers, but I am careful."

Mother shook her head, but I enjoyed the light of defiance in
Yoshiko's eyes.

At last, I had the beginning of a story.

After the interview I strolled up Lexington amid the blur of
rushed commuters and shoppers and Christmas lights, trying to
weave in my mind a fine mesh of Yoshiko's distinctive qualities.
The strong tendrils of her mother's hold were a consideration.
Was her mother the force behind Yoshiko's disciplined genius,
or the tyrant who held the girl captive in hotel rooms around the
world?

That was the thing about mother-daughter relationships—too difficult to read in one sitting, too complex to summarize in a tidy three-hundred word bio. The very woman we relied upon for our survival could also reach into our souls and squeeze so hard we spent the rest of our lives reeling in pain. Not that my mother had consciously tried to wrap herself around me. On the contrary, she'd backed away, claiming to be lacking in the maternal gene, and though my father enjoyed nurturing his job as an archaeologist kept him away from New York for extended periods of times. Hence, I'd experienced a different kind of pain, the sort of the swollen soul, a conscience throbbing with neglect and lack of use, the eight-year-old who brought Oreos in for the class party because my mother didn't bake, the ten-year-old who lied about her birthday to get a free sundae from Applebees, the teenaged girl who slept around because she was the only girl in the class whose parents thought sex was no biggie.

It wasn't until those difficult months around my mother's death—when I'd penetrated the wall of denial to glimpse the inevitable panicked end—that I realized she did care about me. Of course, my mother loved me. However she had spent a lifetime exercising restraint, trying not to appear vulnerable, not to meddle, not to direct my choices. And all along, secretly, I would have loved a little meddling. When you're passably pretty and sure you know it all and growing up on the Upper West Side of Manhattan, your survival relies on meddling from your mother.

But Alice Conner defied convention. When Dad died she quickly sold his beloved country place upstate—the mud hut, she called it—and she renovated the two-bedroom co-op Ricki and I had grown up in. I was just out of college, toiling in a sterile contracts job for an insurance consultant because I needed rent money, and I made the trip uptown to Mom's place thinking I might reclaim my old bedroom for awhile now that she was alone. Turned out I was "Way wrong" on that assumption. The room Ricki and I once shared had been turned into a den, our twin beds replaced by a sofa and entertainment center. And that wasn't all. The chipped, patterned tile of the master bathroom had been replaced by clean white marble with pristine trim for the new Jacuzzi tub and double vanity. The worn carpets had been torn up, the wood floors buffed to a sheen, the walls painted in deep hues so unlike my mother. I remember walking through the newly decorated living room in shock, wondering at the transformation of the white walls into the gem-tones of a Victorian manor house in India with walls and drapes and rugs in ruby red, indigo blue, royal purple. Velvet curtains were swathed over the arches. Votive candles flickered in glimmering clusters of color, and two stained glass pieces hung on the sliding glass doors to the balcony. "Early bordello," my uncle pronounced with a wiggle of his eyebrows, causing Alice to slap his shoulder and show him the books she'd used for research.

"I love the gem-tones," my mother said, running her fingers over the purple and red mosaic tiles of a heavy vase. "These colors make me happy."

But I couldn't believe the outlandish cave of color. "Where did this come from?" I'd asked, thinking of my failed pitch to paint my room blue when I was thirteen. My parents had vetoed paint the color of a robin's egg, and now I was walking through the facets of a medieval jewel. "All those years of white walls—"

"That was your father,"Alice had said as she lifted a votive candle to light her cigarette. "His reaction to his mother's tendency to cover everything with souvenir plaques and cozies and doilies. White is very pure, but eventually it fades to gray."

"Oh, don't we all," Uncle John remarked with a shrug, and I had laughed along, pretending to be jaded and grown-up and independent, pretending that I didn't care that my mother had painted me out of my old room, out of my old life. Twenty-one, and I had just lost my father, and yet my mother was pushing me through a rite of passage I didn't feel ready for, but the renovations had taken place and there was no turning back. "We can't live in the past," Ricki told me when I called her at Brown to complain. "Dad is gone and Mom is moving on."

Gripping the phone, I had swallowed back tears, reluctant to let Ricki mother me. That was my role, my job. I had stepped in to do the mothering when I'd realized Alice wasn't cut out for the task. I was the one who'd told my sister the nitty-gritty of sex,

the truth about boys, the warnings about over-plucking eyebrows, blue eyeshadow and the girls who wore their popularity
like a crown.

Mothers and daughters, sisters, missing parents . . . relationships were a morass of struggle and complexity. Thinking back
to Yoshiko's situation, I wasn't quite sure how to separate my subject from her mother's projections and dreams.

Sometimes you need to wade through the crap and you can't
find a decent pair of boots.

5

A therapist once told me I would not get along with men until I resolved the feelings of abandonment and anger that I felt toward my father. I responded that I didn't feel abandoned, that my father couldn't help it if he had a heart attack, and that I didn't really care that Dad was off at digs for long periods during my childhood. Isn't it okay to love someone and live without them in your life every day?

My boyfriend Carter didn't get the concept of healthy separation either. Over the past few days he'd been on the cell twice a day, wanting to come over, wanting to squeeze in a quicky, wanting, wanting, wanting. "What part about 'Not feeling well' do you not get?" I'd snapped at him. "Would you look at some hot porn and call me next week?"

And *I* had abandonment issues?

Well, maybe just a few. For starters, there was Philip. I vowed never to forgive my ex-husband for screwing around on me. I mean, cheating is one thing, but when you marry a person it's supposed to mean something. Ricki thinks I fell into the relationship with Philip to make up for losing dad. She tells me I was infatuated with Philip, in love with the notion of love and security, two tenants that were threatened when our father died. Sometimes my little sister is too wise for her own good. Of course, I always argue with her, and she gets upset and tells me to be honest. But Ricki doesn't understand that it's not that simple. Some of us are unable to look in our souls and see our motivations, the roots of our pain, the reasons for our personal failures. Sometimes those answers are buried so deep inside us, we begin to doubt their existence.

But pain tests our strength and endurance, and thanks to Philip and Dad and any other guy who'd done me dirt, I was feeling pretty ballsy the next day as my heels clicked over the tile floor of the lobby. Despite equal opportunities and women's rights, the offices of the *Herald* are still a bastion of testosterone-laden, Type-A reporters. Perhaps my lack of testosterone was what put me in the obit section of the paper, but I figured I had enough Type-A to drag myself out of the grave beat eventually. In the elevator I flung back my fake-fur lined coat and glanced down at my black Manolo Blahniks. Power shoes. Few people have the nerve to argue with a girl wearing stiletto Manolos.

As my heels power-clicked along the floor outside the elevator, I sensed through my headachy lethargy that something was up. Instead of the usual conversation clusters around the TV monitors or the coffee machine, editors huddled in their cubicles, glancing nervously over their shoulders. The doors at the end of the hall were closed. That meant private talks in the offices of the publisher and editor in chief, and in a newsroom, almost nothing is private.

I swaggered down the hall in a perverse swell of excitement. I enjoyed the controversy of closed doors. It usually meant someone was in trouble or someone was leaving. Either way, it signaled that a position was opening up, leading to a mad scramble as every editor tried to use the opening to leap to a higher spot in the food chain. Closed doors had served me well in the past. Years ago as an intern, it meant a move to assistant editor and a few promotions to work on the Sunday Magazine, then Wine and Dining. Then, when Robert Feinberg moved from obits to health editor (a backwards leap, I know, but where *does* one go from the Death Squad?) I'd wedged one Manolo into Marty's door and gotten a toehold on Robert's former spot. Yup, closed doors were usually a good omen for me.

Spotting Ed Horn over by the fishtank, I stopped in my tracks, my long coat lapping at my ankles. With his bow tie and polite demeanor, Ed Horn was a city desk writer who was rumored to have joined the *Herald* when the newsroom was a sea of clacking typewriters. With tenure like that you don't worry about getting fired, and I trusted Ed since the day he saved my skin and stopped me from plotting the demise of my arch rival, Genevieve. "Don't waste your time and energy," he'd told me. "A bad reporter will sink himself. You don't have to puncture the raft." Probably good advice at the time, though the evil Genevieve was still afloat and drifting into my side of the pond.

"Good morning, Piggy," he said as he tapped fish flakes into the tank.

In response, Piggy wriggled up to the water's surface, her golden-skirted fins whispering around her.

"Good morning, Jane," he said just as brightly, though he didn't turn away from the tank.

"Good morning and good grief," I said, lowering my voice. "What's up?"

"It appears that Ms. Grodin is fed up with the feeding frenzy of being a food editor."

I cracked a grin. "She what? You mean she's quitting?"

"Moving out to Arizona, planning to do PR work for a spa out there. She says the air out there is so much cleaner. Makes the pounds melt away."

Amy Grodin was going to need a major dose of air to melt down her weight gain, but I bit my tongue before that sentiment slipped out. Ed didn't deal well with catty, and I wasn't good at handing it out in a tactful way. "So they're looking for someone to review restaurants and critique the occasional recipe," I said, visions of expense account dinners dancing in my head. I could just see that Gold American Express card sliding across the fine linens at The Gotham. Ordering up a storm at Le Cirque. Steaks at Smith & Wollensky's. Star-gazing at Joe Allen's. Sampling the exquisite marriage of Japanese and Peruvian cuisine at Nobu's. "You know, I used to work in Wine and Dining. I think I want that job."

"And give up the Death Beat?" Perplexed, Ed adjusted a cord on the fish tank's filter.

It's true, when I'd landed my current spot there'd been a frenzy of excitement, partly due to the readership of *Herald* obits, partly due to the personal challenge. But now that I could sum up a person's life in three hundred words or less, ennui was setting in. I sighed. "Face it, Ed, most obit writers are journalism wannabes or dusty curmudgeons on their way to retirement."

"I beg to differ. Obit writing is a gift—a calling for natural story-tellers. Like you, Jane. And at the *Herald?* You come from a position of power: a newspaper with world-famous obits."

"I'd rather be sampling the achievements of world-famous chefs. What's the dirt on Amy's gig?"

"It's a tricky position," Ed went on. "The food critic needs to guard his or her identity carefully. It requires vast knowledge of international cuisine and food preparation. Then there's the matter of sampling nearly everything on the menu." He patted down his pockets. "I'm fishing for my Tums just thinking about it."

"Who's in line?" I asked him.

He tapped on the glass of the tank. "It's a tad early to specu-late, but Genevieve is speaking to Martin at the moment."

Genevieve! No, not her! No one was less deserving. The guy with the sandwich cart had a better handle on food than Genevieve Smythe. I had to move fast if I wanted to save face. Not that food editor was the perfect job for me, but at this point I needed to block the enemy. Defensive maneuvers. I needed a plan in place when Marty's office door swung open.

"Thanks, Ed," I said, hitching my coat up around my waist. Then I sped down the aisle, zigzagging around the cluttered cu-bicles of the fashion editors to my modest little home, a cubicle with a few small reproductions of impressionist paintings tacked to the board alongside the grids of schedules that I tried to ig-

nore. I slung my coat over the fake wall and saw the glaring red
of an editor's pencil mark shrieking from a piece of copy on my
desk. *What the hell?* A rewrite? I almost never got a rewrite.
Flopping into my chair, I picked up the piece—an old profile
from the vault.

The profile of Antoinette Lucas, network reporter and breast-
cancer-research advocate, wasn't edited at all, but the entire
body of copy was circled in red with a note from Marty that said
"See me." Since it was my first "See me" since I'd started at the
Herald, I was skeptical that Marty Baker was calling me in to laud
my appropriately placed modifiers. Under that, my profile of the
artist Zachary Khan was surrounded by a giant question mark.
Not a typical editorial query.

Suddenly, I sensed someone watching me. Lifting my head, I
spotted Genevieve looking over my shoulder. I swatted at her
with the papers in my hands.

"Ouch!" She stepped back, the fluorescent lights catching the
gold highlights in her pixie-cut yellow hair. Christmas bulb ear-
rings dangled in her ears, and I felt sorely tempted to stick her
finger in a socket and light them up. "Looks like Marty's on the
warpath," she said.

"Oh, really?" I turned the papers facedown on my desk. "He's
been questioning your work, too?"

"Not me," she beamed. "I just noticed those pieces in your in-
box."

As in, you were snooping around in my stuff? I wanted to say it, but
instead I squinted at her as if she were speaking in an ancient
tongue. "Really?"

"Anyway, he wants to see you. Better run." She was so full of
giddiness, I half expected bubbles to float out of her mouth.

I leaned back and propped one high-heeled boot on the visitor's chair. "I'll take care of it," I said casually. "And next time
keep your mitts out of my in-box."

She gasped in mock indignation. "I had a reason—"

"Sure, you did. Just like you have a reason to disappear. Okay?
Okay." I opened a folder and pretended to become absorbed in

the notes there—mostly a scribbled Christmas list and an expired list of chores: Bank, Cleaners, Pedicure, Pick up film from two years ago at CVS. . . .

At least the diversion sent Genevieve bouncing off to her cubicle, which fortunately was a safe distance away, behind a pillar and on the other side of a TV monitor.

I snatched up the red-marked pages and froze. What next? Should I run into Marty's office and face this head on, or take a moment to compose myself and come up with a reasonable strategy. A smart woman would take these rewrites and put a spin on the situation. Yes, this is proof that I'm not really cut out for writing obituaries, and at the moment I'd be so much better at describing eggs Benedict and fresh strawberries with hand-whipped cream. . . .

"Jane?" Marty leaned over the wall of my cubicle. "Did Genevieve tell you? I mean, do you have a minute?"

I plunked my Manolos off the chair and grabbed the copy. "Oh, sure," I said, following him into his office and realizing I would have to wing it. Marty was one of the few editors with a swell, glass-walled office—the kind you see in movies; the kind of office from which the editor monitors his workers, pacing nervously and shouting into the phone. A great office, though Marty wasn't like any of the stereotypical, adrenaline-charged editors. Low-key, quiet, and unassuming, Marty would have been ill-suited for his job if he weren't so damned intuitive and smart. He could smell when a story was cooking and he had a strong sense of both the commercial and societal value of a piece.

Marty asked how I was doing and thanked me for doing the interview on my sick day. As I sat across from him, fielding the pleasantries, I flicked around a loose cuticle under the arm of the chair, wondering if I should attack now for a promotion to food editor or wait to be invited.

Once you hit thirty, you stop waiting around for invitations.

"You know, I'm glad you asked me in," I said, "because I want to talk to you about the food critic position."

He squinted at me, as if it weren't registering. "Amy's position? Oh. Would you really want that, Jane?"

"Well . . . of course," I said, a little flabbergasted. What, did he think I wanted to be known as the Angel of Death for the rest of my life? "Wouldn't you? I mean, savory meals and wine lists beat death any day of the week."

Marty smiled—a quick, polite smile—then rubbed the top of his head thoughtfully. "I don't know. Writing about food is such a bit of fluff, really. Has fine cuisine ever really had a major impact on anyone's life . . . changed the world? I'd be hard-pressed to cite a meal that changed society as we know it."

"Don't forget the Twinkie," I said.

"Ah, yes, the Twinkie defense. Point taken, but when you mull it over, Jane, the work you do is far more significant. I like to think that our obits pay homage to society by revealing the cycle of life; that we celebrate the human spirit, the trials and victories of the individual, the impact one person has on our global community."

I nodded, hoping that my eyes weren't glossing over at the well-worn speech. "You're absolutely right, Marty, but you have to admit, writing celebrity obits is not for everyone."

"Absolutely," he said. "Though you've proven yourself to be exceptionally perceptive, a master at researching and delineating idiosyncracies."

"Thanks." I guess that meant he'd forgotten my past transgressions. The time a soap opera actress had dumped pasta in my lap when she discovered that I was an obit writer (and thus not someone who could advance her career) and I tossed a meatball back at her. The time I told an octogenarian televangelist who whimpered about seeing the pearly gates to get over himself. The Death Beat hadn't been a smooth run for me; I was ready for a change. "I have to admit," I went on, "I think I'm burning out in this area. Time for a change, and when I heard that Amy was leaving, well . . ." I tossed up one hand, as if to fling home my point, but I could see that Marty wasn't tracking. "I want to be the next restaurant critic for the *Herald*, Marty. I have experience working in the Wine and Dining section, and I've got a great track record here." *Depending on who you talk with.*

Marty leaned back in his chair and pressed a finger into his

cheek as if my proposal had thrown him into a fit of consternation. "You want the food gig?" He stared off in the distance as if
a vision were unfolding—one of those Marty things. As I waited
for him to visit Mecca, I thought that Marty wasn't bad looking.
He had thoughtful green eyes and high cheekbones. A strong
square jaw that was somehow softened by his shiny bald head.
Rumor had it that Marty had lost his hair in college, and I believed it. He was one of those guys who probably played Yoda to
the frat boys, doling out beers and sage advice, helping them
cram for finals.

"You'll have to forgive me if I don't see it, Jane, but, I'm sorry,
I don't. I hate to disappoint you, but I think you're a better fit in
obits right now."

I smiled. So this wasn't going to be easy.

"I won't hold you to that if you want to change your mind," I
teased. "Really. Marty, can you think it over? I'm ready to move
on."

"Wouldn't you like to master celebrity obits first?"

I blinked. Hello? Hadn't I earned the nickname "Angel of
Death?"

"What's yet to master? I think I've been to the mountaintop
and beyond."

Marty reached over and picked up the folder with my marked-
up pieces. "Not quite. I pulled these two pieces from the vault.
My friend is an art dealer and he tells me Zachary's health is failing, and Fitzgerald wanted to see what we had on Ms. Antoinette
Lucas." Fitzgerald is one of the bears on the publishing board. I
don't know what any of those men do, but I find them tiresome,
cigar-smoking fat cats. "Anyway, when I read these I was struck by
a certain trend in your writing. You're a fine writer, Jane, but
reading your profiles I've become concerned by the subtext in
some of them. It doesn't occur when you're writing about men
of intellectual and academic accomplishment." He lifted his
reading glasses and swung them open. "The men of stature seem
to be safe from your scorn; it's the rest of us slobs who feel it."

He smiled, and I grinned, not sure where he was going with
this.

"But in some of your profiles I sense a lack of compassion for your subjects. I see it more in the finished pieces, but also in the early drafts. You're so critical."

"Critical can be good. I can make it work for me." I folded my arms, wondering how this had turned into a critique of me. "You know, *critical* is an asset when you're writing about food."

He shook his head, as if my writing weakness wounded him, then put on his glasses and read from my piece on Antoinette. "'When diagnosed with cancer, she took up the cause and used her influence to raise millions of dollars for breast cancer research,'" he read.

I shrugged. "Has that changed?"

"No, but this description is cool and perfunctory, not what Antoinette is about. Have you met her?"

"Two years ago."

"Very personable, isn't she?"

"We had a few laughs together," I admitted, remembering how Antoinette had told me a few surprising anecdotes about her recovery from the mastectomy.

Marty shook his head. "She's just not coming through here. And Zachary Khan . . . This is so bland. I didn't learn anything about this young man from reading this piece. It's generic, almost boilerplate." He took off his glasses. "Uninspired, though I know you have the skills to make this read like poetry. We can't let the *Herald* appear to be passing judgment, Jane. We must treat every person's death with dignity and inspiration."

I bit back a twinge of guilt. Marty had hit on one of my nasty habits. To be honest, my weakness is for brilliant, gifted men— geniuses who aren't afraid to let their vision of the truth shatter illusions. Sometimes when writing up a scientist or inventor or lawyer, I have to admit, I fall a little bit in love. Last month, while working on the obituary of Roy Sheridan, a legal theorist who, while he was a third-year law student at New York University, fashioned a significant part of the argument used in Roe v. Wade, I was gritting my teeth. How was it that this brilliant man had been in the world and I'd never met him? He'd walked away from legal work in the eighties and traveled the country in a

Volkswagen van with his collie. Now there's a sexy image: brilliance on the road. A combination of Alan M. Dershowitz and Jack Kerouac. Of course, Mr. Sheridan's bio was edited down when Bobby Hatfield of the Righteous Brothers died around the same time, but Sheridan still got two columns, above the fold.

I took the file from Marty. "And you think this writer has a future in obits?"

"She's ripe with possibility," he said. "Possibility to be plumbed."

"I really want out," I said. "I'd rather be sampling crème brûlées."

"Hell on your cholesterol level. You'll thank me someday."

"Put me on a toxic waste investigation. Let me shadow detectives tracking a serial killer. I'll even travel through Rotterdam on a shoestring to write the Budget Traveler column."

"Charming though those options may be, we need you in obits at the moment."

"Marty, please, I don't want to write about dead people anymore."

His eyes opened wide. "But that's the source of your problem, Jane. The people you're profiling are very much alive. That's what you need to capture."

Tucking the folder under my arm, I turned toward the door with a sense of defeat and frustration, but before I could open the door, Genevieve slid down the hall on the other side of the glass and tapped. She opened the door and popped in, her gold hair gleaming in the fluorescent light.

"Marty, I just wanted to leave these new bios with you," she said, nearly curtsying over his in-box.

"What's that?" I asked, eyeing the folders. "You didn't pitch those yet." I turned to Marty. "Since when do we open up bios without pitching them?"

"Genevieve is going on vacation," he said with a shrug. "She'll miss the meeting, so I gave her the green light on these bios."

"Just trying to work ahead," she said dutifully. As she stepped around me I noticed that she was wearing open-toed sandals. Sandals in December, and on her big toenails were tiny red poinsettias.

Oh, to drop a bottle of paint thinner on her feet. They were doing construction on the eighth floor. *What were the chances?* I thought as she sashayed right back out the door.

"Jane?" Marty was on his feet, coming around the desk. "Are you all right? You look a little pale."

"I'm okay." I pressed the folder to my cashmere sweater, wishing the cloying smell of Genevieve's cologne would fade. Well, at least I could breathe through my nose again.

Marty reached out toward my elbow, then pulled his hands back and folded them under his chin. "Compassion," he said, as if praying. "Please revisit your profiles with a new perspective. Especially Antoinette Lucas and Zachary Khan. You might want to meet with them again."

"Right," I said, heading back to my cubicle. Time to order up a side of compassion, hold the tears. Compassion with roasted garlic and butter.

Braised compassion with a side of risotto. And for dessert? Compassion à la mode.

Oh, Marty would regret not promoting me to restaurant critic.

6

"I've had it with the corporate world," I told Carter as we shared a buttery sirloin steak, red in the middle, sizzled black on the outside. My sense of taste and smell had returned, and suddenly I felt a voracious appetite for life again. "The corporate world is so unproductive. The *Herald* office is one huge fish bowl, everyone swimming around aimlessly. Everything private is public. You can't make a gynecological appointment without having the curmudgeons in copyedit know your business."

"I'm with you on that," he said, slicing off a hunk of meat. "They make you come into the office, and once you're there they act like it's an inconvenience to allot you any space. They sit you down at a desk with a divider and a computer and *that's* supposed to be a productive environment?"

"And there's the water cooler. Or the coffee cart. Or the restroom or the smoking area. There's always some meeting place where the staff wastes their time kvetching," I said as I scooped a mound of homefries onto my fork. "A total waste of time, waiting for elevators and subway trains. Commuting back and forth. I'd really love to go freelance and work at home."

"I don't mind going in," Carter said. "I sort of like the atmosphere on Wall Street. The way you can turn the pressure on and off during market hours." I wasn't sure exactly what he did at the brokerage firm, but I had met him while writing a profile on an infamous stock broker who died in jail. I liked to imagine Carter on the selling floor of the New York Stock Exchange, yelling trades and accepting huge bids, but in reality he was probably an unglamourous phone trader. In any case, when I felt his hand slide over my knee under the table, I realized just how much better I was feeling.

"Should we go to your place?" I asked.

"If you don't mind the dog." Carter had an Irish setter—it was a crime to keep him in a small apartment, but this just testified to Carter's lack of awareness and responsibility. "Red is fine, as long as you keep him out of the bedroom." There is something unnerving about having a dog's eyes on you while you're having sex, but let's not even go there.

"Red is a good dog," he said, running a finger along the inside of my right thigh. I closed my eyes, savoring the tingling feeling and the taste of real food for a moment. "He just doesn't like to be alone," Carter added.

I slipped out of my high-heeled mule and strategically lifted my foot to Carter's lap. Gently, I pushed up his thigh, massaging his groin with my toes.

He sighed. "Whoa."

"So Red waits in the kitchen?"

"The kitchen." He nodded, then signaled for the check.

"Let me get you from behind," Carter whispered in my ear, moving back so that my legs dropped from his shoulders.

I flipped over on the bed, beginning to feel as if I were in an aerobics class. Carter and I had always enjoyed sex together, but lately he'd been quick to stop midstride to change positions.

"Have you been reading sex manuals or something?" I asked as he knelt behind me and teased himself between my legs.

"Why, am I getting better?" he asked, reaching forward to slide a hand down my belly.

I didn't want to tell him that he was pulling out just as I had orgasm in sight. "You're definitely more adventurous."

He bit into my shoulder, fingering me at the same time. "I've always had a wild sense of adventure. I was going to be an archeologist."

"Why would you want to do that?" I asked, not wanting to imagine Carter all sweaty and grimy, squatting over dirty bones. I grabbed his hand. "My father was an archeologist. It's not so adventurous."

He shoved my fingertips into his mouth and sucked. "It's a fantasy. The wild side of foreign places, mysterious treasures." He took my moist fingers and brushed them over my erect nipple. "Exotic beauties. Dangerous sex."

"That's a fantasy, all right," I said, thinking that it had no correlation to what my father did.

"How do you fantasize about me?" he whispered as his hands massaged down my torso, teasing the edges of the lips between my legs.

"I'm more into the urban fantasy," I said, trying to think up one quickly since Carter wasn't prominent in my fantasies. "How about Wall Street? Millions at stake. Power oozing from the beads of sweat on your handsome brow as you pace the office with a headset strapped on."

His fingers dipped inside me, and I moaned.

"Boring!" he shouted, nuzzling me with his cock. "Indiana Jones! I am going to throw you down on the jungle floor and ravage you!"

He thrust into me, and I welcomed him with a surge of moist desire. I could give up the Wall Street scenario for a brief rain forest expedition. As I recalled, Indy did have fabulous credentials and taught at a university. I cast Carter as a young Indy racing through a canyon of towering palms, taking me by the hand, pulling up my skirt.

He pumped against me, setting up a new rhythm, and I let my elbows fall to the bed as I crouched in the darkness for my swashbuckling archeologist. "Go, Indy!" I whispered as the heat rose between us.

Afterwards we fell to the bed. Carter groaned and cupped one of my breasts. "You okay, babe?"

"Why do you ask?"

"You just seem, I don't know, a little tense."

I sighed. "It's all this crap at work." I usually didn't get really personal with Carter, but since he'd asked . . . "You know my nemesis, Genevieve? Well, she's stepping all over me, and my boss is letting her get away with it."

"I hate my boss," he said.

"Well, I don't hate mine, but that doesn't mean he's always right. There's an opening coming up—a big one. Restaurant critic. But Marty doesn't think it's right for me, and to be honest, that really hurts. He thinks I'm better suited for obits, and yet he's not satisfied with what I'm writing now. It's totally fucked up."

Silence.

"Do you ever feel that way at work?" I asked him. "Undervalued and overwhelmed?"

More silence.

"Carter?" In the darkness, I saw his chest rise and fall steadily, his eyes closed.

Oh, that just did it!

For once, I opened up to him, and did he listen? He fell asleep!

As I pulled on my clothes, I wondered if Carter and I had outgrown this relationship. Despite my fantasies, Carter wasn't joining Mensa anytime soon. He wasn't one of the geniuses of my fantasies . . . which, in the absence of emotional connection, left us with occasional sex. Jiffy lube, as one of my exes once called it. The ten-minute oil change could be a good thing, but shouldn't there be some consideration involved? A tiny bit of interest? Enough to keep him awake and listening while I was pouring my heart out?

Maybe it was time for a new guy. I'd always been so critical of my sister Ricki for hanging onto her schlumpy realtor. I mean, the payoff of that relationship was diminishing for her, yet she clung to him like ivy on a trellis. Was I clinging to Carter, despite diminishing returns?

"Take a look at yourself, girl," I said, staring into the dark mirror. Too dark to see. As I opened the bedroom door, Red hopped off the living room couch and trotted over to face me in the doorway. I looked back at Carter's prone figure, then turned to Red.

"I hope you two are very happy together," I said as I grabbed my coat and headed out of there.

7

Six days later, I dug into my plastic vial of antibiotics, gulped the horse pill down with water, then slammed the glass down onto the kitchen counter as if I'd just toasted the Russian fleet with vodka.

Six days without a drink. I would have to remember that the next time I worried about being recruited by AA. Of course, I still had a few days left on the medication, but since it was Sunday, I figured that a glass of wine with Emma wouldn't kill me. We had decided to take in a movie, *The Last Samurai,* then grab dinner. Afterwards, we landed at Duke's, where it was so crowded we decided to eat at the bar, where our friend Macy was dispensing white wines faster than quantum speed.

"What's with all these people?" I asked Macy, eyeing the invasion of uninvited guests who swamped my favorite watering hole.

"Duke rented out the back room for a Christmas party," she said. "Then he had the nerve to go skiing with his girlfriend. Noah and I are up to our elbows here."

Emma and I turned to each other and exploded: "His girlfriend?" at the same time.

"Owe me a Coke!" Emma said, squeezing my arm. "What girl-friend? Who's the girlfriend? We've never met her."

"And you never will." Macy placed two glasses of chardonnay in front of us. "He won't bring her around here. The man won't play in his own backyard."

"Well, there's a mystery solved." I lifted my wineglass and held it midair. "Here's to you, Duke, for keeping us guessing."

Macy laughed and shimmied her shoulders. "I had him pegged all along. I knew he liked sisters."

"I might have to take him off my list," Emma said sadly. "If he's serious enough to go away with this girl for the weekend, they might be a couple." Emma had a running list of men she'd sleep with in a minute, which she was constantly revising when one of those men got married. She thought it was pure evil to break up a marriage, and almost as bad to cause a rift in an otherwise healthy relationship.

"You had Duke on your list?" Macy rolled her eyes. "You need to get out more, girlfriend."

"Well, I added him when I had to pull Russell Crowe."

"I thought you replaced Russell with Tom Cruise," I said, knowing that Tom had gone back on the list soon after he and Nicole split.

Emma shook her head. "No, Tom came back on a while ago, and after seeing *Last Samurai,* I'm glad he did."

"Uhm-hm. Mr. Cruise can ride my horse anytime," Macy tossed off as she carried two tall drinks down the bar.

"What are the specials today?" I said, looking up at the chalk-board. Emma ran her finger around the stem of her wineglass, her mind elsewhere. "Hello? Are we eating here, or what?"

"He called me," she said. "This week . . . yesterday, he called me. He wants to get back together."

Tom Cruise? Then the ugly truth hit me. "Jonathan?"

She nodded. "I've been sick about it. I don't even know if I can eat. Can you believe that? All those hours in the gym trying to burn carbs, and now one phone call and I'm fasting."

I squeezed her wrist. "Don't tell me you're actually entertain-ing the idea. Oh, Emma . . . no!"

"He reminded me that New Year's Eve would be our one-year anniversary," Emma said dolefully.

"I see he still has a penchant for drama." I remembered last December, when Emma had first connected with Jonathan. She and I were partying it up in a pack of tourists huddled on Times Square. Emma wore a silly paper crown and I had a wig of foil streamers over my head and the air was so charged with intoxicating spirit that I didn't mind giving up champagne for a few minutes of noisy revelry in the cold.

Emma and I were laughing when the crowd shifted and a bunch of people shoved into us, knocking Emma into one of the blue wooden police barricades. Two cops rushed over and quickly helped Emma to her feet. One of them took a special interest in brushing off her coat. Officer Jonathan Thompson lit into Emma with his blue eyes. She fell for his tousled dark curls, unmarred by a riot helmet, his easy laugh, his street stories. From that moment on, Emma was a hopeless cop groupie. She started watching all the crime shows on television. She waved to every passing patrol car and smiled at uniformed officers hanging out on street corners. She started telling me about Jonathan's exciting days and nights, his "jobs," the chatter of the dispatcher that she heard through his cell phone, his "gun runs" and "ten-thirteens." In Emma's eyes, Jonathan lived on the edge of danger (though I suspected he inflated his superhero stories when trying to impress chicks). Somehow, by having sex with him she felt connected to that exciting underworld, not to mention that seducing an officer fulfilled some weird sense of civic duty.

Bottom line: Emma was smitten.

Personally, I thought Jonathan was a big blowhard, but since she was the one who fell against the barricade and into his arms, my opinion didn't matter much.

"I know you don't see the allure, and I'm sure you could do a rip-roaring critique of him," Emma had told me when she and Jonathan first started sleeping together, "but thanks. Thanks for . . . for not doing that."

And so I'd bitten back my sardonic commentary on this show-stealing, blue-eyed hunk who was far too gorgeous to be soiling

his hands dragging perps to jail. It didn't take long to realize
that Jonathan was acutely aware of his own buff beauty; he possessed a portfolio of head shots which he'd been shopping
around to modeling agencies, and had appeared as an extra on
a few of the daytime dramas shot in New York. In the past few
months I had begun to see him as an actor who had opted out of
waiting tables to bring home a heftier check from the NYPD. I
had also noticed that Jonathan liked the ladies—the big dawg!—
and I was about to confront Emma about it when their breakup
spared me the agony.

Macy returned to our end of the bar and dumped empty
glasses into a bin. "Who died?" she asked casually.

"It's the ghost of boyfriends past," I said. "Emma's ex wants
her back."

"Sure he does. They all do, once they have to spend a night or
two alone." Macy wiped the bar, her silver rings shining against
her chocolate-brown skin. "Men are all horndogs at heart. Once
they miss the sugar, they suddenly have big ol' broken hearts."

"He sounded sincere." Emma twirled an orange curl around
one finger, looking so wistful I could cry. "He wants to get together and talk."

"And you're going to meet him? Why torture yourself, Em?
You don't miss him—you said so yourself," I said.

"I don't miss him," she admitted. "What I miss is being part of
a couple. It's sad to think of spending Christmas alone."

"You're going to be with Ricki and me," I said, "and don't drift
into that Christmas romance shit. Men are horndogs year-round;
they don't suddenly earn halos when December comes along."

"My brain knows you're right, but my heart is telling me to
pick up my cell and call him."

"I won't let you do that!" I snatched her purse from the bar
shelf and hugged it to my chest. "Nobody make any fast moves
here, until we figure this out."

Emma's face puckered in a worried expression. "Remind me
why I can't call him. I need an itemized list of reasons."

"Typical banker," I said, shaking my head. "Do you want me to
be honest?"

"Brutally."

"Number one, you could never rely on him when you were living together. There were nights when he didn't come home, didn't call—"

"Out with the guys," she recalled.

"Whatever. You couldn't count on him."

Emma nodded. "Point taken."

"Item two: Jonathan was a scene stealer. Remember the last party we went to at the Met? He always had a tale that was more grandiose than the next person, and honestly, did you believe all of those police anecdotes he told? I swear, he stole them from *NYPD Blue.*"

Emma frowned. "I think that's two items."

"And also, he wants to be a *model.*" I winced. "High ick factor."

"We love to look at those model types," Macy said as she scooped ice into the blender, "but you can't take them anywhere."

"He was really into himself," Emma admitted. "He used to work out in front of the mirror, watch his muscles pop. I think he got off on that."

Macy and I made an "Eeeew" face at each other.

"And then there's the flirt factor," I said. "He likes to sniff around. Teenagers, waitresses . . . he doesn't seem to be too discriminating."

"Did you notice that, too?" Emma asked. "I thought I was being paranoid."

"Oh, no," Macy said, "I've seen him chasing some ass in here. More than once."

Emma sighed. "He really is awful. We don't belong together at all. And to think I came this close to calling him." She turned to me. "Thanks for being honest. You're really good at sizing up guys."

"Really," Macy agreed. "You have an amazing talent for seeing right through the bullshit."

"Is it a talent, or a curse?" I sat back, folding my arms. "I can't stand my sister's boyfriend Nate. I've decided to tell Carter to take a hike, and I'm just not in the mood to start up with someone new. Men are so much work."

"I hear ya," Macy said, checking her watch. "Hey, I get off at six tonight, and I've got passes to a new club where my friend is the bouncer. You two want to hang?"

"Sounds good," I said.

"I should get home," Emma said. "I've got an early day tomorrow, and I need every ounce of energy to deal with the telemarketing division."

"You're not slipping away," I told her. "We can't have you home alone when Jonathan calls. Let's get this party started."

Emma lifted her wineglass. "Maybe just for a while."

"A while" turned into an eight-hour party, starting at the new club and ending up at a bar where Macy knew the bartender, a mysterious, dark-eyed college kid named Zade. My single glass of wine turned into a succession of drinks, so many that I lost track of the booze, but I clung to Emma, refusing to let her leave my sight and fly back into Jonathan's slippery arms. At one point Emma insisted that she go since it was almost midnight, and I released her as it dawned on me that Macy had already left and the bar was emptying. After that I talked with Zade, and somehow I ended up sitting on the bar and making out with him, the two of us kissing and petting like a couple of teenagers. And then the bar was empty except for the two of us, and he went out front to roll down the gate and I pulled him back onto the shiny laminated wood and kissed him again and let my hand press the crotch of his pants—those loose, printed things that look like pajamas.

He stopped, a little hesitant, saying something about regrets.

"Honey," I drawled, "if you have a hard-on and a Trojan, there's no reason to regret anything."

My brain was foggy, but I remember the dark intensity of his eyes as he pressed me down onto the bar, his body lean and wiry as he did push-ups over me. No regrets. No strings. No problems.

8

Monday morning . . . Ugh.

My head felt huge as I dragged myself out of bed and stepped under the hot jet of the shower. Why did I feel so hungover? Probably the drinking. I should have stopped after the second glass of wine. Or the Irish coffees. And I definitely didn't need that snifter of brandy. Ugh.

I pulled on black clothes so I wouldn't have to make any fashion choices and hid behind a pair of sunglasses, even in the dark of the subway stairs. Maybe I'd feel better after coffee and a cigarette.

Oh, hell, I'd quit smoking. I was never going to feel better.

I emerged from the elevator to the office with my collar turned up and my sunglasses on. With the inflated pain in my head, a day in the bull pen was going to be murder. Oren's psycho laugh would be liked machine-gun fire, and the simplest gesture from Genevieve would trigger annoyance overload. But how do you hide in a sea of reporters? The *Herald* used to have a society editor who wore rhinestone cat's-eye sunglasses every day of her life—and that was years before they became retro. In her time, Lulu Bettincourt was as much a fixture at debutante balls as gilded chairs and white gloves, but Lulu had retired to Florida last year, taking her tinted spectacles to true sunglass territory.

I passed Ed, who was tapping on the glass of the fishtank. "Can you knock a little softer?" I asked, but Ed just stared at the glass in consternation. I longed to collapse at my desk and cuddle my coffee cup, but this was my buddy Ed. "I was kidding, Ed. Ed? Something wrong?"

Truman Nagasian, one of the national editors, popped out of his cubicle. "The buzz is that the president is going to raise the alert to orange," he reported. "We're all kind of freaking out today."

"Really?" I said. "What does that mean?"

"They've heard chatter from terrorist cells," Truman said. "Rumor that there'll be a spectacular attack."

I unbuttoned the top of my coat. "But what does that mean to us?"

Truman shrugged. "Longer lines at the airports?"

I turned to Ed. "Should I be scared?"

"After twenty years spent reporting the news, I find that if you let yourself be frightened by some of it you cannot cope with any of it," said a distracted Ed.

I peered into the tank. Piggy looked, well, like Piggy to me. Bulging eyes, luminescent scales, whispery fins. "Looks normal to me."

"She's just not behaving in her typical fashion," Ed lamented.

I have to admit, I adored the fact that this man could disengage from pressing matters like national security and still care deeply about a goldfish. Even through my fat, aching head it endeared Ed to me. I fumbled in my bag for two Advils, popped them, and chugged down a sip of coffee while Ed relayed Piggy's symptoms to me. We discussed possible fish ailments, I tried to be reassuring, then dragged myself to my cubicle, where I found Genevieve reading one of my pieces.

"What the hell . . ." I winced, wanting to slap her manicured hand away.

"I have a fix for you," she said innocently.

"Excuse me?"

"I know how you can fix this profile."

"Like I give a rat's ass. What are you doing at my desk . . . reading stuff on my desk?" I asked, appalled.

All around us heads lifted and fingers stopped clacking on keyboards. Genevieve had violated the cardinal rule: privacy of the cubicle.

"Well, I was . . . I was going to leave you a note, but then I started reading this. I mean, it was sitting out on your desk and all . . ."

"Next time leave the note in my in-box. Or better yet, e-mail me." *That way, you won't be able to pirate my files away.*

That had been Genevieve's modus operandum since she'd joined the staff last spring. Every time I pitched a new person to profile, Genevieve stole my thunder, claiming that she'd been planning the same pitch at the very same meeting. For a while, Marty let her pitch first at the meeting, which worked for a time; at least, until I suspected that she was spying on me, trying to find my list of pitches. Lately I'd begun to keep my pitch ideas at home or write them in anagram. I had become the Nancy Drew of the obit pages.

I pushed past her, dropped my coat on the visitor's chair, and pulled out my chair. "What was the note about?"

"I . . . it was . . ." She collapsed from the pressure, melting under the disapproving eyes of staff writers. "It's not that important. I'll ask Lincoln."

Translation: You'll rob him blind, I thought as I watched her disappear. She was ruining my already bad hangover day, and it wasn't even ten yet. I turned on my computer and checked my e-mail as I warmed my fingers on my latte. Antoinette Lucas confirmed our lunch for the next day, which was good since she'd made headline news over the weekend and I'd been afraid she would ditch me, feeling too important to spend time with an obit writer. Apparently Ms. Lucas had turned down a lucrative new contract with the network to start her own production company. For once, I was really interested in monitoring the development of this story.

I went over my calendar for the week, glad that Ricki wasn't

coming till next week because I had way too many profiles to in-
fuse with "compassion" before then. I continued my online search
for information on Antoinette Lucas, whose name now yielded
google hits galore.

When the phone rang, I kept my eyes on the screen, my
thoughts in one of Antoinette's college anecdotes. "Jane Conner."

"This is Dr. Parson's office, Ms. Conner. Dr. Parson would like
to speak with you. Can you hold?"

I blinked. Wow, a doctor who called *me*? A doctor I could
speak to without falling into the black hole of a voice mail direc-
tory. "Certainly." I spun away from the computer screen and
propped my low heels up on the visitor's chair. Dr. Parson was
calling me. Maybe he was a mensch, after all.

The line clicked and the doctor came on. "Ms. O'Conner?"

"It's Conner." If I had a nickel for every time that happened.
"Yes?"

"Dr. Parson. I have the test results from your visit here last
week."

I smiled. "All better. I can breathe again."

"About the lump on your thyroid."

Oh. I flashed back to the long, skinny needle.

"You have a malignant growth in the left lobe," he went on.
"You need surgery on your thyroid."

Surgery? Me? It had to be a joke, but the drive in his voice
clutched at my sense of drama and held it tight. I was stepping
into a scene from ER—the big phone call from the concerned
doctor.

"I do?" was my brilliant answer.

"The cells found from the fine needle aspiration are consis-
tent with a papillary tumor."

The music of my medical drama ground to a halt with the
word: tumor. Let's face it, that is one ugly word, and it set off a
quivering sensation deep inside me. Call me a fatalist, but in my
experience tumors were not a good thing. Tumors led to
surgery, which led to gut-wrenching chemo, which led to dam-
aging radiation, which led to people surrounding you with flowers and a morphine drip and asking if they can do anything for

you. That was the way my mother had gone out of this world, and damned if it didn't start with a tumor.

Dr. Parson was still talking, something about the thyroid and how it was best to remove it all, about working with an endocrynologist to regulate synthetic hormones. The tremor rippling through me was shaking my legs now, and suddenly I was acutely aware of the activity around me: laughter from the Sports section, some kind of bet being waged between Oren and Lincoln, a phone bleeping endlessly at one of the desks down near the rest rooms. Dr. Parson spoke of *no need to panic . . . schedule the surgery . . . time off to recuperate . . . radioactive iodine therapy* but I was twenty giant steps behind him, picturing a wormlike tumor.

A gray, gooey squid wrapping around my skinny neck.

A tumor. So that meant he was talking about the "C" word, right? Throughout his explanation, he had not said the word.

I was scared shitless, but I had to know. "Are you talking about cancer?" I asked, my voice cracking, raw.

"Yes, it's a papillary carcinoma, a type of cancer, but something we can treat."

I started to curse but the words couldn't make it past the knot in my throat.

Cancer! *I have cancer.*

I was not ready to leave this world. I'd barely had a chance to live, to really live, and here was this thing, this tumor and surgery, this cancer, taking my life from me.

"Ms. Conner?" Dr. Parson sounded stern. "Don't let this ruin your holiday. In the world of cancers, this is a minor inconvenience."

I wanted to laugh at the ludicrousness of that statement and the odd sense of relief it gave me. How inconvenient to get cancer right before the holidays! I imagined women in his Park Avenue waiting room saying, "Oh, Muffy, how inconvenient! Had I known about this neck thing, I could have scheduled the chin tuck at the same time!"

I doubted that Dr. Parson had ever experienced the "inconvenience" of cancer.

"I can't talk anymore," I told him.

"Don't put it off," he warned me. "We need to take care of this."

Take care of this. Snip it out. Get me in the hospital, in the hands of professionals who would cheerfully monitor my progress into hell.

I placed the phone in its cradle and bit back a feeling of panic as I grabbed my bag and coat and swung toward the elevators. I was well on my way to a meltdown and the office bull pen was not a good place to cry your heart out, fall to your knees and ask "Why me?" (Believe me, I've seen grown women and men break down in the office at deadline; it is not a pretty sight.)

Outside the brass-trimmed revolving door of the *Herald* Building I stepped into the scattering cloud of smoke and fished in my bag for a cigarette. Where the hell . . . ? Of course I couldn't find any. I'd quit smoking last week. Right. Quit smoking so that you don't get cancer.

I wanted to bum a cigarette from one of the other smokers, but I knew if I opened my mouth a sob would escape and I just couldn't let that happen. Clutching my bag to my chest, I listened as Drucie from advertising told a story about her son's Christmas list. "Half the items on the list don't even exist. He's invented these toys—like a hovering skateboard and a snowball sling—and he's drawn illustrations to show Santa's elves exactly how it should be built."

"How old is he?" someone asked.

"Just turned seven. Can you believe it? You want your kids to have their hearts' desires, but really, it's an impossible chore for old Santa."

My eyes welled with tears as people chuckled over the story. Drucie shot me a look over her shoulder, but didn't say anything, thank God. She must have sensed my silent desperation as I realized I didn't belong here. I didn't have any cigarettes, my whole body was shaking so much I probably didn't have the manual dexterity to smoke, and the craving had fled with my peace of mind.

That's when I started running. My hair whipped in my face

and my coat blew open and I was probably going to break an ankle running in these shoes, but did that matter now?

Running was a release, despite the burning in my chest. After a few blocks my eyes were blurred with tears from the cold and I slowed to a fast stroll. I was headed west, toward the Hudson, which sent a nasty wind blustering up Twenty-third Street. It was too fucking cold.

I ducked into a dark bar and paused inside the dank vestibule. Music was playing, not too loud, and two skeletal patrons were engaged in friendly conversation with the bartender, who was leaning back and switching channels on the television.

This would be a fine place to hide. My heels clicked loudly as I dove into the back of the bar, miles away from the men. The bartender came down to bring me a shot of tequila, which I took into the corner booth facing away from all the action. The drink burned my throat as I tossed it back. I hugged myself with a pang of despair. Cancer. Cancer! How did it happen? How did my body whip out of control like that?

My mother had asked the same questions. A smoker all her life, and suddenly her lungs had defied her, revolting with cancerous cells that had worked their way from the lungs to the lymph nodes before anyone knew of their existence. My cancer was in a different place, but what if it started somewhere else and spread to the thyroid from there?

I fished the cell phone out of my bag and called Emma. Two rings, and she picked up.

"Jane, I can't talk now," she whispered. "Where are you?"

"In a bar on Twenty-third Street."

"Drinking before noon? That's a new low, even for you."

"I have cancer," I sobbed, then shoved a fist against my jaw to stop that horrible moaning sound. "I just found out."

"Oh my God, I'm sorry. Oh, Jane . . ."

Her sympathy made me sob again.

"Look, the division manager is here today and I just can't leave right now."

"S'okay." I gulped. "There's nothing to do about it, anyway."

"Hold tight and I'll call you right back."

As I pressed the "end" button and stared at the phone a piece of silver garland snapped down from the edge of the bar. Fuck Christmas; I'd never had much luck during this season. In the fifth grade I broke my wrist ice-skating on Christmas Eve and had to wear a smelly cast until February. Then there were all those Christmases when I was in high school and Mom was going through a get-in-touch-with-your-family phase while Dad was conveniently away on digs. Ricki and I hated being corralled on the train out to New Jersey so that we could learn to love our cousins, the suburban brats who yelled at my mother because she'd bought them the wrong Teenage Mutant Ninja Turtle toy. I smiled through my tears thinking of our last Christmas with the "family," when flu-stricken Ricki threw up all over Aunt Carol's kitchen. Thank God for Ricki and her tendency to vomit.

Tucking the collar of my coat up to hide my misery, I took a sip and tried to play worse-case scenario. That being, I die.

All that came to mind was a blank monitor, a dead television screen.

Was there an afterlife? I wasn't a fan of conventional religion, but I wanted to believe that spirits lived on in some way. "Of course spirits live on," my mother had once consoled me. "Can't you hear your father's voice now? Don't you imagine his approval of your new job? His criticisms of the mayor's new traffic patterns? His roar over the Yankees?" In fact, I had heard his voice, heard my mother's years later, when I was trying to sort through her possessions in the apartment I'd grown up in.

"Purple is such a rich color, don't you think?" she called to me as I pulled up a shade and watched sunlight reveal the mottling of the aged gem-tone paint.

"I've acquired an aversion to paper napkins," she whispered as I sorted through linens and napkins, lace-edged confections stacked neatly in a bejeweled chest she had bought in some exotic place like Bombay or Thailand.

The volumes on her bookshelf were yellowed and old, but it pained me to part with them, the puzzle pieces of my parents' lives: The History of Civilization, Dickens, Tolstoy, Shakespeare,

Faulkner, Fitzgerald . . . along with the contemporary paperbacks my mother had sped through, the work of the "hipster-doofus generation," she whispered.

I had heard Alice's voice when the realtor assessed the co-op. "Keep it in the family," my mother's voice streamed like sunlight through the stained glass hangings. "If not you or your sister, then find a friend."

In the end, Emma had wanted the co-op, much to Ricki's relief and mine that we wouldn't be obliged to live out our entire lives at one address. And these days my parents voices were faded and they called to me less frequently. I still missed Dad and Alice, and in the end all the creaky details of their deaths, the weirdness of funerals and crematoriums had given way to that . . . missing them.

They were gone from the world, and I was on the verge of joining them, ill-prepared though I was.

The cell rang and I answered to Emma. "I'm at a computer," she said. "What kind of cancer?"

"Thyroid."

"I knew that, but there are four different types. Which one is it?"

I raked back my hair. "I don't know. A tumor."

"It's not an anaplastic carcinoma, is it? Also called giant cell? Spindle cell?"

I sighed. "Doesn't ring a bell."

"Thank God," she said. "That's the worst kind. Giant cell has a six-month life span after diagnosis."

I whimpered. "I can't believe this." The bartender looked my way and I motioned for another round.

"We'll figure it out, honey. God, I wish I could cut out of here and meet you."

"Don't worry about me. I'll hang together until you get out of there." The bartender brought the second shot of tequila over. I handed him a twenty and waved him away. "Keep the change."

"I just wish we had more information." Always one to arm herself with the facts, Emma is big on veracity. "How about medullary? Follicular? Papillary?"

"That's it, like the butterfly."

"Papillary?" Emma said quickly. "That's good. Papillary is good."

"Really?" A good cancer?

"It's the most common, usually affects women of childbearing age. Metastasizes slowly."

As she talked it occurred to me that this tumor was growing inside me right now, taking over the healthy cells. The bastard. Obnoxious little worm.

"Listen to this: if diagnosis is made early, most people have a normal life expectancy. Did you hear that?"

"I'm not sure if it's early for me."

"What did the doctor say?"

"Not to let it ruin my Christmas."

"Well, that's good, isn't it? I mean, he can't give you false optimism, right?"

"I thought he was just trying to spread Christmas cheer and all that crap."

"He can't!" Emma insisted. "He's not allowed to do that. Remember when your mother was dying? They didn't mince words. That one surgeon was so callous, he just told her to go home and get her affairs in order. This isn't so bad, Janey. Why don't you look it up online?"

"I can't."

"There's so much information here. I think it will be helpful. But I've got to go or the division manager will sink me in my review."

"You go," I said. "We'll hook up later."

As we hung up I stared at the shot glass in front of me. There were no answers there, that much I knew; only a way to delay the intensity of the pain.

As if a ghost were passing through the bar, another prong of the garland gave way, and now the string of silver dipped onto the floor like a drunken remnant of holidays long ago, of Christmases chock-full of unfulfilled expectations and stress. And now I had an even better reason, with Death knelling for me in this very merry season. Merry fucking Christmas. Had there ever been a time when I didn't hate Christmas? I sunk back in the booth and tried to remember a moment from my childhood. We'd always baked cookies and fruitcake with Mom, but then as I recall Ricki and I were little pains in the asses, stealing candied cherries and haphazardly blotting colored sugars onto butter cookies that ended up resembling edible Jackson Pollack paintings.

Philip's face knocked on my memory and I remembered that one magical Christmas when I felt genuine joy: my first Christmas out of college, when Philip had asked me to marry him. I was such a sap back then, mushy-gushy. I fell hard for Philip, opened myself to him, wrote fucking poetry for him. So totally blindsided, never suspecting that he was banging the girls he flirted with.

Later, I found out that on our wedding day he had his mitts on half the girls in our bridal party. Philip was a major horndog, but I didn't see it, couldn't see it. If love is blind, then it's a sport for morons, and back then I was the Queen of Moronica. Engaged for Christmas, married on Christmas Eve of the following year. It was a short marriage, over before the following Thanksgiving, and it certainly threw a pall over the holidays for me.

Christmas. If this was going to be my last, how did I want to spend it? What did I want to do with the rest of my life? What was the one thing I would miss the most?

Only one answer came to me: Love. To have really loved someone with all my heart and soul . . . that was the one important thing I hadn't accomplished.

I buried my face in my hands. Oh, God. I was still the Queen of Moronica.

9

Paralysis set in quickly. My body shut down in those days after the diagnosis.

I paced the apartment in my nightgown, unable to escape the pain that welled up when I lacked the energy to tamp it down. Sleep was the only escape, but it eluded me without the help of drugs, and I felt reluctant to surrender my life, whatever was left of it, to total stupor.

So I paced, then huddled on the couch, shoulders sagging like an old woman, feet tucked to my chest like an infant. I spent hours contemplating the lines on my hands, wondering which one was the life line but not having the strength to research it. I worried about leaving my little sister alone in the world. I cursed myself for accomplishing nothing of lasting value in my lifetime. I contemplated after-life in the smooth surface of an Entenmann's frosted cake on my kitchen counter, wondering at the peace I might find reincarnated in the soft vanilla sponge beneath that smooth fudge icing. Ridiculous, I know, but to be baked in the molecules of sweet heaven seemed a far better place than the turmoil that roiled in my body.

That Christmas, Emma Dee saved my life.

The day I got the diagnosis she dove into thyroid research like a medical student cramming for finals. She surfed the Internet, phoned all her doctors, and grilled her cousin Keith, an actual med student. When she met me for dinner one night after the bad news, she brought printed pages from the Internet and a copy of *Thyroids for Dummies* that she'd picked up at the Barnes & Noble down the street.

"A gift for you," she said, smiling over the book.

I nodded, but had neither the strength nor the energy to take the book and open it. "Does it say anything good?" I asked.

"About your cancer?" She nodded enthusiastically. "The statistics are great! It's like a ninety-nine percent recovery rate."

My cancer . . . that was a creepy thought. Didn't want to own it. But I pushed it to the back of my mind as Emma and I ordered pad thai and chicken satay, crab dumplings, and mussamen curry at our favorite Thai restaurant. "Thai food is the perfect cure for a hangover," Emma had insisted when I suggested calling off our dinner. "Besides, you can't be alone tonight. I won't let you."

Actually, sitting here in our favorite corner behind the coral-tasseled drapes and the giant gold Buddha, I almost felt normal again. I almost felt like any other New Yorker who would wake up early for work in the morning, drop a third of her salary on a morning latte, and bitch about the surplus population of holiday tourists. That afternoon, as I'd stood sobbing in the shower, I'd made a deal with myself to keep this cancer thing at arm's length. I wasn't going to think about it or research it or face it until I absolutely had to (which for me would mean the morning of my surgery). The truth? How long can you stare into the jowls of death without totally losing your mind?

"So did you call the doctor back, like we agreed?" Emma held a shrimp aloft in her chopsticks. "Are you doing a consult?"

"Thursday afternoon. He wants me to give him dates for the surgery. He needs to book the O.R."

"And you're just going to do that?" Emma gaped. "You're going to let the first doctor that comes along perform surgery, without a second opinion? What about his record? You don't even like this guy!"

I shrugged. "I just want it over."

"I can't believe you, Jane." Appalled, Emma lowered her chopsticks. "I've seen you shop for shoes. You have to wear half the size sevens in the shop before you make up your mind. Don't you think you owe it to yourself to shop around for the guy who's going to cut open your neck?"

I batted a crab dumpling around in brown sauce. "It's not like shopping for a pair of Jimmy Choos. God, I wish it were that easy." My jaw caved in, giving way to that dangerous quiver.

"Oh, honey, I know it's hard."

I shook my head. "I don't want to shop for surgeons. I don't want any of this."

"I'll go with you," Emma said. "I'm going with you to the consult with Dr. No Personality, and I'll find an ENT to give you a second opinion." She stabbed my forlorn dumpling with a fork and handed it to me across the table.

I took the fork, but I was losing my appetite. "I don't want to go. I can't even think about this without falling apart."

"So let me do the thinking," she said. "I'll be your business manager. Don't worry about a thing."

I nodded and popped the dumpling in my mouth. Thank God for Emma.

The next day at work I was pleasantly surprised by the smooth tenor of the morning. Ed handed me an article he had downloaded and printed called "The Trials and Tribulations of a Restaurant Critic." Marty welcomed me back—I'd told him I'd gone home yesterday with the sinus thing again—and complimented me on my draft of Yoshiko Abe's profile. Oren asked me for some advice on his profile of Maude Kramer, the oldest known resident of New York City who was approaching 109. Her advice for a good long life? Wake up every morning with a smile, work hard, be kind to people, and don't harm anyone. "I think she's onto something," I told Oren, "except for the morning deal." I was not a morning person.

Late that afternoon as I headed out for my interview with Antoinette Lucas, I realized that the office would be a great source of escape for me this week. No one there knew about my cancer, and Genevieve would be on vacation all week. Aside from the consult with Dr. Parson on Thursday, I could pretend to be a normal person all week: *Jane, Uninterrupted.*

As I plodded up the stone stairs to the Brooklyn brownstone that housed Antoinette's new office I was a little annoyed that she had declined my invitation to lunch, telling me she was consolidating her time lately to get her new production company going. I had hoped to take her someplace really swell then write up the meal and present the review to Marty as a sample of my skills and insights into the culinary world. Although Marty didn't want to move me now, this opening was something I could focus on to the exclusion of everything else, something I could dig my teeth into and put a jaw-lock on until the rest of the editorial board gave up and let me run with it.

The doorway was strung with real pine garland strewn with tiny white lights and red cranberries, and the trim glowed in the gathering dusk, accented by new flakes of snow—one to three inches, if the forecast was correct. I rang the doorbell, feeling as if I had stepped into a Dickensian Christmas tale.

I was surprised to see Antoinette herself open the old walnut door. "Snow?" She peeked out and blinked. "Isn't that glorious! It makes the city look like a Christmas card."

"Until your favorite Manolo Blahniks go ankle deep into an ice puddle," I said, holding out my gloved hand. "Jane Conner."

"I remember you, Jane." Antoinette wiped her hands on a dark green Wagner College sweatshirt, then shook. The last time I'd seen her she'd worn a turban to cover the effects of chemotherapy, but now her brown hair was back, styled in a short pixie cut. In jeans and the oversized sweatshirt she resembled a young Audrey Hepburn playing a carpenter's apprentice. "Sorry, but I've been putting up wallpaper, trying to make our new space inhabitable. Come on in."

As she led me up two flights of stairs, past makeshift tables, drop cloths, and half-painted rooms, sound bytes of Antoinette through the years flashed through my head. Antoinette Lucas, one of the youngest women to snag the news anchor position at a major network, asking an interviewer why her gender should be an issue in her job; Antoinette and her famous silences as she sits back and lets subjects confess and spill and break down; Antoinette in maternity clothes, refusing to name the father of her child; Antoinette brushing away tears as she tells of her greatest fear, that death would take her from her children.

I followed her to a back room on the third floor where the lemony-orange walls, soft lighting, and brightly colored woven carpets combined to a cheery, warm effect. "What a cozy space," I said, dropping my bag to sink into a buttery leather chair.

"This shade of paint is called 'Nacho Cheese,' " she said. "When I heard that, I just had to have it. I finished this floor a few months ago so the kids and I could move in. We're sort of holed up here and working our way out, room by room."

I inquired about her children, about her recent career move away from network television, and about her plans. She responded thoughtfully, providing a few anecdotes that I knew would read well. Despite the energy that seemed to spiral around her as she spoke, her eyes bright, her head bobbing, she was much more relaxed than she'd been in our last interview, less frenetic.

"So you're stepping behind the camera in an attempt to ease the demands on your time?" I said.

"I know, I should get out of television if I want a minute to myself, but the media has been good to me, and I love it. I appreciate the power of television to reach a wide audience, and as a producer I'll have more control over my schedule."

"Will you continue to produce pieces related to breast cancer?"

"If there's something in that area to be reported, but I won't be tied to that." She smiled. "I'm proud of my mission to build public awareness of the disease. At least, it used to be my mission. But the whole cancer scare made me realize that life can go by like that." She snapped her fingers and I felt a little sick, thinking my life was going to be snapped away, too. "Lately, I've been yearning to do something else, explore new topics, maybe even produce a comedy."

"And what synthesized your career shift?"

"Actually, it was a total stranger—and my daughter. We were out having brunch here in Park Slope, and two women across the restaurant recognized me and started waving. 'That's the breast cancer reporter,' one woman explained to the waitress. My daughter turned around and asked me what that meant, and honestly, it launched a period of self-examination. Is that who I am? A disease spokesperson? I don't want to be defined by a disease. I mean, breast cancer? I want to kick cancer's ugly butt."

Listen to this woman, Jane! I told myself. *She's fighting her disease, fighting instead of hiding!* I hadn't cracked open the thyroid book that Emma gave me, hadn't done any online research, and I'd been fantasizing ways to avoid the consult with Dr. Parson. I was a big, fat, lily-livered chicken. See Jane run. Run, Jane, run!

"I'm glad we had this opportunity to talk," I told Antoinette. "You've changed since our last interview."

"So have you." She leaned forward, her dark eyes full of light. "What's different about you, Jane?"

Tears stung my eyes as the answer struck like a blow to the chest. Cancer.

Oh, no! This was not the place! But I was already succumbing to Antoinette's famous silence. I was already crying, lower lip quivering, face scrunched up in that froggy look I despised.

I swiped at my eyes with the back of one hand and Antoinette was holding tissues out to me, whispering: "It's okay."

Pressing the tissues to my hot tears, I didn't see any way out of this beyond confession. "I was just diagnosed with cancer. Thyroid cancer."

She nodded. "I'm not well-versed on that."

"Neither am I," I sobbed.

"But you're scared. I understand that. It's frightening to realize there's an end to this voyage."

I nodded, trying to breathe more evenly.

Antoinette leaned back in her chair. "That was one of my biggest revelations. None of us gets out alive."

I sobbed again, then laughed as her words hit me. She was

right. We were all here on a limited warranty. "I never thought of
it that way. We're all going to die. I just never thought it would
happen to me."

"Mortality can really suck," she said. "But when you know that
life is limited, you realize how much more valuable it is. It really
helped me live for the moment. Awareness of death is the ultimate wake-up call."

"A wake-up call . . ." With a deep breath, I began to see it, and
my recent mantra of "Why me?" morphed to "Why now?" and
"Why this way?" I pressed the tissues against my eyes. "God knows,
I needed a major kick in the butt."

"Consider yourself kicked." Antoinette leaned back in her chair,
still keeping eye contact, still maintaining the connection. "And
let me know how it goes, Jane. Maybe now you'll start to enjoy
the ride."

10

I was no longer kicking and screaming when Emma dragged me to the consultation with Dr. Parson that week. Actually, I'd begun to develop a sort of morbid fascination with thyroid cancer, as if I'd been invited to a train wreck and, though I knew it was risky, I couldn't help but climb onboard.

As a result of Emma's prodding I now knew the four types of thyroid cancer: anaplastic, follicular, medullary, and papillary. In the lottery of carcinomas, apparently I had gotten lucky: papillary cancer is eminently treatable, and patients usually have a normal life expectancy if diagnosis is made early. Emma's cousin, Keith, had told us that undiagnosed papillary cancer is often found during autopsies of patients who have died of unrelated ailments such as heart disease or stroke. Since this type of thyroid cancer has no symptoms, people can live their entire lives without being affected by it. Keith's med school stories were of some consolation, though I was still reserving enthusiasm.

Dr. Parson welcomed Emma and me to his office, then launched into a lecture about the basics of a thyroid. As I watched his pretty cherry lips move I wondered about this organ in my body that I'd never even been aware of before. Consider the thyroid, a flat little nob in the neck. My cancer was not related to cigarette smoke, not related to any known factors in my environment. So why had it betrayed me after all these years? Why me? Why now? *Et tu,* thyroid?

Dr. Parson cut off his lecture to take a pompous I'm-an-important-doctor call, and Emma leaned over to me and reviewed his lecture. "On a scale of one to ten? I'd give him three wormy apples. Thyroid for Preschoolers," she whispered. "Do you like this guy?"

"I find him humorless," I answered, "but is comedy really a prerequisite for a suitable surgeon? I mean, do I want a successful surgery, or someone who can kill at Caroline's on a Saturday night."

"Point well taken," she said as Dr. Parson returned to us.

"So let's talk about the treatment," he said. "We recommend a total thyroidectomy. After the surgery you'll follow up with an endocrinologist who will determine your daily dose of Synthroid. And then there'll be treatment with radioactive iodine. Let me explain how the thyroid responds to iodine—"

"We know all about the magic bullet," Emma interrupted. "How thyroid tissue sucks up iodine, so you give the patient a small pill containing radioactive iodine. Any remaining or metastasizing thyroid tissue absorbs the iodine and gets nuked in the process. I was concerned about damage to other organs from the radiation, but I've read that the procedure has proven relatively safe. Jane will need to stay out of public places for forty-eight hours while the radioiodine is working through her body since it could harm children and pregnant women. Oh, and I also read that she should suck lemons or tart candies to maintain salivation during that time."

Dr. Parson was staring at Emma as if she'd just voted him off *Celebrity Mole.* "I see you've done your research," he said, turning to me. "Any other questions?"

"Actually, we have a list," Emma said. "How many times have you done the surgery before, and what's your success rate?"

Dr. Parson frowned. "I've done the procedure many times, and I've never lost a patient on a thyroidectomy."

Emma nodded. "We'll want a second opinion. Who would you say is the grand master of thyroid surgery in New York City?"

"There's no such person." Dr. Parson was clearly annoyed with Emma and her list of questions. "It's a simple procedure. No controversy here, but you can get your second opinion. Just don't delay too long. In fact, you might want to book a date with my receptionist. I do surgeries on Thursday mornings at Murray Hill Hospital."

As we were dismissed, Dr. Parson tried to soften the blow with a warm smile and words of encouragement about the longevity of patients with my disease. Emma smiled back, but I could see the truth in her eyes. Dr. Parson had not made the team.

Working off a list of participating providers from my insurance company, Emma and I called upon three ENT docs. I was disappointed that there wasn't a single female doctor on the list, but Emma scolded that I must leave sexism out of this and search for a skilled surgeon.

A week later, I realized we'd met our match when Dr. Ken Scotto walked into the exam room and welcomed Emma's list of questions. He wanted to examine me, but I held up my hands to ward him off. "Don't even think about plunging one of those probes up my nostril," I told him.

Dr. Scotto smiled. "You don't enjoy our distinctive brand of torture?" he teased as he pressed his fingers to my thyroid. "Yep, there it is."

As Emma handed him the pathology report from the biopsy, I studied his long, somewhat calloused fingers. A friend had told us that Dr. Scotto had "beautiful hands," which I realized was not literal; the fact that he had removed a neck tumor the size of a grapefruit and left barely any scar put him high on the list.

"What about the vocal cords?" I asked him. "Do you think they'll be damaged?"

He shook his head. "You might be a little hoarse for a few days after the operation, but nothing permanent."

I cocked my head, reassured by the pressure of Dr. Scotto's hands on my neck. He wore a wedding band on his left hand, but a girl could fantasize. "So I'll still have a chance to sing on Broadway?" I teased.

He smiled. "I can't promise that."

Emma and I exchanged a look. "Quick, call Julliard," I said.

She nodded. "They'll need a new understudy for *Wicked.*"

"Cancel my road tour, and we can kiss that lucrative voiceover work good-bye."

Dr. Scotto grinned as he flipped through my chart. "It shouldn't harm your writing career. You'll just need a little time off. A week at least, probably two, until you're able to sing in the shower."

We booked Dr. Scotto for the middle of January.

11

By the time Ricki arrived for her Christmas visit I was ready to take some time off, seize the moment, and squeeze out every glittering charm New York had to offer in my limited lifetime. Even if thyroid cancer didn't send me to that "great writer's workshop in the sky," I was going to go eventually, from a heart attack or a car accident or some flukey event like a hair dryer falling in the toilet or a bolt of lightning or a paper cut that swelled into an infection of monstrous proportions. I wrote about these things every day; how was it that I'd imagined I'd maintain my humanity without a human exit from this world? Just self-absorbed, I guess.

Her brief tenure in the south had made Ricki nurturing and mellow at a time when I didn't mind being nurtured just a little. Together we soaked up the Christmas experience like two wide-eyed tourists in the Sugar Plum Fairy's Land of Sweets. She dragged me onto the ice at Rockefeller Center, and we laughed every time I went down.

"So much for my triple Sow-Cow," I said.

Ricki skated up to me and smacked ice shavings off my jeans. "I think you sowed when you should have cowed." After skating we sipped expensive wine at Morrell's, then sprang for tickets to the Christmas show at Radio City Music Hall, complete with Santa's 3-D Sleigh Ride and the Rockettes dancing their chorus line dressed as wooden soldiers.

By day we posed for photos at Macy's Santaland, sat for make-overs at Sak's, scarfed up candles and candies and ornaments at Bloomingdale's Christmas department, and lined up our shop-ping bags under our table as we sipped high tea in the lobby of the Plaza. At night we donned the dresses we'd scored that day and carried ourselves regally down the aisle of Broadway theaters. In one week we saw *Wonderful Town, The Producers, Wicked* and *Hair-spray.* "Only feel-good musicals," Ricki insisted, contending that I'd experienced enough catharsis for the year. She kept me on a positive track, looking forward with hope and laughter.

Only once had we cried together about my diagnosis—the time I called her to spill my fears. I'd felt bad about dumping the news on Ricki over the phone, but not having much choice I had called her one night and closed my eyes against the tension in my chest. While the cartoon kids of *Peanuts* explored the mean-ing of Christmas on my TV, I told Ricki we needed to talk about something awful.

"That ENT I saw?" My voice sounded small, childlike, but I was unable to pull the volume up with my usual bravado. "He did a test. He says I have thyroid cancer."

"What?" Ricki sucked in air. "Janey? Oh, no. I can't believe it."

"It's true," I said, relieved to have the most hideous words out. "I need surgery after Christmas. And the prognosis is good. Just scary."

"I just, just can't believe you've been going through this." Her voice wavered. "What can I do? Are you okay? Are you in pain?"

"No pain at all. No symptoms. Don't you worry, honey. I'm going to knock this thing on its ass."

"Oh, Janey . . ." Her voice was fraught with that familiar catch, the flicker of pain that I'd come to recognize over the years when girls in the third grade were making fun of her, when she'd skinned her knee in the park, when a teenage boy had lied to talk her into having sex, when our father had fallen to the table with chest pain and never recovered. It was my job to keep that sound from Ricki's voice, my job to protect her. A sudden memory hit, a green spring day that had burst upon us after a stretch of cold, gray winter. We were kids—maybe seven and ten—and in our rush to get to the park before dark we had grabbed our roller blades and left padding and helmets behind. I remember digging into the pavement, shooting ahead with intoxicating speed, laughing and horsing around with my little sister while our mother sat on a bench reading. Ricki knocked me on my butt and in retaliation I whipped her around, sending her rolling away, off-balance. She went straight down, landing on her bare knees, shrieking in pain over her bloody, scraped knees. Mom closed her book and assessed the damage with a frown. "Nothing broken?" she asked, pinching Ricki's legs gently through her fierce wails. Still sobbing, Ricki shook her head frantically, her cheeks stained with sooty tears, her pain evident.

I knelt beside her and slid my arms around her waist and held her tight. "It's okay," I told her. "I know it hurts, but it's going to be okay," I soothed, pressing her face into my shoulder. Her chin trembled against me, and I held her tighter to absorb it all. Not so much the pain of the scrape, but the alarm, the sense of losing control, of the world spinning beneath you without an anchor to hold you down.

She sobbed, then hugged me back, allowing me to sooth her. As we followed Mom back to the apartment to clean up Ricki's cuts, I remember wondering why our mother hadn't known that Ricki needed someone to kneel down and hold her. Weren't parents supposed to know those things instinctively—the precise laundry list of what their children required? It seemed odd that she was unable to mother us in the classic sense, but I didn't question her love, which poured through in other ways with a roomful of flowers on our birthdays, trips to museums around the country, autographed copies of treasured books like *A Wrinkle in Time*. Alice Conner cared for her children in the way she thought appropriate, but her aloofness left a gap that I walked right into with open arms, becoming Ricki's champion, nurturer, and caretaker.

The slightest sound on the line jolted me back, reminding me that my sister was crying on the phone.

"Nothing to be upset about," I'd said as panic rose within me and bombarded my thoughts like legions of angry bees. If something happened to me, who would take care of Ricki? Who? Who would be her family? I had to stay strong, for her, but my body was revolting, my throat thick, my eyes burning with quickly pooling tears. "It'll be okay," I said hoarsely.

"Oh, Janey, I'm sorry!" she sniffed. "I'm such a baby. Here you've got this scary news and I'm blubbering over the phone, but that's only because I care about you. You're my big sister and I've always relied on you and . . . and now it's my turn to step up and fend for you. I'm not going to let anything happen to you. Do you hear me?"

I squeezed my eyes shut and let the hot tears roll down to my chin, knowing that there was nothing Ricki could do, but also knowing that I needed to hear her pretend she could save me. "God, I wish you were here," I said, wanting to lean into her, to sink against her slender shoulders and hide there for awhile. I sniffed. "This is bad phone news, I know, but it couldn't wait anymore."

"Don't apologize. You should have told me sooner," she said. "Do you want me to come up? I could get a flight out of Raleigh-Durham."

"You can't leave now," I said, the practical side of me emerging. "It's your big season. I'll hold out till you get here for Christmas. But you have to come this year. This thing, this cancer may not be fatal, but it's made me realize that we're not here forever. We've got to seize the moment, make things count."

"Oh, God . . ." There was another catch in Ricki's voice. "I know you're right. You are so right, Janey, and I wish Nate could see that. Sometimes I feel like time is spinning by and I'm just keeping my hands busy weaving snowflake potholders. I know it's what I do, but there's more to life—juicier things that seem to be lingering beyond my reach while Nate is floundering at pulling his life together."

"It will come together," I told her. "I see lots of juicy things in your future."

"Right now it's your future we have to secure, Janey. I feel a little selfish, but I don't know what I'd do if anything ever happened to you."

I took a deep breath, brought back to reality at the image of my sister the former girl scout weaving a potholder. "We're going to take care of each other," I said firmly. "It's what sisters do."

Ricki got to work decorating my apartment, stringing lights on the balcony and draping garland over each picture frame. As the season progressed, I thought less about dying and more about living in each moment. I tossed out my worn socks and lingerie, cleared out the sad soldier boots from the back of my closet, then sprawled on the floor to update the address book on my e-mail.

"What are you doing?" Ricki asked as she wired shiny gold and burgundy beads into a circular wreath of real spruce branches.

"Getting rid of some dead weight, old boyfriends." I deleted Carter with a quick click. Jeff and Darren and Austin met the same demise. "Ba-bye," I said in a goofy voice. "Ba-bye, now!"

Ricki laughed. "Breaking hearts at Christmastime?"

"No hearts were involved, believe me. And I'm through with having sex for the sheer fun of it. I'm going to find some meaning in life . . . if it kills me."

Ricki gasped. "Would you watch what you say?"

I closed the address book. "You've got to appreciate the humor in that. I'm going to live life to the fullest."

Ricki smirked. "You are one odd duck. But I'm glad you're taking this so well. And you know what else? I'm sort of glad Nate didn't come along on this trip. I thought I'd miss him, but it's fun with just the two of us."

"Ain't that the truth."

"Jane. You'd like him if you got to know him."

"Don't talk to me in that stern schoolmarm voice. I would like your boyfriend if he treated you right, but what the hell was he thinking, dragging you down to that cottage in the middle of nowhere?"

"I like living in the Outer Banks, and putting a few hundred miles between Nate and his ex-wife was the best thing that ever happened to us."

I looked up from my laptop. "Do you love him, Ricki?"

She took a deep breath. "I really do."

"But . . . ? There's a catch, right?"

"I'm not sure Nate is as into it as I am. I'm not sure he experiences anything in life with the same intensity I feel."

"Do any men?" I flopped back on the floor, trying to think of just one man who felt things intensely. Maybe it was the reason I was drawn to intellectual types; I hoped that there might be something potent brewing beneath the surface.

"I think Dad did," Ricki said. "The way he withdrew before a dig, preoccupied with working out the logistics and mystified by the possibilities. And then afterwards, 'the return to civilization,' as Mom called it. Dad was all sunburned and bearded and smelly. Mom used to tease him that he peeled off another layer on each dig."

"Like an onion," I added, smiling. "I can't believe you still remember that. You were only eighteen when he died."

"Practically grown up. Or at least I thought I was. Thought I knew everything, now, eight years later, I know less."

"Well, I'm pushing thirty and I know squat." I stretched my arms lazily toward the ceiling. "Oh, to be stupid and content. You always talk a good game. Are you happy?"

She smiled. "Most of the time. And when I'm not, I just work harder."

"Like Dad."

"Honest work soothes the soul," Ricki defended, twisting a piece of spruce into the ring.

"Tell me you turn life's lemons into lemonade and I will throw your wreath out the window."

"So I should take a cue from you? 'Lower your expectations and you'll never be disappointed.'"

"Did I say that?" I grinned. "I used to be fucking brilliant."

"Jaded."

"Realistic."

"Try cold," she said. "But you've changed. Welcome back to the human race, Jane."

I turned away to hide a smile. "I've gone soft," I mumbled as I stared at the lights of the little tree Ricki had set up and admitted to myself that soft wasn't always a bad thing. A soft pillow, a soft bed, soft skin. Soft could be okay in the right forum.

A soft heart? Maybe that was another word for compassion.

12

Tuesday morning, the day before Christmas Eve, I braved the morning cold and scattered snowflakes for a trip to the *Herald* Building. Although I was still on vacation, I'd received two urgent voice-mails from Marty, who said he didn't want to leave a message but wanted to talk in person. Since Ricki and I had ten o'clock facials scheduled at Elizabeth Arden, I decided to pop into the office and score a few bonus points with the boss.

The elevator doors opened to an unusually quiet floor. Ed wasn't gazing out the window by Piggy's tank. Instead, the tank was cordoned off by yellow tape—crime-scene tape—and Piggy's illustrious body floated sedately on the water's surface.

"Oh, no." I pressed my warm coffee cup to my cheek, then noticed the chalk outline on the counter beside the tank—a crime-scene-style outline of a fish.

Behind me, reporters for Crime Beat snickered behind their copy, the bastards. "Where's Ed?" I asked Carolyn Putzel.

She nodded toward Ed's cubicle where he was tucked in, his head hung low, his spirit broken.

"Ed, what happened?"

He peered at me through smudged spectacles. "I'm not really

sure. She hasn't been herself lately, but I thought it was temporary . . . a phase."

I shot a look at Piggy's body afloat in the tank, feathery fins sloshing on the surface. "Do you want me to take care of her?"

Ed sighed. "Would you? I haven't the stomach for it."

"No problem." I went over to the tank and ripped down the crime-scene tape. Someone snorted, and I turned to see Don Mancuso smirking. I held up the tape. "Lose something?"

"Where's your sense of humor?" he asked.

I gathered the tape in a ball, stuck it on his desk, and snatched up his half-empty coffee cup. "Where's your sense of compassion?" I answered as I swept Piggy up in her net and plopped her into Don's latte. I glared at Carolyn and Don. "I'm going to the ladies' room to send Piggy off to a watery grave. When I get back, that chalk outline is going to be gone, right?"

Carolyn pushed out of her chair and snatched two tissues. "I told you it was too much," she razzed Don.

I was already marching toward the ladies' room, keeping my hand steady to avoid the slosh of fishy latte.

"You were a good fish, Piggy," I said before I flushed. As I imagined the fish slipping down the pipes and into underground waterways the size of the Lincoln Tunnel, I felt a pang of sorrow for Ed. Piggy had been his escape in the office, a source of contentment and consolation when the events he reported were chaotic and frightening. I couldn't replace Piggy, but I could salute her.

I checked my watch, wondering if I could push back my facial. . . .

"It's so good of you to come in, and during your vacation . . ." Marty said, pressing his hands together in a gesture of prayer. "Thank you, Jane." He walked around me, closed the door, then spoke in a lower tone. "What I didn't want to say on the phone is that Zachary Khan is dying. My friend in the art world tells me that it's quite serious."

"And I haven't revised his profile." I winced. "Sorry, Marty, but he's flat-out refused to see me. He's holed up in his studio loft and his partner fends everyone off. I talked to his partner, Tacitus, a few times, but I didn't get anywhere. The facts are up to date, but—"

"Zachary called here," Marty interrupted. "He's ready to give an interview, but time is of the essence. I can pass the profile on to Genevieve, but I wanted to give you a shot if—"

"I'll do it," I said without thinking. "I've always wanted to meet him." And I couldn't stand to give Genevieve the satisfaction.

"But tomorrow is Christmas Eve, and you're still on vacation," Marty protested.

"I'll see him today, if he'll let me. It won't take me long to write now that the background research is done."

Marty sat back and scratched his smooth head, looking relieved. "If you're sure you don't mind . . ."

"You really know how to play me." I smiled. "That passive-aggressive routine might not score points for you on the editorial board, but it's the only way to make me fall into line."

The hint of a smile tugged at his lips, his eyes glimmering as he handed me a pink message slip with the artist's number. "Do you think?" He looked boyish, like a wide-eyed kid considering batting strategies at his first Little League game. How old was Marty, anyway? I'd always thought of him as a bit of a curmudgeon, but was he actually that much older than I was? That Woody Allen demeanor could be deceiving. "I've been trying to be more assertive lately," he said, "but I've been told that my attempts are falling somewhere between whiny and bitchy. You should have seen me put my foot down when the copy department wanted to roll back our deadlines. The guys from sports e-mailed me a headline that said: BAKER SLAM-DUNKS DEAD-LINE."

I laughed as I headed for the door. "Sorry I missed that. You can't take a few days off around here without things changing."

"The world is always changing," he said, standing behind me. "Perpetual motion. Sometimes we're moving too fast to see it."

"Such a cosmic observation, Marty." I turned back to see him leaning against the doorframe, arms folded, sleeves of his charcoal shirt rolled up. How could I have worked for the man for three years without realizing he was exactly my type: a sardonic, brilliant man who flexed his intellectual muscle instead of raising his voice? I swallowed hard, wishing he was still just a boss. "Hey, if I don't see you, merry Christmas."

"Enjoy," he called as I walked back to my desk, feeling like a school kid.

I made an appointment to visit Zachary Khan in his loft that afternoon. Before I left the office, there was one more thing, for Ed. I could imagine the pink-coated lady at Arden crisply yelling that I was late for my appointment, but I shut out the pressures of the day to focus on my profile.

PIGGY, 2001—December 23, 2003

A bright aquatic gem of the newsroom died suddenly today of unknown causes. The golden-finned scarlet fish of unknown species was raised from a guppy by reporter Ed Horn, who provided a home with an abundance of clean water, fish flakes, and wisdom. Over the years Piggy became the Zen-like center of the newsroom, an ethereal diversion, the sole source of quiet peace in a mosh pit of advice. Perhaps Piggy had one advantage over all other fish, for she was dearly loved. Her friends will miss her, but we send her on to distant waters with a fond farewell. Swim on, friend.

It was the most sentimental obituary I'd ever drafted. As I printed it out and dropped it onto Ed's desk, I knew I'd be mocked by my colleagues for weeks.

What the hell. If I wanted their approval, I'd bake them some Christmas cookies.

13

"I can't believe he's seeing you," Tacitus said sternly as he threw the elevator gate open and motioned for me to follow him down the hall to the maze of paintings hanging from chains on the ceiling of Zachary Khan's studio loft. "He's seeing no one, and suddenly he tells me to call the Angel of Death from the *Herald*. Well, before you try to trick me with that you-can-trust-me voice, let me say that I don't like you, and nothing you do is going to change that."

"I appreciate your honesty," I said.

"I don't understand it. This poor boy spent last week behind an oxygen mask, and now he opens the door to a walking, talking menagerie of bacteria?" He turned back to assess me. "A prayer to the power of the goddess Lysol."

"I'll try not to breathe while I'm in the same room with him."

"Better yet, put your hands up, sister," he said, taking a small bottle of hand-sanitizer from his pocket.

I held out my hands, he squirted, and I rubbed them together. The antiseptic stung my sinuses, but I doubted that Tacitus wanted to hear my complaint.

"Okay." He turned away and moved past the paintings, not

waiting for me to follow. "What are you, anyway? Some two-bit deathmonger looking for a list of everyone Zachary slept with?"

"I don't write for the Society section," I said, finding it hard to move past the enormous canvases that Tacitus seemed immune to—the layers of paint richly applied with a pallet knife; studies in crimson and magenta, russet, and gold. Once Zachary had attained financial success he had started to hold on to his works of art. Rumor was that his dealer was considering a lawsuit but feared the negative press that would follow someone suing an artist who was dying of AIDS.

"So what the hell do you write, then?" Tacitus bitched. "Fortune cookies?"

"Now there's a job I hadn't considered," I said thoughtfully, still engrossed in a series of colorful bursts in a field of indigo. "Zachary knows why I'm here. I'm doing a profile on him, and I'd rather do it with his cooperation."

"Listen, sister"—Tacitus spun round to face me—"If you've got a camera in that bag, you can turn your fanny around and hightail it out of here."

Meeting his fiery eyes, I cracked open my leather bag. "Just a notebook."

"Tacitus, are you harassing my guest?" came a voice from beyond the maze of paintings.

We stepped around an abstract gold sculpture of lightning bolts to an open area of the loft where bookshelves, a fireplace, and two overstuffed sofas formed what was once a cozy living space, now dominated by a hospital bed. Zachary Khan was a warm, mocha glow in a sea of white sheets. Despite his weight loss, he resembled the man I'd seen in photos—spiky black hair, wide, expressive mouth, and dark eyes in brown ridges that makeup artists would kill for.

"I'm glad to meet you." I stepped toward the bed, not sure of the etiquette of interviewing someone so sick—a first for me. "I'd shake your hand, but I don't want to give you cooties."

"Damn straight," Tacitus said, nodding toward the sofa. "Have a seat."

But the furniture seemed miles away. I moved into a rectangle of ivory sunlight by the wide windowsill. "Mind if I sit over here? So we can talk without shouting."

"Suit yourself," Tacitus said. As he checked the IV line, the catheter, the items on the bedside table, I began the interview with a few questions from my list—the perfunctory warm-up questions to get Zachary talking. He skipped over his childhood in Philadelphia, told me a few art school anecdotes, and then answered my questions about other living artists he admired.

"I could go on about politics in the art world for days, but anybody can tell you about that," Zachary said. "I don't want to waste time; don't have time to waste. Besides, I get the feeling you and I can connect on another level. Are you sure we haven't met before?"

"I would remember meeting you," I said. "But you're right . . . let's just talk."

"Okay." He closed his eyes. "I've been dreaming of tunnels with bright light streaming in. So trite, I know, but the light is quite enticing."

"Can you describe the light?"

"Shades of white: ivory, cream, golden white, cornflower silk."

"Can you two change the topic?" Tacitus interrupted. "None of that passing to the light. Nobody here is passing to the next world anytime soon."

"Oh, don't say that, T.T. I'm ready. I pray for a good death."

"Stop that. You're tired today, but tomorrow will be better." Tacitus tucked a blanket under Zachary's feet. "You've rallied before, babushka. Just relax for now. After Christmas we'll do Bermuda again. Rent those little mopeds. See the sun set over the hills."

"Not this time, T.T."

His eyes bright with tears, Tacitus squeezed Zachary's hand, then turned away and ducked behind the curtain, presumably off to weep.

My sense of decorum told me I should go, that I did not belong here; I was an intruder interrupting the last days and moments these men would spend together. But I remained in my spot on the low, wide windowsill, riveted to this moment, strongly connected to Zachary for some inexplicable reason. I felt less like an observer and more like a fixture of the room, like the elbow joint of the pipes that brought water to this floor: a necessity, an organic part of the whole, but not a big deal.

"He's afraid of death," Zachary said.

"So am I."

"Really?" Zachary bit into the word as if it were juicy forbidden fruit. "The Angel of Death lives in fear of the subject of her profession? If I had more energy I'd be genuinely amused. It brings to mind the image of a dog chasing its tail."

"Well, don't go spreading that around, palsy." I put my notepad on the sill and pulled my knees up to my chest. "I've got a reputation to uphold in this town."

"Too late. I'm going to spill all at my next cocktail party." He coughed, then swiped a folded tissue over his brow. "Oh, Christ, I think I've got a fever. This body . . . once it served me well, climbing ladders and scaffolds to paint walls and enormous canvases. I used to scale that pole in the corner, hold on with my feet and one hand while I painted with the other. But that body is long gone, and I find it difficult to stay connected to this limp shell I've become. It's not me anymore."

"Do you feel as if your body has betrayed you?"

"Not really. It's more like the body has completed its job and is ready to be transformed."

"Transformation?"

"To ashes," he said. "Dust. This time next year, if I'm lucky, I'll be enriching the soil around my mother's tulip bulbs."

"And what if you're unlucky?"

"That would be another torturous year in this body."

"So you believe in an afterlife?" I asked.

"Absolutely. I can't believe in a healthy, creative light just going out. The spark—that energy?—it must go somewhere. And I have a very healthy spirit. Inside my soul yearns to wander, but it's trapped in a body that can no longer walk, let alone ride a moped over the hills of Bermuda. The thought of that is exhausting, and I don't want to be tired anymore. I want to ride, I want to fly . . . and that is not going to happen in this body."

"Then you're not afraid?"

"I'm ready to morph. Just praying for a good death."

"A good death?" I thought of my own glimpse of death's door and felt a shudder. "That's a contradiction of terms."

"Is it?" Zachary smiled. "I'll get back to you on that one."

14

The next morning, at the dawn of Christmas Eve, I left the coffee brewing beside a note for Ricki telling her that I'd be back from the office by lunchtime. I hadn't planned to go in—any sane person would hammer out her work in bed and e-mail it to the office—but I had been composing and revising Zachary Khan's profile in my head all night, and I wanted to block out the noise of life from the comfort of my square, bland cubicle and focus on Zachary.

Through the night he had haunted me, though not in a creepy way; his intense, dark eyes had soldered our connection and his mission to escape the confines of his body tugged at my heart. I had prayed for his good death—imagine me, praying. To whom was I appealing? I wasn't exactly sure. God almighty, Baby Jesus, Mary the Virgin Mother, Tacitus's Goddess of Lysol—I sent Zachary's request up there for any deity with the power to make it happen.

On days like this the paper operated on a skeleton crew, and I was grateful for the quiet office. Logging onto the computer, I saw that a few of my file pieces had run over the weekend: Felix Kaspar, a figure skater known for his jumps, TV-actress Madlyn

Rhue, and John Dreves, a master crystal maker who had de-
signed the olive bowl for Steuben Glass. Were they at peace
when they died? Mr. Dreves had been ninety; was age a function
of accepting the end of this journey? All this time spent writing
obits and I now had more questions than answers.

I settled in quickly and started shaping Zachary's profile. As I
filled in anecdotes from his time in art school, I thought of Marty's
criticism of the old draft—that it could be the profile of any
artist dying of AIDS. I wanted to make Zachary come through; I
wanted readers to celebrate his beautiful soul. There was his
art—those compelling layers of color that had captured my interest. Could we run a color photo of a painting? The obit pages
rarely were treated to color ink; I'd have to rethink that one.

But color was a crucial element in Zachary's work. I pressed
my coffee cup to my cheek, thinking of how my mother had
fallen in love with color after two decades of white walls with my
father. Those ruby reds, sapphires, purples. "The gem-tones,"
she called them. The day my mother died, as I paced beside her
big hospital bed in the apartment, I realized how much the paint
had faded, the bold pigments succumbing to sun and time and
occasional scrubbing, their hues now chalky and garish. But the
morning sun cut a path through the floor-to-ceiling windows,
slicing through the stained-glass piece that hung there. A swatch
of color touched the white sheet over my mothers toes—red and
gold and purple and green.

"Look, Mom," I said, running a hand over the image. I went to
her and squeezed her hand. "You're getting colored sheets."

Her eyes opened, strained and distant, but she peered down
at the colors. Talking was nearly impossible over the respirator,
but she squeezed my hand. Such a small gesture, but I was glad
for the acknowledgment, relieved to know that she'd seen the
colors that made her happy before she died.

I was approaching the end of a relatively inspired draft when I
sensed movement on the floor.

"Jane? What are you doing here?" Marty asked, stopping at my
cubicle.

"Right back at ya, boss." My fingers were still flying over the keyboard as I glanced up and soaked in the healthy pink of his complexion set off by a burgundy shirt and a ridiculous dancing-Santa necktie. There's something so appealing about a man who makes an attempt to dress well but desperately needs a woman's assistance. I pulled back my fingers before they plucked out total gibberish and wondered if I could really have a crush on Marty.

The boss man. Martin Baker, editor in chief. I'd never let myself get involved with a coworker before, but then, this seemed to be the appropriate time in my life to start breaking some of my own damned rules.

"I didn't expect you in today," Marty said, taking the seat that I usually rested my feet on. "For God's sake, Bob Cratchit, it's Christmas Eve."

"I wanted to get this done today. I had a great interview with Zachary Khan yesterday and I wanted to write it up while it was fresh in my mind."

"Excellent." He put a folder on my desk. "I was just going to put these in your in-box. Some of your recent pieces."

I flipped through the profiles, relieved to find them clean. No edits. No giant "SEE ME" written in the margins.

"You've done some fine work lately. I like the new dimension in Antoinette Lucas's profile, and the rewrite of the violin prodigy gave me goosebumps. How did you put it? 'The child's performance brims over with insight, and yet she has not had a chance to experience life beyond her schoolbooks, hotel rooms, and rehearsal halls.' You really captured something there."

I nodded. "Good. So I'm back on track?"

"Absolutely. I don't know how you managed to respond to my criticisms, but you have quickly evolved as a writer. You found humanity. You make the reader care about your subject."

"Well, finally! What's a girl got to do to make a reader care."

Marty smiled, his green eyes alight with something I couldn't read. "What did I tell you, kid? Compassion."

I swear, at that moment Marty was the most attractive man on the planet, bald head, ridiculous tie and all. Smart, intellectual, low-key Marty. He positively glowed amid this pedestrian office of oversized desks and overused PCs. I wanted him naked now, in the copy room, but somehow I sensed that proposition would scare him off before we'd had a chance to forge a real relationship.

A real relationship. I had evolved.

From outside came the chime of a church bell, and it summoned the image of a funeral in my mind. Zachary's funeral. Zachary's ashes nurturing a bed of luscious tulips in bold reds, crisp yellows, regal purples.

"Are you still interested in becoming our next restaurant critic?" Marty asked, pulling me from my thoughts.

I scratched my head, realizing that it would be hard to make a move now. I wanted to learn more about people, meet more of my subjects. I had a major surgery coming up, which wouldn't make this the best time for a career shift. I wanted a chance to use the tools Marty had revealed to me. "I don't know that crème brûlée would hold my interest now," I admitted. "That is, don't know if it's interesting enough to write about. Definitely interesting enough to eat."

"I was just about to pack up and head out," he said, glancing up at the wall clock. "Can I coerce you into a cup of Christmas cheer? I know a friendly little place down the block that serves a great egg-free eggnog."

"Sounds great. I've never understood how raw eggs could be part of an American tradition. Isn't that salmonella feed?"

He nodded, helping me with my coat. I liked the way he touched my shoulder: firmly but gently.

"Remind me to tell you about the Christmas party that almost took out our entire editorial department one year," he said. "After that, I switched to the pasteurized variety."

As we walked together to the elevator I grinned, hoping the light in his eyes was for me. It had to be, right?

I had my answer when the elevator doors closed on the two of us, and Marty leaned forward and touched my shoulder again. "Merry Christmas, Jane," he whispered. His face hovered near mine but he held back, polite, restrained.

I leaned closer, longing to kiss him, wishing he'd kiss me. "Are you holding back for the security cameras? Afraid of a workplace harassment suit? Or just reluctant to give security a show?" I waved to the camera in the corner. "Hey, guys! José, how's the little one?"

Marty let out a laugh and the mood vanished, but I wasn't going to let my opportunity escape. I linked my arm through his, surprised by the smoothness of his overcoat and the solid feel of his biceps.

He drew in a breath, then placed his hand over mine, firmly, intently. It was a start. And who knew what would happen after a glass or two of eggnog? After all, it was Christmas Eve.

Signs and Symbols

December, 2004

Ricki

15

"Away in a manger, no crib for a bed, the little Lord Jesus lay down his sweet head . . ." I sang along with my friends as we strolled down one of the more charming streets in town. A crisp wind blew in from the ocean side, but we weren't going in that direction, especially since most of the oceanfront homes were empty this time of year. By the time December's jetstream brought Arctic air dipping down over North Carolina, most vacationers had long abandoned us, leaving Nag's Head to the locals: a spicy mix of homegrown residents, expatriots, transplants, and retirees.

A light breeze feathered the fringe of my scarf. No, we weren't expecting even a single flake of snow, but I felt Christmasy nonetheless, surrounded by friends spreading holiday cheer in a tradition that predated Charles Dickens and Samuel Clemens through a quaint coastal town strung with electric lights.

"Sing it, ladies. Sing it like ya mean it," Cracker teased in an exaggerated southern twang. Hailing from Atlanta, Georgia, Cracker wore his southern charms like a boater in the Easter Parade. He was thin and tall, unabashedly sarcastic and catty, and was rarely seen wearing anything but casually worn jeans and loose cotton shirts. When someone asked him if he minded being bald, he replied: "I like to think of it as taking a hiatus from hair." A former chef, Cracker had come to this island for a summer job, which turned into a year-round hobby—a typical scenario for the castaways here on OBX, the Outer Banks. Cracker was in a committed, long-distance relationship, which left him free to play Will to my Grace.

Our group paused in front of the police station, which was decked with a wreath blinking in red and white. My assistant, Adena, and I had installed the wreath earlier that day, and I was glad to see that someone in the station house had remembered to plug in the lights.

As we sang, two officers emerged without jackets, acknowledging us with stiff smiles.

Beside me, Cracker waved. "There's something about a man in a uniform," he told me under his breath. "That's what I want under my tree this year."

"Oh, right," I said. "I'll just tie one up with a cranberry bow."

"Love the image," Cracker growled in his crocodile voice. "Be generous, and I'll let you keep the short one with the mustache."

"Thanks, but I don't think either of us will be at a loss for pretty packages under our trees." Cracker had Serge Montoyez, an accountant who was still a few years away from retirement and could only afford to spend summers and holidays here at the beach, and I had Nate, who was tied up at a business dinner tonight. Although it annoyed me that he was missing this, I knew he'd be waiting for me at home when the caroling ended. Maybe he would have a fire lit and amber sherry sparkling in the little cordial glass. Yes, Nate was every girl's Christmas dream . . . but my stray thoughts were pulling me way off key. I nudged Cracker with my elbow, then moved closer to Georgia, hoping to blend in with her sparkling voice.

Georgia Brooks swung her waist-length blond hair behind her to lean close to me. "See the blazing yule before us, fa-la-la-la-la . . ." she sang, holding a pretend microphone out to me. Georgia was one of those natural beauties—a true blond with slender legs and a Miss America smile, which she shared avidly. Sometimes a chatterbox at times, occasionally an astute people-watcher, always a pip, Georgia was good to have around.

We'd been caroling for an hour—my idea—and the whole time it was clear that Georgia was carrying us since she was the only one who both knew all the words and could almost carry a tune. Cracker and Ben knew two songs, Lola and her husband Tito knew the tunes but none of the words; and though I knew the lyrics to every Christmas carol ever penned, I had trouble staying on key.

"Merry Christmas!" we called to the cops when the song was finished.

"Have a good one," they called back. "Stay warm, now."

"Forget about warm . . . I'm feeling downright hot," Cracker muttered as he flapped the lapel of his jacket.

I smacked his shoulder and skipped ahead to a stop sign twined with glittery garland—another bit of trimming from my shop. This year when I'd offered to replace the town's weathered Christmas decorations, the mayor had been a tad skeptical at first. "I'm not quite sure we can afford you," he'd said, rubbing his creased forehead. Then I'd told him I planned to do the job free—my small way to give back to the community that had helped me build an embarrassingly successful business—and I think Mayor Treemore had begun to see me as more than some fast-talking entrepreneur from up north. "Where to next? Miller's One-Stop or back for hot cider and cookies?"

"Not Miller's," Georgia said, and Lola agreed emphatically. Probably because they both worked at the small general store on Highway 12.

"Please, let us sojourn to Ricki's place," Cracker said dramatically.

"I wouldn't mind going back to the senior center," Tito said. "It was nice and warm there."

"All these years and you can't take the cold," Lola teased her husband, wagging a nail studded with a rhinestone at him. Tito Hammond had moved to North Carolina from Hawaii after a visit to his grandmother had led him to meet Lola. "He didn't have a shape like the Pillsbury Dough Boy back then," Lola often teased him now, but it was clear that there was still magic between the two of them. Lola's family is from these parts—Lumbee Indians. She's in her forties and, a mother herself, Lola often feels compelled to mother me, but with her wild red-tinted hair, exotic nails, and New Age pursuits, she is nothing like my own mother, God rest Alice's poetic New York soul.

The senior center had been our first stop; it was also part of my usual rounds on Wednesday nights when I dropped off fruit punch and leftover cookies from Bitsy's Bakery. One of the seniors had invited me there to teach crafts last year during the slow January season, and the weekly session had become habit partly because Mr. Winslow reminded me of my Dad, who'd died before his time, and I found it reassuring to hear him talk about air and water currents, high and low tide, and birds indigenous to the North Carolina coastline. Mr. and Mrs. Tafuri, Jasper Hendricks, and Dinah and Sara Ellery were used to seeing me, but their faces had lit up when the rest of the crew filed in tonight.

"Let's go back and sing for the seniors," Tito said.

"They did seem to appreciate us," Ben added.

"That's because half the people are tone-deaf," Cracker said. "And the other half are just plain hard of hearing."

"Why don't we head back to the shop and warm up?" I suggested. By the shop, I meant The Christmas Elf, the boutique I'd opened up two years ago, after Nate and I had landed in this salty wilderness. "We can go back to the senior center next week."

"Next week?" Cracker moaned. "You mean we have to do this again?"

"Oh, listen to you, Cracker," Lola said, dismissing him with a wave of her spangled mitten. "You seemed to enjoy doling out the punch to the ladies at the center."

"Can I help it if Mrs. Tafuri reminds me of my dear old granny?" Cracker dug his hands in the pocket of his suede jacket and trudged on into the wind.

Lagging behind a bit, I watched their outlines as they traipsed beneath the glimmering lights of a landscaper's shop, the cape-style roof framing them against a purple sky overlaid by fast-moving black lace clouds. Cool but no precipitation, that was my forecast, though it never got too cold here. Temperatures stayed moderate—though for the locals anything below seventy was considered downright chilly.

Here in the Outer Banks, the sky sometimes reaches out and grabs you. Like the October dawn when I woke up on the deck bathed in orange light, the sky awash with fiery red and the amber striations of aurora borealis reflected in the calm ocean. Or the time Nate and I saw a waterspout out on the bay hurl gray plumes into the massive ceiling of clouds like an angry fire hose. Nate ran downstairs to call the police, but I stayed out on the balcony to watch, somehow confident that I was a spectator of this event and not a potential victim. We'd fought over that one; I called Nate a chicken, he called me a nut job. Come to think of it, that waterspout had stirred up a good amount of trouble between us.

That time it was my friend Lola who smoothed things over, telling me that Geminis like Nate could be difficult to live with. "You know," she told me then, "Gemini is the sign of the twins—often two sides of one personality. Some people think it's positive and negative polarity at the same time." Talk about torn. She had reminded me that, while Geminis could be witty, logical, and spontaneous, they also tended to be nervous, restless, and superficial at times. That was Nate: she couldn't have described him better if she'd hired a copywriter from the Lands' End catalogue.

Lately Nate had tended more toward edgy and restless. When I told Lola I thought it was the stress of his pending divorce, she agreed. "The ex-wife is trying to trap him," she'd said sagely, "but she has no idea how elusive a Gemini can be. The metal of Gemini is quicksilver; it's shapeless. Try to hold it and it flows through your fingers."

The image of a silvery Nate dripping through Gina's manicured hands made me smile. As I strolled, collar up against the wind, I wondered if quicksilver burned.

Yes, Gina was a bitch, which you might expect me, the other woman to say. Fortunately, Gina was hundreds of miles away now, and I had friends who would defend me against her to the end. As Lola's tinkling version of "Silent Night" drifted back, I lifted my face to the velvet sky and counted my blessings. Despite my holiday state of mind, I wasn't naive enough to think that good things could be earned. I was damned lucky to have found a man I wanted to get home to and a calling that brought me satisfaction and exponential profits. Taking inventory, I had to admit, life was good.

I gasped as a flare shot through a distant corner of the sky—a glimmering burst of light.

Ahead of me, a few friends reacted with "oohs" and "aahs."

"A shooting star!" Tito exclaimed.

"Did you see that?" I pressed a hand to my heart, reeling from adrenaline. "We have to make a wish! Everyone, quick!"

"A wish?" Cracker scoffed. "Damn, Ricki, you're more superstitious than my ninety-year-old granny."

"Don't knock it," Georgia said. "If there's a tiny chance that it'll work, I say go for it."

"Right." I clenched my hands and eyes and searched for my heart's desire. My life was fine, really, but Nate could use a little help. He'd been so moody lately, impatient, sometimes uncooperative. Like scheduling this business dinner on the same night that I'd organized the caroling party, then telling me that he didn't think it was appropriate for a grown man to attend such an event.

"Wait a minute," I'd said. "Is that one of those new age affirmations, like 'real men don't eat quiche'?"

"It's just not a guy thing, okay?"

"But Cracker and Ben will be there."

Nate had snickered at that. "I rest my case."

"No, the case is not closed. This isn't an isolated incident, Nate. I sense that you're pulling away. Is something wrong? I mean, besides crazy Gina and the divorce and all that."

"Nothing is wrong," he'd said testily. "At least, nothing that won't be solved once this mediation is over. I told you, I'm trying hard to make the divorce final by Christmas. Now would you stop taking things so personally and accept the fact that we can have different interests in life?"

Which had made sense at the time. It made all the more sense when Nate moved close behind me and slipped a hand under my sweater. Nothing could drive a point home like a hard, swift passion.

I really did love him. So I made a wish for Nate to find himself. If he could weather this rough patch he was going through, things between us would be better than ever. With all the wild sizzle of that careening star I sent my wish up for Nate. I wished so hard that I fell off the curb, my ankle twisting inside my new hiking boots.

"That must be some wish," Ben said, steadying me as I pitched toward the pavement.

"No doubt thinking about Mr. High Maintenance," Cracker growled, shaking his head. "Tell me you didn't waste your wish on him, Ricki. All the stars in the heavens couldn't set that man on track." He has never liked Nate, and although Nate never complained I sensed that he didn't appreciate Cracker's sensibilities: his rawhide-dry wit, buttery warmth, and inner strength tougher than year-old beef jerky.

"Thanks." I squeezed the sleeve of Ben's denim jacket, trying to maintain equilibrium. Strong, quiet Ben to the rescue. Maybe he would help me change the subject. "So Ben, what do you know about stars? You used to be a scientist, right? Was that shooting star really a giant sun that was burning out, or what?"

Ben grinned. "You mean, similar to the way I burned out in my career?" Rumor had it that Ben had left a successful career behind to open his surf shop here in the Outer Banks, but this was the first time he'd ever come close to mentioning it. I blinked, afraid I might miss this revelation from the enigmatic Ben. We'd all speculated about his age and his background. With a thick head of silver hair, olive skin that tanned beautifully but didn't seem to crease, and a musical frame of reference that spanned from the Rolling Stones to Good Charlotte, Ben was ageless—a man out of time. "And actually, I was an engineer, though I can pick out a few constellations." He pointed up toward the sky. "See over there, sort of above the line of the tower on the firehouse? That's the North Star. That brings you to the line of the Big Dipper." He drew a short diagonal line with his finger.

I followed the line of stars, slightly awed. "You know, people have charted stars for me a million times but I always forget how it works. How did you learn to do it?"

"Boy Scouts."

"Speaking of the Big Dipper," Cracker interrupted us, "where is Nate tonight?"

"He had a business dinner," I said, trying not to sound defensive.

"Oh, of course," Cracker said. "Wednesday night at the Rodanthe Rotary. That's so bogus."

Was it me, or was Cracker bringing the mood down, taking shots at my boyfriend? "You know, Cracker, I give up on you and Nate. You're probably better off keeping your distance, but if you got to know him I think you'd understand him. You might even like him."

"When a pig flies."

I wanted to go over and wrap his scarf around his face until he became a muffler mummy. At least that would shut him up. I think Ben sensed the tension between us; he kept talking, which is not Ben's style at all. Usually, Ben is the strong, silent type, as intrusive as an end table.

"Actually, the Big Dipper is not a constellation," Ben went on, and I realized he had spoken more tonight than he ever had in the past year. Maybe he was trying to cheer Cracker up, too. "It's part of Ursa Major, which means "Great Bear." But it is a popular star group, probably because it's so easy to spot. You know, in Southern France they call the Big Dipper 'the Saucepan.' In Great Britain it's a 'Plough.' And for runaway slaves, it used to be a symbol of freedom because it led them north as they traveled by night. Did you ever hear that spiritual about 'following the Drinking Gourd'?"

"That's right," I said, my thoughts still floating among the stars. "A symbol of freedom. Hard to believe that there's something we share with people around the world, people throughout the ages. The same stars. Isn't it amazing?"

"I find it more amazing that you can hang a wish on the death of a star," Cracker muttered.

"Call it superstition, but I definitely felt something when that star shot across the sky. I mean, in the entire universe there's this huge action, this enormous thing that just happened, and I can't believe that anything about it was an accident. It's got to be a sign. A sign of good things to come."

"Says *you,*" Cracker said.

"Would you lighten up, Professor Poopypants? Don't you ever look for the signposts along the way? Indications that you're on the right track?"

Cracker shook his head. "Sweetpea, I've been derailed for some time now. When you're speeding down the highway to hell, you don't stop to admire the view."

"She's got a point there, Cracker." Ben squinted at him. "Unless you buy the theory of a totally random universe, you've got to heed the signs along the way."

I have always been fascinated by signs and symbols. "You know," I said "when I was a kid I came across this chart in a children's almanac. Three or four pages of symbols and signs. I was familiar with some of them, like a skull and crossbones for poison, and a little school house with an 'X' for a school crossing. And then there was the universal symbol for 'no'—the old red circle with a slash through it. No smoking! No pets! No diving! But others were foreign and strange to me."

That was back in the days when my life had seemed normal, when I had a mother and a father like the other kids at school, two parents who left my sister and me alone to fight and wrestle and make up and pass a flashlight from top to bottom bunk for reading under the blankets at night. That was how I'd discovered the symbols. I was probably just seven or eight at the time, my sister eleven or so, and she'd tossed the book onto a stack on the floor as if it were useless. "A bunch of crap," Jane had called it, grabbing my attention by using a word that was forbidden in our house.

I'd picked up the book and it had opened before me like panels to a hidden passage.

"I remember scanning the chart," I told the guys, "running my fingers over the rows of symbols and their meanings, so clearly spelled out. And I thought, *here it is, right before me*. Here's what everything means. As if those pages of symbols could explain it all—the secrets of the universe revealed."

Cracker sighed. "Honeylamb, I wish it were that easy."

"No, you don't," Ben spoke up, and Cracker and I turned toward him in surprise. "That's like wishing for light without darkness, or yin without yang. Without the quest for symbolic meaning, the final outcome would lack significance. Part of the enlightenment comes through the journey."

For the second time that evening, Ben surprised me. Apparently there was a beautiful mind lurking beneath that surfer-dude facade. More insight into the man who'd abandoned civilization to mire himself in sand and surfboard wax.

"Something gives me the feeling I am in way over my head." Cracker squinted at Ben. "That's pretty heavy stuff for a expatriot engineer. Who died and made you Obi-Wan Kenobi?"

Ben just gave a stiff smile. "No animals were harmed in the making of this expatriot."

Cracker and I laughed, and I slung an arm around his shoulders, glad that the tension between us had broken. "Can you show me some more constellations, Ben?" I asked.

As we walked, our shoes scuffing over sandy pavement, I thought of how one symbol led to another. The constellations had been named by ancient Greeks, and Greek mythology had its counterparts in Roman legend. In college, my humanities major had opened the door to vast matrixes of symbols and their multifaceted meanings as professors demonstrated how nearly every cult and religion possessed the same archetypes. Most people recognized that Venus was the Roman embodiment of Aphrodite. But to learn that Venus also symbolized the planet Venus, which ruled those born under the astrological signs of Libra and Taurus, and represented the angel Ariel, or possibly Mary Magdalene's womb . . . to learn that it was associated to the colors pink and green, to the stones rose quartz and pink tourmaline, which symbolized romantic love and friendship . . .

As my friends jumped over the candy-cane striped curb of our parking lot, I smiled at the vision of my shop, its cedar shakes and gingerbread trim lit up like a gingerbread house. Maybe it was my fascination with symbols that drew me to this unusual occupation: proprietor of The Christmas Elf. There were so many symbols for Christmas: stars and bells, mangers, candy canes, gingerbread men, fat red bows and pine cones dusted with silvery snow, mistletoe and holly, poinsettias, evergreen trees topped by white angels. My shop offered an abundance of decorations, samplers, and knickknacks bearing those symbols, along with a few more modern items like holiday CDs and watches and clocks that chimed carols on the hour.

The shop happened by accident, really. I'd followed Nathan Graham, the love of my life down here to . . . well, to be with him. Just as I was getting out of grad school at Brown, Nate had decided to try his fortunes as a realtor here in this predominantly summer community. At that time he'd been separated from Gina for about a year and believed that the move would give him the space he needed. I couldn't agree more, having been the "other woman" for awhile, putting up with Gina and Nate's kids living just a few blocks away in Providence. Somehow, packing the car and a U-Haul trailer and rolling south on I-95, I had realized that the trip was the beginning of a bonding adventure for Nate and me.

The Outer Banks would be our place. Our home.

Since Nate had his spot at Munchin Realty, he'd already secured a basic one-bedroom cottage a block off the beach in Nag's Head. While he lined up summer rentals, I kept busy unpacking and decorating the place, which required a few coats of paint, borders, and numerous trips to Pottery Barn, Pier One and local beach shops for accessories. For a while I was in my element: turning a drab, poorly insulated shack into a cozy four-star bungalow with built-in hot tub and Japanese garden. But once our cottage became worthy of a spread in *Better Homes and Gardens,* boredom set in.

I remember those early spring days, pressing through the wind as I walked miles along the beach, impatient for summer to come, longing for fulfillment of my career aspirations. There I was, a Master of Fine Arts, marooned on a deserted island among a community of sweet-talking, slow-moving people who eyed me as if I were a cute alien. In truth, I was a fish out of water. This long, narrow barrier reef island is dotted by ethereal lighthouses and isolated from the mainland by its very nature. The only access is by a bridge to the north or a ferry system to the south, boats traveling between Cedar Island, Ocracoake, and Hatteras. If you want to get anywhere you have to travel for miles on Highway 12, which takes you through every town as well as stretches of preserved wetlands like Pea Island, a strip of tall grasses and dunes where lumps of fog sit on the road even on the sunniest days. We're far from the mainland, yet loaded up with satellite TV and hot tubs, with plenty of stores and shops and a Brew Thru, where you can drive right in and stock up on liquor without even stepping out of your car. It's a land apart, and it took me awhile to adjust with my east-coast, Yankee priorities.

One afternoon I was nursing a beer at The Crusty Captain when Cracker leaned over the bar and told me one of his customers was interested in my work. People were friendly, but Cracker was the first person I'd really met in town, and I'd brought him a couple of Christmas ornaments I'd been crafting out of pine cones, ribbons, and glitter glue—just something to do to pass the time since the pine cones fell right in our back yard. "Her name's Ms. Raven, and she told me she'd buy a whole carton of your doodads for her gift shop down in Hatteras. But I told her you were just making them for your family."

I remember that moment well, my jaw dropping as my heart sparked. "She would give me money for these things?"

Cracker grinned a snaggletooth smile that, along with his growly voice, reminded me of a crocodile. "She offered ten dollars for a dozen, but I think we can get her up to fifteen or twenty."

And with a box of pine cones and a bartender's crooked grin, my business was born.

Right away, I expanded my repertoire, using hot-glue guns, Styrofoam balls, beads, sequins, and ribbons to fashion an array of ornaments, which Nate started selling from the reception area at Munchin Realty. Then, when Nate saw the summer tourists pull out wallets fat with disposable cash, he quickly found me a retail space of my own in this gray-shingled cottage, just across the parking lot from the strip of stores containing The Crusty Captain, Ben's Surf Shop, and Miller's One-Stop General Store—and The Christmas Elf was born.

"Great Gussy, Ricki! Hurry it up before your jingle bells freeze!" Cracker called from the porch of The Christmas Elf, where the rest of the carolers streamed inside.

Back in reality, I quickened my step to catch up. The shop had been kept open by my part-time assistant, Adena, a quiet student at Carteret Community College who now was ladling hot, spiced cider for Georgia and Lola. Ben and Tito were already settled in on the sofa, and Cracker stood cranking the cords on the Christmas cuckoo clocks, one of his daily rituals when he stopped into the shop.

Strains of Handel's "Hallelujah" chorus filled the cinnamon-spiced air as I slipped out of my winter gear and joined Adena. "How's it going?" I asked, slipping a red and green striped apron over my head.

"Great!" Adena smiled, her naturally rosy cheeks a good match for her disposition. She was pretty enough for a Rockwell portrait, if the artist wouldn't mind including the row of piercings that ran up her left ear. "A few customers from Devil's Kill dropped by, and we got a large phone order from Oregon. Oh, and someone wants the poinsettia quilt. I told her we'd hold it until Monday."

"Did you hear that?" I called to Georgia. "Sounds like your quilt will be sold."

"Woohoo!" Georgia beamed. "That'll be like found money."

Georgia had made it with some church friends in a quilting bee, and I'd agreed to sell some of their rich, warm works of art on consignment. "I'll be sorry to see it go."

"We've got another one almost ready for you," Georgia said, beaming. "It's covered with Christmas snow scenes."

"I can't wait to see it." I turned on my cell phone and saw that I had three calls from Nate. They must have come in while we were caroling. I hit the speed-dial and he picked up.

"Hey, hi!" I said. "We just got back from caroling and I saw that you called."

"I can't talk now," he said. "I'm having dinner with Chet."

"Oh. Were you calling about something important?" I asked.

"Just killing time. I'll see you later."

"Okay, bye." I tried to sound cheerful as I clicked off, but nobody likes to hear that she's a time-killer. I would have to give Nate a little talk, but for now I tucked the stress away and smiled over the shop, which was brimming with pink faces, fragrant spices, and lively chatter.

I took a sip of warm cider, then went to my craft table to turn on the hot-glue gun. I'd been working on snow clouds, a berry garland, and glittering Christmas stars—decorations for the Christmas pageant at the elementary school, an annual event in Nag's Head. I figured now would be a good time to finish so that Adena could deliver them in the morning.

"You finished with that scenery yet?" Cracker asked, lifting his cup of cider as he leaned against a bookshelf near my table.

"Just about. I need to glue a few more ornaments to the garland and add some laminate to the star. Wouldn't want glitter falling in the shepherds' faces."

"Mm-hmm." He narrowed his eyes. "You and Nate going to be attending the pageant this year?"

"I wouldn't miss it," I told him. "I don't know if Nate will be free, though."

"Mm-hmm."

I felt his gaze heavy on me. "What? What's that about?"

"It's just that Nate seems to be absent a lot lately," Cracker said. "If he doesn't watch it, the man might miss Christmas completely."

"Now that would be a shame," I laughed, but there was some truth to Cracker's words. I'd sensed that Nate was withdrawing from me, but in fact, he was holding back from the entire community, our family here. What the hell was going on with him?

Surveying my friends in the shop, I realized I'd had a good run in my almost three years here. Cracker's bar was right next door, and when he wasn't manning the bar he was often hanging out here, adjusting the clocks and critiquing my projects. Georgia and Lola stopped in every day between their shifts and breaks at the grocery, and now that it was his slow season, Ben had recently taken to bringing me coffee each morning, then reading his *Washington Post* in the rocking chair, beside my gas fireplace strung with garland and Christmas stockings, until noon when he suited up and caught some waves.

Having grown up in New York and been educated in Providence, I had been a little put off by the slow pace here. Everything from the mail to the traffic seemed to move three notches slower than in the rest of the world, which could be maddening when you come from the land of fast food and speeding trains. But over time I'd grown accustomed to the laid-back atmosphere here: the slow smiles, the friendly conversation with the kid pumping gasoline, the elderly ladies who graciously counted out their pennies, the strangers who insisted on holding doors for me, the friends who stopped into the shop just to say hello and chat.

I'd found a home here, but I wasn't so sure that Nate felt the same way.

What was going on with him, anyway? He kept promising the divorce would be final by Christmas, but he'd been so moody and distant lately. Part of his funk had to be because Gina had been stalling for so long. I felt that pain, too. We'd all been waiting for that stubborn woman to cave so that Nate and I could get married and think about starting a family. Nate had been out of Gina's house and living in another state for more than two years now; you'd think the woman would let go. But every time Nate and Gina seemed close to reaching a settlement, Gina would throw another wrench in the works. Like sending the lawyers photos of Nate and me together in a restaurant. Or demanding the right to move to England or Borneo with Nate's two kids. The woman was impossible! Granted, there are two sides to every story, but if I had been married to Gina, I'm certain I would have locked her in a closet by now.

Cracker picked up a small ornament that had tumbled from my table and handed it to me. "Sometimes I get the feeling that Nate isn't happy living here."

"That's not true," I said quickly, automatically. "It was Nate who initiated this move, Nate who accepted the job with Munchin Realty. Of course he likes it here. He's just under some pressure right now."

"Mm-hmm." Cracker nodded. "Like a pressure cooker. Only, if you don't let the steam out, you know what happens? Those things explode."

Dipping my paint brush in sealer, I tried to block out unpleasant thoughts and soak in the dulcet tones of Perry Como's Christmas album, the laughter and conversation, the warm atmosphere of friends and sparkling lights and smiling Santas. Dabbing the brush over the giant, glittering Christmas star, I thought of the wish I'd made earlier.

Oh, Nate, please pull yourself together.

We had so much to look forward to, if he could just put the past behind him and look ahead. Follow his star.

Finishing up the laminate, I lifted my brush and eyed the glittering piece of cardboard. A Christmas star could work wonders. If only Nate would look to the sky.

16

When I got home that night, Nate was asleep on the couch, the television blaring across the room, an empty wineglass on the end table. I switched off the TV, turned on the gas fireplace, and leaned over him to kiss his forehead.

His eyes opened, catching me as if I were an annoyance.

"Hey, sweetie," I said, straightening without kissing him. "Long day?"

He tossed up the blanket and sat up, as if I'd just blown a reveille. His light brown hair, mussed by sleep, shot straight up behind his head. I wanted to reach over and smooth it down for him, but he hated when I doted. "What time is it?" he asked.

"Just eight-thirty. The caroling went well. We totally rocked at the senior center. We're going again next week, if you want to come along."

Nate rubbed the back of his neck. "I don't think so. I've got a lot going on."

"All week?" I didn't mean to press him, but someone needed to pull him out of his self-absorption. "Can't you take one night out of your schedule next week and go caroling with me?"

"What's eating you? You're worse than a nagging wife!"

"I . . ." Oh, no, not the nasty wife comparison! When he said things like that I felt my ultimate goal of happily-ever-after zooming light-years beyond my grasp.

Frustrated, I raked my hair back and told myself to let it go. Keep quiet. *Remember the wish you made on that star, and let it work its magic on Nate.*

"It's nothing," I said with restraint. Then, I lost it. "Actually, it's just that . . . This is my busiest time of year, and still I manage to find time to go caroling and work on a few volunteer projects."

"The point being?"

When Nate snapped that way I just wanted to flick him, just to inflict a little pain, to humanize him and remind him that he isn't entitled to behave badly just because he has dark, seductive eyes and thick hair that calls out for feathering by female fingers.

To be totally honest, my first attraction to Nate was physical. When I spotted him across the room, looking so together in his dark slacks and sports jacket and necktie, I remember staring blatantly. Just staring in awe. It wasn't only his shiny brown hair and velvety dark eyes, the shadow of stubble that glazed his jawline or his tight, tightly wound body; Nathan Graham had a presence that was unmatched by anyone else in the room. A certain vibe that made it clear this man was not a student or a professor or a beleaguered administrator. Nathan Graham was a man who chased after anything he wanted.

And for a time, that thing was me. I sat abruptly in the navy velvet Queen Anne chair, reminding myself of that time. My surprise at being the chosen one. The thrill of the chase. The joy of surrender.

Yes, it had all started over Nate's good looks, but lately I'd been working hard not to succumb to the lure of the physical. I tried to pretend those dark eyes didn't tug at my emotions so that my voice wouldn't wobble when I popped the big question: "You haven't given me an answer about Christmas yet. Are you coming to New York with me? I have to let Jane know."

"Why? So she can set up that lumpy sofabed in her living room?"

"That's not fair," I said, hating the way he argued. "You only slept there once, and it's nice of Jane to put us up. But if you'd stop snapping and listen a minute, I've been wanting to tell you that I made a reservation. Three nights at the Waldorf-Astoria, just the two of us."

"That'll cost a fortune!"

"I can afford it. The Christmas Elf is doing really well, and we never really took a vacation this year, so I figured that—"

"You already made reservations?" He pressed his hands over his ears, as if it was too painful to absorb. "You made the decision for me, without even asking me?"

"Nate . . ." I know, I know, he just woke up and here I was sounding whiny, but I couldn't help myself. "Why can't you make a commitment here? I'm just asking for Christmas, not your eternal fealty." I would have to work on the fealty part in the new year. "Are we going to spend Christmas together or what?"

He pressed his hands over his eyes. "You know my life is in a total state of flux! The mediator keeps yanking my chain, and I've got papers to sign and maybe even a court appearance to make."

"On Christmas Day? I don't think many divorce mediators schedule court hearings on December twenty-fifth, Nate."

"Of course not," he sneered. "You're always so dramatic, Ricki."

"Am I?" I stood up and turned away before he could see the wimpy expression on my face. "Is it dramatic to want to know whether we're spending Christmas together?"

"Of course we are," he said. "What else would we do?"

"Well, we weren't together last year," I pointed out, thinking back to the Christmas I'd spent with my sister in New York. Jane had been going through a scary health crisis, and I'd actually been relieved that Nate wasn't around to get in the way and distract me from cheering her up. But he didn't have to know that. "Actually, Nate, we've never spent a Christmas together." I shot him a lethal look. "I just realized that. You've always been tied up with Gina and the kids."

"And there you go again, twisting things around until it's all about you. I never hid the fact that I had two kids from you, and

I thought you agreed that Christmas is for children? Granted, my kids are older, but they still need their dad."

Just cut my heart out, why don't you? I thought, hating the way he twisted my words. "Christmas is for children, Nate," I said quietly. "But that doesn't mean you have to act like a child."

"See what I mean? You always go for the drama."

I feigned interest in my snow-globe collection, sorely tempted to smash one against the wall, but since they had sentimental value I contented myself with shaking the globe of Manhattan till the wax snow swirled furiously. "I'm not sure whether it's drama or just stating the facts. The facts being that for almost four years, for the whole time I've known you, you've been on the verge of getting a divorce from Gina. I think I've been supportive, and I've pretty much tried to stay out of it, but here it is, years later, and . . ." My voice was hoarse, but I couldn't stop now. I slammed the snow globe onto the shelf, taking a dink out of the wood though the globe didn't crack. "Four years that we've been together and somehow, after all this time in which you've claimed to be so in love with me, you're still married to someone else."

"Oh, here we go. At last, we get to the real problem."

"And you call me dramatic?" I swung around to face him. "Be honest here, Nate. There's something grossly wrong with this picture."

He raked his hair back into place, his eyes dark and distant until he lifted his chin and connected with me. "Babe . . ."

I folded my arms, determined not to cave.

"You've been great," he said. "Nobody's denying that. And I know I'm totally stressing over everything, but the truth is, the divorce is going to be final soon. We're in mediation. Mediation! Do you know what that means? Gina can't put the brakes on anymore."

I'd heard this story a million times before, the old "Big Bad Gina" song that Nate played whenever he wanted Ricki to do the sympathy dance of seduction.

Well, not this time.

"You know," I said, "I'm beginning to wonder how much of

this is Gina and how much of this is you, Nate. Maybe you don't really want to be divorced." Was I saying this? Really saying it? I hadn't really allowed myself to think it until recently. But something Cracker said had hit me . . . about Nate not being happy here. Did Nate regret leaving his old life behind?

Nate shook his head. "You're talking crazy, girl."

I stood my ground. "Perhaps the possibilities of life after Gina frighten you. Have you ever considered that? Maybe holding on to your paper marriage is a way to ward off future commitments—things like marriage and kids . . ." *And happily ever after,* I wanted to add.

"Oh, to hell with that!" He shot off the couch and crossed, suddenly in my face. "Don't put words in my mouth, Ricki. Don't ever tell me what I want."

"Why not? Someone's got to tell you. Obviously, you're mired in indecision. Totally lost. A miserable man stuck in a miserable situation."

He rolled his eyes. "Oh, right! If it's so miserable, why are you still here, then? Nobody's got you chained to this cottage, you know."

Furious, I pushed him away and stormed into the bedroom, not sure whether to start packing a suitcase or to barrage him with pillows.

"I must have hit a nerve," he called from the doorway. "Right? You're not leaving because there's something you like here, is that it?"

"No!" I grabbed a square gold-tasseled pillow from the bed and flung it at him. "No!" I tossed up the quilted red star. "No! No! No!" Decorative green pillows bounced off his chest and shoulders.

Nate caught the last pillow and lowered his hands, eyeing me with a hint of satisfaction. "You sure?"

I sighed. "Damn you! Why are you such a workout, over and over again? You do this to me every time, Nate. You're so mushy about commitment and I hate that about you. Always sending out mixed signals so I have no idea what you want."

"Come on, Ricki." He moved closer. "You know what I want."

He pulled my sweater over my head, tossed it away, and ran his hands over my bare skin, working over my shoulders and back, around to cup my breasts.

I was a sucker for bare skin massage.

"This is what I want, and you know it," he said, squeezing hard, then kissing each nipple through the thin fabric of my bra.

I hated fighting with Nate, but somehow our arguments usually spilled over into incredibly passionate, practically primordial lovemaking sessions in which we both greedily staked our claims and arose victorious. As he pushed me back onto the quilted red comforter and pulled down my bra, I closed my eyes and enjoyed the sharp sensations that rushed through my lower body.

"I hate you," I whispered as I worked my fingers through his hair.

He yanked open my jeans and dipped a hand down into the moist folds there, making me toss my head against the covers and groan. I dug my fingers into the plush comforter. "I love you."

His eyes were dark as he smiled up at me. "Now who's sending out mixed messages?"

17

The next day as I leaned over the bed to kiss Nate good-bye, I was still worried about him. Great sex was, well, great, but our issues remained.

Fortunately, there was no time to mull over personal matters as today was December second, which meant that the Christmas season was in full swing and The Christmas Elf would be a wonderland of sugar-coated, tinsel-covered insanity until I closed the doors on December seventeenth.

As I unlocked the shop door, Lola waved at me from the window of Miller's, giving me the "big, wide" symbol for packages. I ran across the parking lot to pick up the delivery she'd signed for: three huge cartons, which Ben helped me lug over. He disappeared while I listened to the phone messages, lit up the place, and turned on some carols. I was on the phone with the woman who'd reserved the poinsettia quilt when he reappeared with two steaming cups of coffee.

"It is a gorgeous quilt and I have to admit we're going to miss it, but I'm sure you have the perfect home for it," I told Mrs. Papadopoulis. I mouthed a "thank you" to Ben, watching him settle in to read the newspaper by the fireplace before I turned away to set up the Styrofoam forms for some custom-ordered wreaths. The wreaths required handmade angels with heads made of large pearlized beads, halos of tiny gold beads, and skirts made of crystal beads, and as I strung them together and sang "Let it Snow!" along with Bette Midler, my spirits lifted. There is something therapeutic about being in this industry of renewal and good cheer. When the message is "Peace on earth, goodwill toward men," you can't nurse your own worries for too long.

By midmorning, the shop was bursting with people and activity. Nate had called twice to chat, but I was so busy I couldn't focus on his details about new listings and storm damage to local streets, especially when Bitsy arrived with the gingerbread slabs. "Sorry, honey, but I've got a major construction project here," I told Nate.

"What are you talking about?" He seemed impatient.

"A gingerbread house for the school pageant."

"Why don't you have Adena do it?" he asked. "It's what you pay her for, right?"

I glanced over at Adena, who was loading up boxes with merchandise and bubblewrap, trying to fill orders before the UPS driver swung by. Nate didn't seem to understand the volume of work we had as Christmas approached.

Besides that, a group of preschoolers from Tuckaway Day Care clustered on the rug, constructing Christmas gifts for their parents out of foam pieces and flat, glittering faux gems under the guidance of their teacher, Diane. The shop was really hopping at the moment.

"We're really busy," I told him. "I'll call you later." Sliding the phone into my pocket, I turned to Bitsy. "Let me help you unload," I said, following her out the door and to her van.

A few minutes later, we stood at my craft table, gloved and aproned and ready to frost and decorate the surrounding gingerbread. Ben had taken it upon himself to wait on the customers who'd stopped in, chatting them up and giving them personalized attention while Bitsy and I focused on architectural issues.

"I'm not sure this will hold up once we've got it put together,"

I said, gently lifting one of the slabs of gingerbread that Bitsy had baked in her industrial oven. "And even if we do, will the house survive a move to the school?"

"Good point." Bitsy whirled the electric beaters around the bowl of frosting one last time, then turned them off. "We may have to strike the mansion and subdivide."

I nodded. "A gingerbread community. Seems like the only way. But can we cut the panels?" I tested one slab of gingerbread with my fingertip. "Seems moist enough, but it seems a shame after all your hard work."

Bitsy was already cutting efficiently with a sharp knife. "That's the way the cookie crumbles," she said wryly. "Don't worry. If we need to cover up rough edges I've got plenty of extra frosting."

While she held two roof panels together, I caulked the seams with frosting. Then Bitsy moved on to assemble another house as I methodically applied "snowcapped" shingles to the roof. As I worked, I overheard the children fielding questions from their teacher.

"And who is going to visit your home on Christmas Eve?" Diane asked her group.

"Santa Claus!"

"And how does Santa get in?"

"Down the chimney!"

"But Miss Diane, my house doesn't have a chiminee."

"That's *chimney,* Joey. And I wouldn't worry about it. If you've been a good boy, Santa will find his way in."

"He wasn't that good," another kid said. "Not as good as me."

"Was so!" Joey protested. "I'm always good, but I told you. Santa can't come because there's no chiminee."

I lifted my head from the frosting bowl for a look at Joey. Was it possible he was telling the truth?

"Come on, now," Diane said, tousling the boy's sandy brown curls. "I know Santa visited you last year. Didn't you get a train set?"

Joey squinted at her. "That was my *old* house. It had a chimney."

"Finish up your work," Diane said. "And you can ask your

mom to bring you here on Saturday if you want to meet Santa in person."

I winced as I pressed down a row of gumdrops. "That reminds me, Adena," I called to her. "If the S-A-N-T-A suit doesn't come today, one of us will have to drive into Raleigh-Durham to pick it up tomorrow." I needed that thing by the weekend so that Nate could charm the local kids into a few more weeks of good behavior. When he'd suggested wearing the Santa suit last year, it had successfully lured families into the shop. Although I no longer needed to draw more business, the appearance of Santa had become one of the seasonal highlights of The Christmas Elf: "As much a part of Christmas as stockings and eggnog!" said the *Nag's Head Herald.*

"I'll be bringing my grandchildren," one of the women in Ben's group told me. She wore a white turtleneck with a glittering holly pin that I recognized from last year's inventory. "They thoroughly enjoyed last year."

"Will you serve eggnog again?" her friend asked, this one decked in a charming sweater embroidered with Santa's reindeer flying up the lapel. "My husband loved your recipe. He must have had three cups."

"Eggnog," I said aloud, more as a reminder to myself to pull together the details for this weekend's Shopfest. "Absolutely. It's funny, most people don't care for eggnog, but that recipe changes their mind."

"What's your secret, darlin'?" Holly Pin asked.

I smiled as I pushed back a strand of hair with one shoulder. "Vanilla ice cream. Got that recipe from my friend over at The Crusty Captain, only I leave out the rum so the kids can enjoy it."

Just then there were shouts from the kids. I turned to see what the commotion was about and managed to jab Bitsy's sleeve with a smear of icing.

"Sorry," I said, handing her a paper towel as Diane explained that it was okay, the kids could pick up the spilled container of beads together. Diane and Ben corralled the kids, and Adena answered the phone while I washed my hands so that I could take care of the ladies' purchases.

I waved and smiled at the kids as Diane had them recite a big "thank you." She led them to the door, then paused. "Joey, where is your coat?"

The boy held out his arms, where a light navy sweatshirt hung unzipped. "This *is* my coat."

Diane kneeled down to zip him up. "Honey, you've got to wear something heavier next time. It's windy out there."

"Wait," I called, rummaging through one of the bins. "Here. This might help." I unrolled an acrylic scarf, red background with a white snowflake. "Would you like to wear this, Joey?"

He put his hands on his hips. "Don't you have one with a snowman?"

"Joey . . ." Diane moaned, but I quickly searched through the bin.

"A blue snowman." I leaned down to wrap the scarf around the boy's neck, trying to cover his ears. "How's that?"

"Cushiony," he said. I smiled.

Diane touched my arm. "Ricki, I'm not sure you'll see that again."

"That's okay. Joey can keep it, as long as he promises to stay warm." I patted Joey's shoulder. "Just remember your coat next time, okay?"

Pleased with himself, Joey grinned then muttered, "Thank you, Ms. Wicki." Yes, he really said "Wicki," and I felt my heart melt like honey in hot tea.

"You're very welcome," I called as Diane led the group out the door in a big daisy chain of mittened hands.

"My goodness, everything does happen at once, doesn't it?" one of the women said.

"I love it that way," I admitted as I punched in the price for her wooden nativity scene. "People are part of the magic of Christmas."

The woman leaned over the counter and nodded knowingly. "People *are* the magic of Christmas. The people you love," she said. "Your family. I do hope you count your blessings."

"I do," I assured her, trying not to acknowledge the catch in my throat. My family. I hadn't much thought about it, but my friends here in Nag's Head had really become that. Aside from my sister, whom I thought of as my lovable evil twin at times, I had felt no real connection to the world until I'd come here. It was easy to be anonymous in New York, easy to be another bobbing face on campus, another student ID number on the lists of grades. But not here.

"We're not really related," Bitsy pointed out to the ladies. "But maybe that's why Ricki puts up with so much from us."

"It's true," Ben said. "I keep dreading the day Ricki tosses us all out the door so she can get some work done."

"That'll never happen," I teased. "I can't work without background noise." I handed the holly pin woman her change, and she reached across the counter and grasped my hand.

"I am serious, dear. It's rare to find such a family in this world."

Sincerity gleamed in her watery blue eyes, and I found myself covering her hand with mine, squeezing it gently, listening to the voice inside me that said: *Take a moment. Make the connection. Seize the day.*

As the ladies made their way out, calling their good-byes, I thought about the wonders of Christmas spirit. That was what kept this place running—the whirling, swirling pixies that warmed hearts with their cinnamon breath and merry carols. My little Christmas shop had acquired its own personality, something bigger and better than I'd ever envisioned. Go figure.

The shop was quiet that evening when Cracker stopped by to check in, crank the cuckoo clocks, and snag some free cider before he had to go next door and open up the Crusty Captain. When he saw the newly constructed gingerbread village, his jaw dropped.

"Sugar, I think you've outdone yourself this time. If that isn't the most charming little cookie town. Pure munchkin euphoria."

I smiled up from the bin of old decorations I was using to decorate the fragrant, fresh-cut spruce Ben had brought me late this afternoon, and I was rushing a little to add some homemade ornaments so it wouldn't look so bare. "The village was mostly Bitsy's creation," I said. "She showed me how to make these trees out of candy canes and Hershey's kisses. Clever, isn't it?"

"Smart 'n' tasty." Cracker inched his fingers toward the chocolate paved sidewalk, but I smacked his hand away.

"Don't touch. It's for the school pageant." I tossed him two kisses from a bowl on the counter.

Cracker caught them in one fist and smiled. "That's right. The pageant is tomorrow night, isn't it? I don't usually attend, but for this mouth-watering wonderland I just might make an appearance. Show some community support."

"That's the spirit," I said. "Nate and I will be there."

"Oh, dear." Cracker folded his arms. "Does that mean I should reconsider?"

"You don't have to sit with us. Nobody says you have to like Nate, though I'd love it if the two men in my life could just be civil."

"Talk to Mr. Nathan Graham about civility. I saw him at the Texaco this morning and I swear I had to work him over to get out a greeting. The man was glued to his cell phone, ignoring everyone in sight, pacing like a maniac, arguing like a she-devil. I do believe he would have driven off with the hose still in his gas tank if Hank hadn't come out to take command of the situation."

I winced. "Poor Nate."

"Poor Nate? Don't you have pity on the rest of us—the innocent bystanders who must tolerate his lack of civility?"

"Nate's feeling down about his divorce right now."

"Yes, but must he inflict his agitation on others?" Cracker asked. "I'm only telling you this because you love the man, Ricki. God knows you're not responsible for his behavior, but his lack of civility is off-putting at times."

"He's just in a bad place right now." I bit my lower lip, not sure how much to reveal to Cracker. He was a close friend, the kind of friend you could dump on, but it's hard to express your feelings when you're not entirely sure of them.

Cracker unwrapped a kiss and popped it into his mouth with a knowing, "Mm-hmm."

"What's that supposed to mean?"

"Oh, honey, you can tell old Cracker. Do you know how long I've been mending the world's problems from across the bar? I am the Dr. Phil of the lovelorn."

"Lovelorn?" I squinted at him. "Have you been reading historical romances again?"

"Tell Cracker. What's the problem?"

I stepped up on a stool to hang a clear glass icicle on a high branch. "It's not that big a deal. Just that he keeps picking arguments at home." I stepped down, sighing. "And me, fool that I am, I argue right back. And the weird thing is, we're not arguing about details of his divorce or custody of his kids or anything like that. We're arguing about Nate's attitude toward the divorce. His inability to push it through. That passive-aggressive bullshit."

Cracker rolled his eyes. "Nothing new about that."

"But somehow it's beginning to seem like a new problem, like my problem." I hung a glittering pine cone on the tree—one of the first ornaments I'd made before the shop had opened, and it made me feel a twinge of nostalgia for that sweeter, simpler time. "Sometimes I worry that he's losing interest. That the thrill is gone."

"I thought you two had a sizzle goin' in the fry pan."

"We do," I said, a little freaked that I was following his metaphors. "But it still doesn't mean he isn't straying. What if he's having an affair, Cracker?"

He pushed down an arm of the spruce to shoot me a look. "Who would fool around with him?"

"Well, I did, back in college," I admitted. "Don't you think Nate's attractive?"

"Good looks got nothing to do with it, sugarlamb. You fell for Nate because he was forbidden fruit. Another man's wife."

"Well, not quite. I mean, they were separated and getting a divorce and everything." That much was true. Had I thought Nate was truly involved with his wife, I would not have gone near him. Scout's honor. A home wrecker I am not, partly because of scruples, partly because I figure if a man is willing to be stolen away, then no woman will ever have a secure hold on his heart. "The legal matters weren't supposed to take so long, though. Whoever heard of a nice, friendly divorce that lasted four years?"

Four years. Had Nate and I really been together that long? Four years. When we'd met, his youngest daughter Molly had been a freckly nine-year-old, still playing with dolls and holding hands with her dad. Now she was a basketball player with a fierce hook shot, a shape that made boys gape, and a strong loathing for spending summers in the Outer Banks with her dad. Poor Nate. He tried to be a good father, but his ex-wife wasn't very supportive of his efforts, dishing the dirt to Molly and Kaitie whenever she had the chance. For my part, I tried to keep my distance from Gina; tried to give the girls space and time alone with their father. I did my best, though there was no getting around the fact that I was the intruder—the unwanted future "step." With these obstacles, it was amazing Nate and I had made it this long.

I thought of the first time we'd met, at a college job fair, how Nate had seemed more seasoned and laid-back than the eager rugby types at Brown who wanted to plumb more than my mind before we'd even shared a cup of coffee. After years of fending off requests for meaningless sex, I'd found it entirely refreshing when Nate had asked me out for a weekend afternoon, inviting me to accompany him to an exhibit of Fabergé eggs scheduled to leave Providence the following week.

An afternoon of art, tea, and stimulating conversation.

So began my first adult relationship, a connection based on mutual interests, social interaction, and (much later) great sex. At the time, Nate had been deeply involved in commercial real estate in Providence, so he knew most of the tony restaurants and cafés. He had been instrumental in finding space for the proprietors in Little Italy and Fox Point, and consequently had a standing reservation (and a discount, I think) at the city's hot spots. I'd been impressed by the way he had a finger on the pulse of Providence—a social reference so different from my student colleagues, whose expertise didn't reach beyond the list of pubs that had two-for-one drinks at happy hour—and by the fact that he knew the city so well, knew its rich history and its stately buildings.

Our first few outings were purely platonic. Nate took me on a walking tour of Providence's historic East Side, showing me the excellent examples of restored eighteenth-century mansions and homes. Another time we walked the "Mile of History," a concentration of original Colonial homes along Benefit Street, splendid sites of early Federal and nineteenth-century architecture. Nate seemed so at home in those neighborhoods that I drew a sort of psychological connection, envisioning him as the master of one of those fine city estates. In my mind, he was one of Providence's favorite sons, and I felt special to be strolling along the river with him, catching the ArTrolley on Gallery Night, or dining out in a Portuguese restaurant where the staff treated us like royalty. Nate seemed thrilled to be with me—he admitted that he had been lonely since he'd parted with his wife—and he acted as if I were the most amazing woman on the planet. He started naming things after me: a "Ricki smile," or a "Ricki look," or "that Ricki sigh." In Nate's world, I was the "It" girl, and honestly, I loved being the feminine center of his universe.

Not that such euphoria came without its price.

More than once I'd stumbled over Nate's baggage—his guilt over the emotional withdrawal of his two kids. There were Nate's financial woes, the prospect of losing his million-dollar home to Gina, the divorce lawyers' fees, the cost of financing two households.

But when you're falling in love, your sweetie's torturous troubles compel you to love him more, to defend him from his adversaries, to buoy him up from the depths of sorrow and buffet him against the winds. I couldn't fight Gina, but I could offer Nate half of my bed and a drawer in my bedroom dresser in my apartment, which was a million times better than the bachelor pad he'd signed the lease on. By the time I was starting my final year of grad school, Nate and I were a couple.

"Mm-hmm?" Cracker's suspicious hum brought me back to reality. "Do you think there's ever such a thing as a nice, neat divorce?"

I waggled a glittery pinecone at him. "They hadn't slept together in two years."

"Mm-hmm."

"Don't you believe that?"

"It doesn't matter what I believe, Ricki. Let's focus on the situation at hand, which is the fledging interest of your man. When is the last time you had sex?"

I gasped with mock exaggeration. "You want me to kiss and tell?"

He lifted his eyebrows. "Hello? I'm the one who knows about your marathon in that vacated beach house in Rodanthe. The horizontal tango for, what, two days was it?"

I laughed. "It would have been three if that agent hadn't shown up unexpectedly to scope out the place."

"Mm-hmm. But we digress. The point is, you're worrying about all the wrong things, sugar. You think his eye is straying, but let me remind you, we're talking about Mr. High Maintenance here. Mr. Loud-Talking, Cell Phone-walking, Highway-Passing, Sports Car-Revving . . ."

"Okay, okay," I said. "Stop holding back and tell me how you really feel."

"Oh, honey, don't get me started or I'll be hissing and tearing up your upholstery."

"Minus the claws and the hissy fit, please."

"That man is just preening for some extra coddling and attention. So why don't you head on home now? Adena is coming in soon, isn't that right?"

I checked the clock that had a different colored ornament on each number. The small hand was creeping toward the purple "six" ornament. "She'll be here in a half hour or so."

"So when she gets here, give yourself the night off. Light some candles so you can set the mood, feed him a nice warm meal and, you know . . . butter his beans."

"Ugh, dinner! My cupboard is bare. There just aren't enough hours in the day, you know?"

"I could send you home with some of my famous corn chowder," Cracker said. "But then, soup isn't enough of a meal for Mr. High Maintenance, is it?"

I sighed. "Now, see that? Prissy. And we were on such a nice track for a while."

"Prissy?" Cracker folded his arms. "I may be dramatic, occasionally catty, but never *prissy*. Now if we can keep this all dignified, I'll help you. But you can't make me like him."

"That's okay," I said. "Leave the liking to me. You just hang around and spout off great advice."

"My specialty. Is that a yes or a no on the soup?" Cracker asked. "Because Miller's has some nice-looking salad fixings that would go well with the chowder."

"Yes, please," I said, thinking that it would be a marvel if I could actually get out of here before six o'clock tonight. Leaving early during the busy season . . . It was absolutely decadent, but Cracker was right in his backhanded way. I'd been so focused on spreading Christmas cheer, I hadn't really been sharing myself with the person I loved most.

Well, that was about to change.

18

The worst thing about resolutions is that when you can't follow one through, you feel like a failure. That night when I got home, the cottage was dark. I kept calling Nate's cell but he didn't pick up until the soup was hot, the salad dressed.

"I'm home early!" I told him. "I've got dinner ready."

"You're kidding? I'm on my way to Avon." A good hour south of us. "I just assumed you'd be working late, so I decided to drive down to this site."

So my big evening fizzled into a big "Oh, well."

By the time Nate came in, I was asleep on the couch. I remember Dave Letterman saying: "I don't know what that means," and the audience roaring as I clicked the remote and stumbled through the living room. The bathroom floor was ice-cold, but I forced myself to brush my teeth and rinse my face, knowing the activity would be enough to wake me up just enough to ruin my sleep. I hate when that happens, but I was too tired to stay up, and Nate was already in bed, possibly asleep if the sound of his steady breathing was any gauge.

"You awake?" I asked softly.

"Mmm."

I turned off the light and slipped under the red plaid quilt. My side of the bed was cold, and I eased closer to Nate and nudged my chilly feet into the warm aura surrounding his body. It was a ritual of ours in winter, one of those patterns couples fall into when they've been together a while: I always prodded him with cold toes and he always withdrew, grousing, "Get those icy feet away from me, you witch."

Not wanting to wake him, I moved tentatively, trying to steal warmth.

To my surprise, he reached down and pulled my feet to him. "Come here, you." He tucked my feet between his thighs, folding them into furry warmth. Sweet heaven.

I sighed, loving the feeling, charmed by the implications.

It was more than a gesture, more than a small exception. I knew it was a sign that something had changed. He was opening himself to me, accepting me wholly—cold feet and all. Nate wanted to be my protector, my champion against the cold.

A sign? I could only hope that my wish was beginning to take hold.

"So how did your evening go?" Lola asked the next morning when she and Ben appeared with three coffees and the morning papers.

"It sort of *didn't,*" I said sheepishly, biding time as Ben slipped over to the rocking chair by the fire and settled into his usual spot to read. That was the problem with living on a small peninsula where everyone knew everyone else's business. When I'd stopped into Miller's to pick up a salad last night, I'd told Lola about my plans, and now it was good manners for her to follow up. "The next time I try to stage something with Nate, remind me to let him know in advance."

Perching on a stool by my worktable, Lola seemed to get the picture quickly. "Do you want to talk about it? And what's that you're working on?"

"An emergency costume for tonight's pageant. Turns out they're short one elf."

"It's so nice of you to do that for the school," Lola said. "And you don't even have a kid in the show."

"I enjoy it," I admitted as I traced a holly-leaf pattern onto green felt. "Though I'm stretched a little thin this year." With my work on the school pageant and decorating the town, I was falling behind on mail orders, but there was still time before I had to use rush shipping.

"So what did you end up doing last night?" Lola pressed.

As I gave her the nutshell version the door bells jingled and a carload of customers streamed in. "Merry Christmas!" I called, then lowered my voice for Lola. "By the time I reached him on his cell, it was too late. So he drove to Avon, and I sipped soup in front of the TV and watched *Rudolph the Red-Nosed Reindeer.*"

"Isn't that just the way things happen sometimes?" Lola said. "My kids love that movie. Corey always feels sorry for the elf who wants to be a dentist."

"So do I," Ben called from behind his paper. "It's no fun to be trapped in the wrong profession."

Sometimes I forgot Ben was there, like a loyal hound by the fire, until he added the occasional thoughtful remark.

Lola crossed her arms and tilted her head toward him. "Ben, it's a good thing you managed to get out of your mistake before it was too late," she teased. "A lot of people don't have the guts to make a major change in their lives."

"Is it guts or sheer idiocy?" Ben lowered his *Washington Post.* "That's a matter of some debate. Some of my old friends think I threw away the best part of my life. A solid job."

"Wow, do I hear my mother's voice!" Lola cupped a hand around one ear. "When I married Tito he was working in a pizza place, and my mother tried to stop the wedding. She kept asking me, 'Why would you want a man who doesn't have a solid job?' For Mama, it was all about job security."

I squeezed the scissors, cutting through the felt with satisfying precision. "I've always been lucky in that area. Since I minored in education, I knew I could teach. I just never needed to."

Ben folded the paper in his lap. "My job security is about fifty yards that way," he said, pointing toward the door. "The Atlantic never shuts down. Yeah, I've got a few boards to recondition now, but once the weather warms up, the people come, and they need boards and wet suits and surf shirts and sunglasses."

"You own the surf shop next door?" asked one of the customers, a thin man with wispy gray hair and gangly arms. When Ben nodded, the man introduced himself and mentioned that his nephew ran a shop down in Key West.

"Paul Gaber?" Ben smiled. "Pleasure to meet you. I used to rent sail kites from your son." While Paul Gaber's wife browsed, Paul and Ben settled into the chairs to chat by the fire.

Lola reached into her pocket for her tarot deck, her newest New Age preoccupation. Lola was a student of astrology and tarot, always seeking wisdom through the movements of the planets and the symbols in the cards. Although I'd studied the tarot deck years ago, I gave it up. The cards were too addictive back then, and sometimes I found their vivid symbols dark and intimidating. "Busy today?" Lola asked.

"Nonstop. I've got mail orders coming out my ear, plus all the foot traffic here," I said, realizing that I had another school group coming in and a busload of teachers from Raleigh, as well as the women from Georgia's quilting bee. "Then there's the school pageant tonight, and tomorrow is the first Saturday in December: my Shopfest. Which reminds me, can you put a few gallons of eggnog and vanilla ice cream on hold for me? I have to serve eggnog tomorrow."

"No problem." Lola fanned the cards over the table and shuffled. "When things settle down, you have to let me throw some cards for you. Looking at your chart, I see a crossroad coming up for you. A turning point. Any idea what that's about?"

"A crossroad? Does that mean choices?" I asked, intrigued and wary. "Hey, when did you do my chart and what else did you see? I mean, what's in my future?"

Lola smiled, gathering up her cards. "Listen to the song."

The carolers on the CD sang: "Oh, tidings of comfort and joy."

"Comfort and joy," Lola repeated. "The very thing you give, you shall receive."

"That's so sweet." I trimmed the holly leaf, pleased with the sharp points and curves. Lola's prediction was a lot better than I'd expected, but I wanted to hear more. "So what else is in my chart? Do you see Nate? Any kids down the road?"

She touched the puka shells at her neck. "Of course you'll have kids. Every woman needs her children."

Good news, I thought, though it wasn't clear whether Lola was thinking of my astrological chart or simply spouting off edicts of the world according to Lola. I wanted to ask her, but then the doorbell jingled again and a new group of customers appeared and I was lost in the act of juggling conversation, creativity, and commerce.

That afternoon I was juggling a shop full of customers—mostly my busload of teachers—while working through the list of e-mail orders when the door bells jingled and Georgia appeared, greeting all the shoppers as if they were family. Georgia is such a social creature; always so cheerful and silly. I secretly harbored plans to steal her away from Miller's in the next year, if The Christmas Elf could afford another full-timer.

"How's it going, honey?" Georgia called to me. "Your candy-cane curb has been lined with cars all day, so I know you've been busy. Brought you some hot chicken tenders. Martha's on the fryer today, and she always does them just right." She took out a cardboard box and waved it under my nose.

"Thanks." I dropped a Santa tablecloth into one of the mail packs and snatched the chicken from her hand. "What time is it? After three already? The day goes so fast when I'm busy. I promised Mrs. Joel I'd be over at the school by seven and . . . Thanks for the food, honey! If it weren't for you, I'd be fainting in the tinsel."

"My pleasure," Georgia said, pushing me back onto a stool. "Now you just take a break and I'll help you out here for awhile. What were you doing, filling orders? And I know how to run the register, too. Lord knows, I do it all day at Miller's."

"Just for a minute," I conceded, sitting and balling up a napkin. "Don't want to get chicken grease on any of the merchandise."

"Oh, I love this song!" Georgia said. "All I want for Christmas is you!" she sang as she sashayed up the step stool to reach an ornament from one of the top bins. "Hey, how are you?" she asked a couple browsing through the trees, except when Georgia spoke it came out: "Haryew?"

Confident that she had things under control, I moved to the computer chair and logged on. "Eighteen new orders?"

"Good for you!" Georgia said.

"That's just in the last ten minutes." I stared at the screen. "This is phenomenal! Fantastic. What am I saying?" I smacked my hands against my cheeks. "I'm going to be up all night."

"I'll help you," Georgia offered. "I can stop by after the pageant if you want. I'll even bring Daniel. Maybe the Christmas mood here will soften his old Grinchy heart a little." Daniel was Georgia's boyfriend, a good-looking artist who shared Nate's malady: Failure to Commit. The greater difference being that Daniel was home-grown; his parents owned hammock shops here in Nag's Head and in Avon, and, as Daniel liked to say, he was "easing" into the family business.

"And I'll give you a hand," Ben called from the CD section. "You know my business is slow. No problem closing up for a few days, and my surfers can reach me by cell if they need me."

"You've already helped me so much," I said, blinking as two more orders came in. "I really appreciate it. This is just . . . really exciting and a little scary."

A few minutes later Cracker appeared with three spools of packing tape. "I was over at the hardware store and thought you could use some extra," he said, "before people buy it up to send off their Christmas gifts."

I threw my arms wide in amazement. "I was just running out! You're an angel!"

"Honey, I'm no angel, but I'm happy to propagate the myth," Cracker said as he attacked a stack of brown boxes.

Just then the door bells jingled and as I looked up my pulse quickened. Nate. He didn't stop by here too often, but I was happy to see him amidst this seasonal insanity.

"Hey, honey!" I waved him over past the glittering trees and the bins of cranberry and pinecone garland to the small computer station. Once he saw me Nate plunged his hands into the pockets of his cashmere coat and averted his eyes, not a good sign. Little alarm bells rang in my head as he made his way through the crowded shop. Something was wrong. Nate was not happy.

"What happened? You look so sad."

He raked his hair back with one hand. "How soon can you get away from here? You need to get packed. We're hitting the road in the morning."

I squinted at him, trying to figure out what I'd missed. "Is there a hurricane coming? Why would we leave?"

"Providence," he said, as if it were obvious. "I've got to meet with the mediator Monday morning, and I figure I might as well spend Sunday with the girls. Molly has a basketball game Sunday night, and I told her I'd be there."

I picked up a decorative pen and pressed the faceted star into my palm. Nate had always been inconsiderate, but he wasn't usually so oblivious to my world. "Nate, I can't go to Providence now."

"Why not? Why wouldn't you want to go?"

"This shop!" I sputtered, a little too loudly.

I noticed the people around me suddenly turning away, trying to pretend they weren't eavesdropping, and Georgia started singing, "Star of wonder, star of light . . ." in her hoarse, off-key voice. But Nate didn't seem to care that we were making a scene. He just stuck me with that cold, dark stare, implying that I'd lost my mind.

"Come on, Ricki. You're the boss. Go over to that door and hang up the closed sign. Or put your assistant in charge for the weekend. That's why you hired her, isn't it?"

"Nate, she's a college student," I said, feeling defensive. "And she's part-time. And in case you've forgotten, tomorrow is the Shopfest, my biggest weekend of the year. People drive in from out of state for this weekend. You promised to play Santa again, remember? Honey, we just can't go this weekend." I checked my watch. "It's not five yet. You can still probably reach the mediator and reschedule for later in the week."

"No, I can't," he snapped.

I sat back in the chair, jarred by his anger. "Maybe we should talk about this in the back—"

"How would it look for me to postpone after I've pushed this thing along for the past year?" he said. "Do you want *Gina* to think I'm losing my resolve?"

That comment hit me in a vulnerable spot. "This is not about . . . her," I said, realizing that we were segueing into a full-scale argument in front of an audience. "It seems to me that since you're an equal party in this negotiation and you live out of state, the meeting can be set at a time that's convenient for you."

"Forget it. We're going."

"I'm sorry, but I can't." My face flushed hot with anger and embarrassment. I hated Nate for springing this on me, hated him more for playing it out in front of my friends and customers. My pulse thudded with a sickening intensity, hammering away at me with the same indifference I saw in Nate's eyes. He refused to accept the weight of my commitments here, my investment in this business, my emotional ties to this community. "Open your eyes, Nate. I've got a shop full of people here, a show tonight, a huge weekend planned, and I can't drop it all to be your buddy while you rush home to fight with Gina."

"Don't you see I'm doing this for you?" he asked indignantly.

I pressed the starry pen deeper into my palm, wishing its sharp facets were the only pain I felt. "Actually, I'm not getting that part, why I'm supposed to be thrilled about dropping everything for the horrendous drive up to Providence." I lowered my voice. "And after all this time, don't push your divorce on me, Nate. It's not about doing a big 'favor' for me; it should be about putting an end to a relationship that didn't work out for you."

"Semantics." He waved me off. "Fine."

I took a deep breath. "Okay, then. Do you want to meet me at the school or should I pick you up at home?"

He squinted at me, his face so puckered it lost its appeal. "You know what? Don't bother. I'll probably just start driving tonight."

He turned and, with a swirl of his glamourous coat, he was striding toward the door.

"Nate?" I stood up, calling after him. I wanted to push past the customers, run to him, take his hand and beg him not to go. *Please, just stay, honey. You can fly up on Sunday night. You can change the appointment. Would you try to be flexible, just this once, for me?*

But I didn't chase after him, didn't beg or grovel, didn't make another attempt to reason with him. Instead, I returned to the computer and gripped the edge of the table, trying to pretend that the information on the monitor held me in fascination while scattered thoughts raced through my mind like storm clouds. Nate was leaving. I had to get ready for the Christmas show. Nate blamed me for his unhappiness. Tomorrow was Shopfest and I had no Santa.

"Hey, honey." Georgia massaged my shoulders. "You okay?"

"On a scale of one to ten? I feel like a big fat zero." It was difficult to breathe. "I'm so embarrassed," I whispered.

"Why should you be? You didn't do anything wrong, and no one's holding you responsible for Nate's bad behavior."

Although I knew that was true, I couldn't shake the gloom that hung over me.

"If you need me tomorrow, I'd be happy to come. I bet Miller will give me the day off if I ask him."

"That'd be great," I said. "But can you play Santa?"

"I'm good, but not that good." Georgia folded her arms and shot a look around the store. "I'll bet we can find a tall, stout man who can fill that Santa suit. Uhm, Cracker? Stop hiding in the garland there."

Cracker peered out from behind a lavender Victorian tree. "Just who are you calling stout?"

"See?" Georgia gestured toward him grandly. "What did I tell you? A volunteer!"

Smoothing down his sweater, Cracker turned to the two women behind him. "Do you think red makes me look fat? I've always avoided plaids for that reason. Oh, God, I should have paid attention when Serge was on that South Beach Diet. Is it lots of fruit—or no fruit at all?"

"I'll be Santa," Ben said nonchalantly as he stretched packing tape around the seam of a box. "I've already got the hair and I'm a pretty good listener. Though I may need to borrow a few pillows to fill out the suit."

"Not to worry!" Cracker rubbed his hands together delightedly. "We'll stuff you full of Christmas goodies at the pageant tonight. My man Ben gets first dibs on a big slab of gingerbread."

"How about you, Cracker?" Georgia asked. "You're not off the hook."

"I can't play Santy Claus, but I make a mean batch of eggnog, which is a must for the Shopfest. I'll whomp up a big bowl of it and keep it coming all weekend," Cracker promised.

"Super!" Georgia beamed, reaching over to take a basket of ornaments from a woman waiting at the register. "I'll tell Miller I need the day off. We're going to have a great time tomorrow."

I blinked, intrigued and a little awed at the activities swirling around me. Did I just recruit a staff for tomorrow without saying a word? The prospect of seeing Ben in the Santa suit brought a smile to my face, despite my bad mood over Nate, damn him. He'd struck a blow to a vulnerable spot, but right now, with the customers and the pageant and a few customized wreaths to assemble, I didn't have the time or energy to plumb the pain.

Ignoring the dead air in my lungs, I went to the register beside Georgia to wait on the next customer. "Thanks, guys," I said, trying to keep my voice light. "You're really saving my skin."

"We'll get you through the weekend, honey," Cracker said. "What are friends for?"

19

"We are the children," the kids on stage sang, swaying in the red, green, and white felt aprons I'd stitched for them. "We are hope!"

Sitting beside Georgia, who gasped at every adorable sketch in the school Christmas pageant, I felt myself choking up over their song. Unlike the similar bit of sludge that Michael Jackson had slung out a hundred years ago, these lyrics tugged at my heartstrings, reminding me that children were the future of the world. Taking in their little pugged noses and toothless grins, I wanted to bask in their innocence and simplicity. I wanted to have a pure heart again, a heart unmuddled by vicious ex-wives and blustery boyfriends who abandon you when you need them most.

"Away in a manger, no crib for a bed," the children sang as the players in the nativity scene began to gather. A white-veiled Mary winced as Joseph took her hand. Together they followed two donkey-hooded children who danced under the sparkling silver and blue star I'd made.

"Aren't they the cutest?" Georgia nudged me. "I just love their little chirpy voices. Better than the choir at my church, and our choir is good. Professional quality. Hey, are you coming to church with me for Christmas?"

She'd been after me to visit her church for months, but the hellfire and brimstone reputation of southern churches had held me at bay. "We'll see."

"Oh, look! Here comes Isabel," Georgia said, turning to wave down the aisle to her niece, who was dressed as an angel.

Shepherds moved onto the stage, the trim on their purple and blue costumes sparkling under the stiff white lights. As the children tucked the baby-doll Jesus into the manger and sang "Silent Night," I mourned my own lost innocence.

When did my life become tainted? Of course, it didn't happen overnight, but somehow I'd become one of the women I'd always felt sorry for: an entrepreneur who chased her business voraciously while waiting on a man. And somehow, since my business capitalized on Christmas, my life seemed worse than the norm.

I was relieved when the principal took the stage to thank the little performers and to invite everyone to the school cafeteria for punch and goodies. Introspection can be a dangerous thing when your heart is in a tangle.

Inside the cafeteria, children were yipping and crowing over the gingerbread village. A few little girls jumped excitedly as they pointed to their favorite parts. Boys smacked their foreheads and raced around the table to check it out from every angle. Parents and teachers nodded with admiration.

"Nice work, partner," Bitsy said, clapping a hand on my shoulder. "They seem to like it."

"They love it!" Georgia gushed. "It's so magical, you almost hate to see it broken apart."

"Ah, but it's meant to be eaten," Bitsy said. "Can't hold onto beautiful things forever. Got to enjoy as you eat. Seize the moment, that's what I say."

That advice had been chasing me around lately, but somehow, without Nate, I didn't feel quite ready to seize. My moment was on hold, my happiness a pretty package dangling beyond my reach.

Not that it wasn't gratifying to see the kids tear into their gingerbread tiles. With help from a few parents, the village was divided and doled out in decorative squares to the children who had formed a line. I recognized some of the kids from Diane's preschool group, as well as their older siblings, parents, grandparents, friends, and neighbors. Mr. Winslow had hitched a ride with his neighbor, whose daughter was one of the angels, and he summoned me over to warn that a storm was blowing in.

"A whopping nor'easter!" he rasped, his hands splaying out to emphasize the enormity of it all.

"Not a hurricane?" I asked, studying the light in his eyes.

"Oh, no, no! This is a different storm system entirely. You have your winds blowing up from the northeast, pulling up the warm, moist air from the Gulf Stream."

I sat down on the folding chair beside him, knowing there was more. "Okay, and then what?"

"Well, as the northeasterly wind pulls the storm up the coast, it meets with cold, arctic air blowing down from Canada. When the two storm systems collide"—he smacked his hands together—"you've got a rainy mess."

I nodded, wondering if my father would have aged as gracefully as Mr. Winslow, settling into a community, keeping up with his hobbies. My father had just turned fifty-eight when he died quickly of pancreatic cancer. Honestly, I didn't miss him all the time, not until certain "Dad" qualities turned up in people around me, people like Mr. Winslow. "So what's your prediction on this?" I asked. "I've got loads of people driving in from the mainland tomorrow."

"Mmm. Could be dicey. Wind is already kicking up out there, but it may be that the precipitation holds until tomorrow night."

"I close at seven tomorrow," I told him. "Could you stave off the rain till, maybe, six-thirtyish?"

He winked, his furred brows arching. "I'll do what I can."

As the party began to wind down, my energy began to sag along with the "Merry Christmas!" banners. "I'd better get going," I told Georgia.

"And what are you rushing home to?" she asked. "Listen honey, why don't you come on home with me? We'll hang. Grab some dinner. Drink some wine while we watch old videos."

"I appreciate the offer, but I need to get some sleep for tomorrow. Plus we're supposed to put up our tree this weekend. Which reminds me . . ." I winced, peering through the glass wall of the lobby to the wavering trees in the parking lot. "That wind looks nasty, and our tree is leaning against the wall out back. What do you think the odds are that Nate brought it inside before he left town?"

"If he's anything like my Daniel I'd say you'd better find yourself a new tree. But you shouldn't be decorating your tree all alone this weekend. You shouldn't be alone at all, Ricki. Come on over to my place."

"No." I touched her shoulder. "You're being so sweet about helping out tomorrow and I really appreciate it. But really, I just want to get home and crash."

Reluctantly, Georgia helped me into my coat. "Now you drive safe, okay?"

I smiled, thinking back to how that had thrown me when I'd gotten here—constant reminders to get home safely. The questions brought on when someone caught you frowning. The veracity of people inquiring after your thoughts. It was all so downright . . . personable.

At the door I came across Diane, looking every inch the concerned preschool teacher as she held onto Joey's shoulders. "I don't think it's safe for you to walk home, Lila," she told a girl who had the same wide brown eyes and sandy-colored hair.

Although the girl couldn't be more than ten or eleven, she took Joey's hand with authority. "My mom says we have to walk—there's no one to pick us up tonight."

Diane leaned down so she could be eye-to-eye with the girl. "I realize that, sweetheart, but I'm sure your mom didn't count on this storm kicking up. How about if we find you a ride?"

"I'm heading out now," I said. "I'd be happy to drop you somewhere."

Lila raised her shoulders defensively.

"It's okay. I know her," Joey said, smiling up at me. "She's Wicki."

"I know her, too. Ricki Conner, this is Lila Salem," Diane introduced us, then confided that she'd drive the kids herself, but she was late for a doctor's appointment.

"I'm happy to give them a ride," I said, "if it's okay with Lila."

The girl shrugged, peering at me curiously through her bangs. "Whatever."

Outside in the parking lot, I looked at my little VW convertible and turned to the kids. "I don't have a car seat," I said aloud, thinking of the machinations my married friends up north went through whenever they needed to load kids into a car. "How old are you, Joey? And what's the rule here? I didn't even think of that."

"It's okay," Lila said, folding the passenger seat up while Joey slid into the back. "He doesn't use one."

"Oh, you're a big guy, huh?" I teased as I got into the car. In the mirror I saw that Joey was smiling, but Lila looked pained as she reached for the seatbelt. A less well-mannered child would carp: "Just drive, lady!" but Lila sat back in the seat and steamed quietly behind her bangs while Joey observed how the wind was bending the trees and rolling a metal trash can right across the parking lot.

At least one of the kids in my car didn't hate me.

I switched off my CD of Christmas carols for fear they'd annoy Lila, then followed her directions south on the Croatan Highway. With one major highway cutting a swath through the center of this narrow strip of land, the Outer Banks is easy to navigate, though sometimes a little creepy after nightfall. Lila directed me to the south end of Nag's Head and had me turn right onto a dirt road that seemed way too narrow for a car. My headlights washed over a graveyard of junked cars, their rusted chassis scattered in odd clusters, as if their busted headlights were eyes and the grills mouths that could whisper messages to each other as their frames sunk into the mud. Did I say creepy? I couldn't imagine these kids walking down this lane, even in the best of weather.

Quickly I twisted my focus back to the road, but not before my car hit a rut.

Joey laughed at the huge bounce of the VW. I gritted my teeth and slowed down, trying to find the lights of a house on the horizon.

But the landscape was bare of any real structures as the dirt road in the beam of my headlights gave way to sand and muck and tall swamp grasses that danced wildly in the wind.

"Which way?" I asked, pressing on the brakes gently.

"This is fine," Lila said, unbuckling her seatbelt. "We're just over there. Come on, Joey."

"Over there" turned out to be a narrow path through the tall grasses. I could barely make out the rusted frame of a portable trailer—the kind that popped up once you parked. What could be inside? A sleeping compartment? Certainly not a bathroom or kitchen, and even if there were such accommodations, there were no water or electric hookups back here.

"Are you sure you'll be okay?" I asked, trying not to sound judgmental but worried that this was not a safe place to leave two children.

"I said come on!" Lila reached over and unbuckled Joey's seatbelt, then reached forward to collapse the front seat. "Thanks, Ms. Ricki. Move it, buzz."

Wind whistled into the car as she pushed the door open and melted into the evening. Joey leaned between the two front seats and patted his new scarf in the light above the mirror. "Bye," he said reluctantly, then followed his sister out into the dark.

I sat there tamping down disturbing questions as the children disappeared among the tall grasses. Had they always lived this way? How did they eat and bathe? What did their parents do for work? Did they even *have* parents?

Mostly, I felt that someone should be intervening here—that someone being government agencies—and I could not fathom why that was not happening.

Eventually, realizing that Lila and Joey were not going to emerge from the swamp grass, I put my sand-pelted car back in gear and rolled out of there. I pulled onto the Croatan Highway and headed north, longing for reassuring signs of civilization. The Dairy Queen. The Multiplex. The children who would be exiting the elementary school shielded from the wind under Dad's coat or holding hands with Grandma.

But the school was now deserted and dark, of course. Anyone with a lick of sanity would be taking cover from this storm at home. Mr. Winslow was right about his nor'easter. This monster was roaring into town with a fury.

The traffic light above my car blinked red as I looked to my right, wondering if the DQ was still open for a quick bite. Something teased the space at the edge of my headlights—a rope wavering in the wind. The garland I'd strung around the street sign had come loose and now it was slicing through the air.

Again, that feeling that *somebody* should fix this, and in the rushing storm and flying sand I didn't want that somebody to be me . . . but there were no other cars on the road and it was my decoration, my responsibility. I threw the car into park, shielding my eyes from the sand as I stepped out of the car. My hair flipped around my face, blown straight up, plastered back and pulled to the side as I hurried to the sign and chased the dancing garland. I managed to catch it before it whipped me in the face, but the plastic tie-back was nowhere in sight.

Cowering in the wind, I gripped the garland and wondered if it all came down to this—this cheap tangle of plastic tinsel. *This* was the great demonstration of my work? *This* was my contribution to the community? *This* was the sum and measure of my life?

I yanked the string hard, once, twice, finally ripping it off the signpost. Tossing it on the seat beside me, I drove home locked in resolve to take two Tylenol P.M.s, change into my jams, and sip chicken soup till I passed out.

That plan changed as I stepped into the cottage and discovered the electricity was out. I fumbled my way to the fuse box and flipped switches to no avail.

So I was alone in a dark, isolated cottage—the stuff of a suspense novel. I fumbled to the door and stumbled over something heavy—the empty tree stand. Where was our tree? I hadn't noticed it leaning against the garage on the way in.

Back outside, I circled the house. Not a trace. How far could the wind blow that thing?

I found it down on the beach, lolling in the surf, ruined.

For the first time in my life, I didn't want to believe in symbols and signs.

20

"So you've had a rough night, sugar," Cracker said as he buffed the wooden surface of the bar with a soft rag.

"I've had better." I had told him about Lila and Joey's dilapidated home, the power outage, and my runaway Christmas tree, figuring that was enough bad news without going into my sham of a life and a relationship. A girl's got to maintain a little privacy.

"I can't believe that you walked all the way here, though. What if our power was out, too?"

"I would have banged on the door and demanded that you stay open by candlelight."

"Now that I would have liked to see." Cracker tossed the rag over one shoulder. "I'll help you put up your tree, if you want," he offered, his voice suddenly sympathetic.

"I think it's a lost cause." I took a sip of chardonnay and plunged into the worst-case scenario. "What if I don't put a tree up at home this year? God knows, I've got a dozen of them set up at the shop. I mean, how much Christmas does one person need?"

"Get outta town. You told me yourself you can never get enough Christmas."

"Well, perhaps I've reconsidered."

"Ooh! Big talker!" Cracker folded his arms. "Have another glass of wine and then we'll see where you stand."

"Or if I *can* stand," I said, knowing that was more big talk. Although I enjoy an occasional glass of wine, I've never had much of an aptitude for alcohol. Two glasses of wine and my body simply shuts down, lips sealed tight. Pathetic, I know, but I couldn't even bury my troubles in an alcoholic stupor.

Behind me the door opened and I turned to see Ben rush in, his hair tousled and stark against his black leather jacket.

"Windy," he remarked, joining me at the bar.

"A nor'easter," I said, oddly happy to see him. Maybe if I surrounded myself with friends I could put off thinking about the things that were bothering me. Wasn't that the point of a night out?

"Really? It seems to be moving through quickly." He grabbed the remote and clicked the TV mounted by the ceiling to the weather channel. "Is that what blew you in here?"

I laughed. "Well, yeah, pretty much, but I've been in here before. I used to be a regular when I first moved to the OBX."

"Before you were gainfully employed." Ben took the bar stool beside me, his eyes on the TV. "What's for dinner, Cracker? Got any crab chowder left?"

"Just enough for you two," Cracker confided, glancing over one shoulder at the occupied tables in the corner. "You want that now, or should I heat up some bread for you?"

Ben turned to me. "What do you say?"

I lifted my wineglass, settling in for the long haul. "Bring it on, bread and all."

As we broke into a crusty loaf of bread and made small talk, Lola and Tito sneaked in, called a hello, and took a table in the back. "It's date night," Cracker explained. "They're here every Friday, just the two of them. They make the kids eat pizza while they step out for fine dining."

"That's sweet," I said.

"Sweet? It's a necessity when you've got a houseful of kids. People need time alone."

Savoring a bite of sherry-laced soup, I wondered if I could fool myself into believing that Nate's time away would be good for our relationship. Doubtful, but now that he was hundreds of miles away Nate seemed to be the least of my problems. He'd been bumped from the list by a much more personal dilemma—my insignificant life. My tinsel existence. I was a Christmas Carpetbagger.

Elbows on the bar, I was watching the end of a rerun of *Full House* and thinking about heading home for those two Tylenol P.M.s when Lola appeared beside me, a hand on my shoulder.

"Come join us," she said.

I tried to decline, but she insisted that they'd finished eating and, "I see you're in a bad way, sweetie. Come. I'll read your cards."

Not exactly what I had in mind, but when someone offers to provide a glimpse to your future, the bait is irresistible. "Maybe just a few cards," I said. I excused myself, and Ben nodded as I followed her over to the table, where Tito sat scrolling through the mini-jukebox selections.

"Uh-oh!" He stood up and scooted his chair back. "Looks like Madame Lola is open for business."

"A short reading," Lola told him, reaching into her big patchwork bag.

I tucked a lock of hair behind one ear. "You can stay, Tito. I don't care if you want to witness the tangled web of my life."

Tito held his hands up, his thick fingers spread defensively. "Oh, no, I try to avoid tangled webs, and I'm happy to join my friends at the bar."

Already Lola held the pouch in her hands, its pattern of gold moons and stars in a sea of deep indigo silk reminding me of tales of wizards and witchcraft. From my college studies of the tarot I remembered that mystics wrap their decks in silk and stow them in wood boxes, the theory being that the fine cloth and

wood protect the cards from negative influence. I also remembered the electric charge that sparked the air every time I sat for
a reading.

"Nervous?" Lola shuffled the oversized cards. That was the
thing about Lola; she was good at reading cards, but she was
even better at reading people. With her psychic abilities, she
seemed to know the questions before I even asked them. "We
can throw four cards if you want to keep it simple. One to symbolize you, and one each for past, present, and future."

I nodded.

She laid the deck on the table. "Cut the cards into three stacks."

I realized I'd been sitting on my hands. I separated the deck
into three sections, then pulled my hands onto my lap, trying
not to look too desperate and pathetic but probably failing.

Lola flipped the first card, the Four of Cups, which showed a
naked woman dancing away from a king on his throne. The second card nearly made me choke—the Eight of Swords, showing
a knight slumped over in his horse with eight swords staked in
the ground behind him, eight swords resembling gravemarkers.

Lola must have heard me sucking the air between my teeth,
because she patted my hand before she turned over the next
card. "Oh, don't you worry. This is pain that already exists—it's
in the place of how your life is now. And it's a good thing to talk
about it, get it out there."

The next card was definitely better: the Star, with its image of
a goddess pouring water into a river under a starry sky. "Now
that's more like it," I said, though I couldn't quite recall the
card's meaning. The final card, the one meant to symbolize me,
was the Fool, a man dressed as a jolly jester strolling merrily toward the edge of a cliff.

"Oh, darn. I hate that card," I admitted. "I always used to get
it, and it drove me crazy."

"And why would that be? The Fool is about unrealized potential—the young soul at the beginning of the journey with much
to learn, much to experience. I wish I could draw the Fool now
and again."

"Easy for you to say," I said. "Not so easy when it keeps coming up in your readings on the campus green. One of the less mature guys in our group called it the Asshole Card."

"Of course!" Lola rolled her eyes. "I forgot. You learned the tarot as a way to show off for other Ivy League students."

"Worse than that. We were studying it in one of our humanities classes, and we became tarot junkies. We started doing readings for each other once, twice a day. Then, more. Like . . . every hour. It was as if we could change our fate by drawing the cards more often. I remember once, walking across campus, I stopped to throw a few cards about a test I was taking. Then, once I got to class, I snuck the deck out and turned over a few more. It was that intense."

"Until you learned that you couldn't trick the cards."

"Right. No matter how many times I shuffled, that damned Fool card turned up in my spreads."

"Well . . ." Lola tapped a red-lacquered nail over the Fool. "Here he is again, honey, back to tease you until you learn your lesson from him. But this time, I want you to stop the denial and realize it's telling you that you have great potential you don't see, perhaps capabilities you're currently blind to."

"Mmm." I wasn't going to get up and do a happy dance over the card, but Lola's interpretation made it more palatable.

"So." Lola clapped her hands together and rubbed them vigorously. "The Fool is you, honey. You and your undiscovered potential, whatever that means."

I thought of my sister and her perplexity and disappointment with the fact that I owned and managed a Christmas shop. "You needed an M. F. A to . . . what?" she'd asked. "To sell poinsettia quilts and Styrofoam balls stuck with sequins?" Jane would be thrilled to know she'd been right all along.

"Let's see what else we have here." Lola tapped the card with the woman dancing away from the king. "The Four of Cups," she said, nodding. "This card is in the place of your past. Do you remember what it means from your studies?"

"Not exactly." I frowned. "But I have a feeling that dead soldier in the corner is not a good sign." I was referring to one of the cups, which was spilling red liquid all over the palace floor.

"The overturned cup . . . yes, that's sad, isn't it? A hint of disillusionment, disappointment."

Nate's face came to mind, his brow twisted with anger. "Disappointment in love? In a relationship?"

"Well, you know that cups are hearts, sometimes considered the suit of affairs of the heart, of emotions. And on the Ace of Cups we see Venus, the symbol of love and the beginning of the romance cycle. But by the time we get to four, well, the bloom is off the rose. The Four of Cups represents the stage in any relationship known as the end of the honeymoon. A stagnant period of decline."

"Been there, done that."

"Yes, I think you have. I'd say this is about your relationship with Nate. But no surprises there. You've been stressing about Nate for awhile, sensing that something wasn't quite falling into place. Such as, his divorce."

I looked down at the table with dread. "Which brings us to the scary card. The Eight of Swords."

Lola shrugged. "What can I tell you? This card usually stands for disillusion. See how the knight is deflated? He's fought a battle that he now realizes is futile. Not that you've fought any battles, honey. But it could also symbolize a crisis of conviction, the discovery that something you once thought was noble and honorable proves to be false." She shook her head. "I'm sorry, honey, but I'm not making any solid connections here. Does it make sense to you?"

As she spoke I noticed the lights of my shop reflected in the side window of the bar—the warm red glow suddenly glaring and brash. My shop. I enjoyed working there, and there was no denying that I had a talent for creative Christmas atmospheres.

However, that atmosphere was wearing thin in the real world, where tinsel blew away in a single storm. I hated to think that pinecone ornaments were going to be my only contribution to society. Children in the neighborhood didn't have winter coats, and here I was wrapping the town in tinsel.

Adjusting her puka shell necklace, Lola stared at me curiously. "What is it, snookie?"

"Nothing." I closed my eyes and shook my head. "Just . . . a few priorities I need to sort out." How could the cards know about my disillusion? I hadn't been able to put a word to the way I'd been feeling until that moment, but once Lola said it recognition clanged in my head like the bell down at the volunteer firehouse. *Disillusion.* At least I had a name for it now . . . and a card.

"Well, good. Honey, if you can make the connection, that's all that matters. So . . . here we have the Star card in your future. She's one of the Major Arcana and some people think this is the card of wish fulfillment. This is the goddess of renewal. She restores by means of love and peace."

As I studied the card I thought of the shooting star we'd seen the other night, of my wish, of my worries over Nate's state of mind. The man could definitely use this goddess's waters of renewal. Come to think of it, I'd be happy for a splash myself.

"It's a very nice card," Lola said, patting my hand.

"I can see that. I guess I'm just a little overwhelmed." To put it mildly.

She gathered up the cards and worked them into the deck. "Here's the thing to keep in mind, Ricki. These cards show the situation as it stands today. You can think of it as the astrological forecast, similar to what that Mike Seidel is saying on the Weather Channel. He tells us the weather without any value judgments. Rain: good for the plants, bad for a picnic. That's what the cards do, only they speak to an emotional level. They don't cement your destiny; they only tell you the elements that are at play in your world."

"And these things might change," I said.

"Honey, things change all the time. But here's something I'd like you to do, and this is from Lola. Think of where you'd like to be in five years. What would you like to be doing? Where in the world do you want to be?"

I nodded. Right now, I couldn't imagine leaving the Outer Banks, couldn't imagine life without Nate, but I hadn't projected that far into the future. I sighed. "Something to think about when I get a minute."

"Okay, Lola," Ben said, putting a beer down in front of her. "I see that you've got the cards out, and I'm ready to cash in on that reading you promised. I'd appreciate if you could tell me what to buy my parents for Christmas, and Tito says you'd better say you see a hottie in my future."

"Snookems, how can I refuse when you bring me a beer?" Lola pointed to a chair. "Have a seat."

I started to get up, but Ben gestured for me to stay put as he took the outside chair. "Don't bother getting up. This will be short."

"Do you think so?" Lola teased him. "In my experience, you quiet ones have a lot going on under the surface. You know: still waters run deep."

"My life is a blank slate, a tabula rasa," Ben said with a lazy grin.

"A tabula rasa?" I nudged Ben's arm. Lately he was full of classical allusions, this one referring to the mind before it receives impressions gained from experience. "Geez, Ben, you're taking me right back to grad school days."

"Everyone has a past, surfer man," Lola said. "And this gives me a chance to unravel your mysterious past."

I sneaked a curious look at Ben, wondering about his history—mainly his romantic history. In the years since he'd come to the Outer Banks no one had seen him dating, and Cracker and I had pursued some wild speculation about his past. In New York I would have assumed such a solo figure was gay, but neither Cracker nor I got that vibe from Ben. He seemed to like women and was kind to every person he met, but emotionally, Ben kept the world at arm's length.

We were all dying to know why.

"Mysterious?" Ben folded his arms across his cable knit sweater. "Me? I've always been totally aboveboard."

"We'll see about that." Lola plunked the deck on the table in front of him. "Okay, surfer man. Cut the cards into three stacks."

As Lola turned over the cards I tried to be discreet. Turning toward the bar, I folded my legs and pretended nonchalance, though I couldn't help but listen.

"The Six of Swords, the Three of Pentacles, the Ace of Cups. And let's see your significator . . . the Hermit. How perfect."

"That old man is me?" Ben picked up the card and winced. "I may have snow on top, but at least there's no hole in the roof."

"The Hermit isn't about age. It's about a person who seeks a life of solitude to explore spiritual rebirth."

"My own private Idaho?" Ben quipped.

"I think you know what it's about, honey." Lola tapped another card, and I couldn't help but twist around for a look at the Six of Swords, a card with six people on a boat headed toward a light onshore. "See the ship on this card? It's about a voyage, a journey to an unknown destination, an unforeseen future. This is your recent past—a rite of passage for you. Probably your escape from that other job to come here and start the surf shop."

"Makes sense," Ben said.

"Escape from that other job and . . . perhaps a relationship that wasn't working out?"

Ben hid a smile. "You're tracking."

Lola waggled her fingers at him. "Sometimes it helps me do a reading if you can provide a little information. Helps me make connections."

"Really?" Ben's brows rose skeptically. "And here I thought you were supposed to be reading my cards."

"Was this a marriage?" Lola probed.

"You could say that. Legally, yes, it was. But it's over. In the past."

Lola took a deep breath, as if sucking in the vibe from him. "Okay, then. Now the Three of Pentacles is a work card. It indicates work or skilled labor that will lead to commercial success, but your shop is closed now, isn't it?"

Ben nodded, but I couldn't resist. "Yes, but Ben has agreed to help out in The Christmas Elf this weekend. He's playing Santa."

"Aah!" Lola grinned. "That's it. Because this card usually refers to work performed together with others. Joint efforts and harmonious partnerships."

"Works for me. How about this ace?" Ben pointed to the Ace of Cups, which showed a beautiful, mermaidlike woman drinking from a chalice besides a giant water wheel. "I think this might be the card Tito had in mind."

Lola smiled. "My husband might be a little psychic. You see this woman? She's the Goddess Minne, which means Love. This is the most benevolent card, Ben. It is happiness, love, pleasure, and home. This, my friend, is the jackpot of love."

"Wait a minute!" I protested in mock indignation. "How did he get that?"

Ben smiled. "Jealous?"

"Definitely." I tapped the table. "Come on, Lola. I want a re-shuffle."

"Children, children." Lola shook her head, collecting the cards. "One reading per customer. Besides, Tito and I have to get going. The kids are probably having an X-Box marathon. I need to pull the plug."

We all decided to call it a night. Even Cracker was going to kick out his last two patrons soon and close up so that he could get an early start at The Elf tomorrow.

"Closing up early for you," Lola said. "That's a good friend."

"For Cracker, an early start is anytime before noon," I said. "But I have a feeling I'm going to need the help, especially since the weather seems to be clearing."

"What happened to our nor'easter?" I asked as I stepped out onto the plank board porch of the Crusty Captain.

"Looks like it fizzled into a southwester," Tito joked.

Lola and Tito offered me a ride home but I thought the fresh air would do me good, and Ben was walking in the same direction. We said goodnight, then headed across the highway, figuring it was mild enough to walk along the beach. We stayed on the road, avoiding the man-made dunes built to preserve the coastline, then cut down the path into the cold sand. The winds had softened to a brisk breeze and the sky had cleared to angry dark clouds racing briskly over the horizon. I turned my face toward the Atlantic, awed by the glow of the Appaloosa moon against the water.

"Somehow, you just never get sick of the ocean," I said. "This is such a magical place."

"A magical place with a sordid past."

"Oh, really? How's that?"

He swung around to scowl at me. "Don't tell me you don't know how Nag's Head got its name?"

I shrugged. "Well, no. A nag is a type of horse, right?"

"An old horse. Legend has it that horses with lanterns were used to lure ships close to the shore for pillaging. This was in the early eighteenth century, when some of the landlubbers who called themselves 'bankers' got wind of how profitable pirating could be, as proven by Blackbeard. So the bankers draped old horses with lanterns and walked them up and down the beach at night. Merchant skippers in the waters offshore would see the lights and assume they were coming from other ships, closer to the shore. The skippers would move their precious cargo closer and consequently run aground. Then the bankers would go aboard the stranded ships and steal their cargo."

"Blimey!" I grinned. "That is quite a history. I always knew that Blackbird sailed these waters, but land pirates."

"They still exist," Ben said. "Only now they're called realtors."

"You got that right. But don't rank on Nate just because you feel sorry for me. We should dish about him because he deserves it."

"Who said I feel sorry for you?"

He sounded so earnest, I had to smile. "Okay, we'll skip the pity party for poor Ricki." The girl who was abandoned by her boyfriend. You'd think that you'd outgrow romantic embarrassment in your twenties, but somehow that feeling of no-date-on-prom-night lingers.

I decided to change the subject. "You know, Ben, you pulled some very interesting cards tonight."

"Did I? The illustrations on those tarot cards are so vivid and wild, it's hard to tell."

"But you've got to admit, your future . . . the Ace of Cups? I really envy you. I wish I could trade futures."

"Trade futures? I have a cousin who used to do that on Wall Street, but he had to give it up after a few years. Too much pressure. You think my hair is prematurely gray? Three months on the trading floor and he was completely bald."

The breeze lifted his silver hair, teasing strands over his forehead. His hair looked white-blond in the darkness. "Okay, funny guy. I'll take your tarot cards and your hair, too."

"Nah. You don't want to be the old hermit."

"You'd be surprised," I said, thinking that a life of isolation might be preferable to a life wrought with confrontation and disappointment. Arguments over an ex-wife's hidden agenda, over taking out the trash, over the merits of eggnog versus buttermilk. All day I'd been worried about going home to an empty house, but in truth, the solitude would be a relief.

"Do you believe in destiny?" Ben asked.

"Destiny? I don't know. I hate to think that our futures are set in stone. No, I think life throws obstacles and opportunities in our paths, and maybe that's a form of destiny. But I don't think there's a predetermined timeline that we're all following. How about you? What do you think?"

"I don't know, either." Walking slowly, hands in his pockets, Ben studied the sky. "It's all a mystery, I guess. We've got such a short time on this planet, and we spend so much of it jockeying for position, trying to find a place, a person, a creed that helps us make sense of it. Like you said the other night, like those cards showed us: we look for the symbols and signs that may or may not mean anything."

"I like to think they mean something," I said. "I have to believe that."

"I've got another question for you, but this is one you should take your time with."

"Okay, shoot."

"Are you happy with Nate?"

It was a bit of a shocker, hearing such a personal question after our metaphysical discussion. "Of course!"

"See, now, you weren't paying attention. I told you to take your time and there you go answering without thinking."

I shrugged. "There are some things you just know, Ben. Nate

brought me to this beautiful patch of the planet, led me to my friends here, my Outer Banks family. I wouldn't be here right now without Nate, right?"

"There's a difference between feeling happy and feeling grateful," Ben said. He stared out at the dark water, as if he were trying to identify the clouds gathering in the sky. His silence let me take in the splash of black water against the sand, the rattle of wind in the tall grass of the dunes.

I loved this place. When had Nate and I stopped taking night-time walks along the water and morning jogs down the beach? He was always too busy. I was too tired. And to be honest, I didn't remember when the feeling of happiness had faded, but it had fled somewhere between the push for Nate's divorce and my yearning to move our relationship to another level. But that stage was temporary, wasn't it? We would find each other again, reconnect, when he returned on Tuesday. What had Lola said? A crossroads was coming up. We were just going through a phase. "Nate and I are going through a rough patch," I said quietly. "Which happens, I guess. You know, you can't expect to be happy every day."

Ben tipped his face down toward me. "Why not?"

Wide-eyed, I turned away without answering. Maybe it was a rhetorical question, but it lingered in the wind for awhile. "Were you happy every day?" I asked. "Back when you were married?"

"In the beginning, yes. In the end, there was just no happiness in sight for either of us. That's why we had to end it."

"Was it a bad split?"

"It was all pretty amenable, but it was the hardest thing I've ever had to do. It's hard to walk away when you love someone," he said, his eyes catching mine with a cryptic message. "But we wanted different things. A different lifestyle. I wanted kids, she had no interest in diapers and bottles. I think we each thought the other person would come around eventually, but that wasn't going to happen unless one of us sacrificed our dreams. In the end, it was just too much to sacrifice."

So they had ended it, and Ben had become the hermit, nursing a wounded heart. I reached up and touched the shoulder of his jacket. "I'm sorry."

"Don't be. Pain can be very liberating, and I'm in a better place now. Hell, I've found a slice of heaven here. Sometimes I wake up and hear the gulls outside, the ocean pounding the beach, and it's as if I've been reincarnated into a beautiful new life. I got a shot at the ultimate do-over. But that probably sounds really hokey."

"No, no, it doesn't." Up ahead, the lights of my cottage glowed beyond the dunes on the beach. "I can see that the power is back on." I wanted to hear more about Ben's rebirth, but already he'd revealed more than I'd ever expected, and sometimes you just need to let things unravel naturally. We said goodnight and he waited while I tromped through the sand and closed the cottage door behind me. As I clicked on the gas fireplace and stood at the bay window to catch Ben's shadow moving down the beach, I was haunted by his challenge.

Why not happiness? That was a good question.

21

After the emotional roller-coaster of the past week, I welcomed a weekend jam-packed with activity that would keep me too busy to contemplate my life. Forget what those philosophers say: the unexamined life is a wonderful thing when the pond is too murky for you to see your toenail polish.

And the Shopfest on Saturday was chock-full.

Maybe it was because the weather held, or perhaps it was the fact that we were giving away free eggless eggnog, thanks to Cracker, but by eleven o'clock Saturday morning there was a line of people from the door of our gingerbread shop stretching straight out to the Croatan Highway. By noon, Sheriff Fuller was on the scene, a little bewildered (or so I heard); I never made it out of the store during that interlude, but Cracker told me that the sheriff handled the scene with charm and grace, setting up traffic cones to slow the traffic and eventually closing our parking lot to everything but pedestrian traffic. Ordinarily that would have annoyed Miller, but since the crowds spilled over into his store to purchase sandwiches and drinks, he didn't complain.

Adena had recruited some of her friends to help fulfill e-mail orders, and they worked quietly and efficiently in the backroom. Wearing a Santa cap and singing Christmas carols a tad off-key, Georgia manned the register.

Out in the parking lot, Cracker passed out his eggnog, extolling the virtues of his secret recipe containing vanilla ice cream, pudding mix, and nutmeg. "I've made a few changes to the recipe," he told me on the side. "Tried a few touches from my training in New Orleans. I call it 'Voodoo Eggnog,' bound to be a potion of love."

"I hope you're not giving *that* to the children," I said.

"Only the G-rated version," he quipped.

Sitting in his usual place by the fire, Ben remained attentive as children shared their Christmas lists or simply smiled and posed for a photo with Santa.

Some people came to browse, some customers drove across the state to pick up customized wreaths or quilts, and others made the trip because they said The Elf helped them conjure Christmas spirit. "Can't you just feel it?" one woman told me as I restocked ornaments on the trees in the Winter Wonderland section. "Christmas is in the air!"

After my experience with rebellious tinsel during the windstorm, I wondered about the source of Christmas spirit. Was it as simple as the smells of cinnamon and pine, a mixture of visual symbols and Christmas carols, or was it something more? Something deep inside, something in the soul that reminded us of our short stay on this planet and the fundamental need to share a part of ourselves with the rest of mankind?

That day I became the supreme juggler, restocking bins, ringing up purchases, waiting on customers, checking packages before they shipped, and working on customized orders at my craft table. Around one o'clock, Lola appeared with a generous order of pulled pork sandwiches from Pigman's Bar-B-Q, and we took turns eating in the back room amid giant rolls of bubble wrap, sheets of cardboard cartons, and rolls of red ribbon. Adena's friends worked steadily, some of them tuned into portable CD players as they packed.

Sometime near dusk, Georgia mentioned that a bunch of carolers were outside, and it turned out to be the choir from her church, who lined up on the plank board porch of the Crusty Captain and launched into hymns in three-part harmony.

"O come, o come Emmanuel, and ransom captive Israel . . ." The sweet blend of voices gave me goose bumps as their music filtered into the shop.

"They sound fabulous," I said as I wrapped a delicate snow globe in bubble-wrap. "Wow, they remind me of the choir on a Christmas album my dad used to have."

"They do make a joyful noise," Georgia said as she climbed a ladder to reach into a high bin.

The choir ended up staying until we closed at seven o'clock. After I locked the door, Georgia dragged me into the Crusty Captain, where most of the singers sat at tables, feasting on soup or burgers. Georgia's boyfriend, Daniel, was there, playing Ronnie Spector Christmas songs on the jukebox, and we all ordered food and laughed over the events of the day.

"I didn't think I'd make it," I admitted. "When Nate bailed on me, I thought today was going to be a nightmare, but it wasn't at all. I had a blast, thanks to you guys. And I really mean that— thanks. You saved my sorry butt."

Ben grinned as Cracker slid a bottle of Pete's Christmas Ale his way. "We wouldn't let you down, Sug," Cracker told me.

Georgia grabbed my shoulders and gave a squeeze. "Of course not. Your friends never let you down." As she waved to someone at the door and headed over to chat, it hit me. Friends didn't run out on you at the last minute. Well, perhaps my new friends were superheroes, but that didn't excuse Nate.

As I nibbled on a buffalo wing, I decided to let Nate go for now. He didn't deserve to have me mooning over him, and he certainly didn't deserve my pity anymore. With a feeling of relief, I chased him from the corners of my mind and joined in Ben and Cracker's conversation. I wasn't going to think of Nate until he returned. In fact, I promised not even to speak his name. Bye-bye, Mr. Unmentionable. Good-bye and good riddance.

* * *

On Sunday mornings, Mr. Unmentionable and I normally enjoyed sleeping in. Usually we stayed in our pajamas till noon, sipping coffee and picking at coffee cake. I did the crosswords while Mr. Unmentionable browsed the real estate section of the Sunday *Tribune,* joking about how we might spring for a lavish mansion on the Connecticut shore with helicopter pad and tennis courts, or a prewar condo on Park Avenue on sale for a mere eight million.

But that morning, it didn't really feel like a Sunday as I awoke sprawled diagonally across the bed and stretched lazily. The heat pump was churning and tendrils of frost laced the edge of the window. Must be cold, I thought. I glanced at the clock and blinked. Seven-thirty A.M.? Way too early.

I tried to go back to sleep, but to no avail. As I lay there staring at the ceiling, I wondered what other people did on Sunday mornings. When the answer occurred to me, I felt really stupid. So stupid that I got out of bed, showered, dressed, and got on the road without coffee. Outside, I could see my breath in the air for the first time that season. I stopped at Miller's for a cup to go, and in less than ten minutes I was pulling into the lot of a white clapboard church, its doors thrown open as people headed up the stairs. Taking one last sip, I had a flash of wardrobe anxiety and buttoned my jacket over my Donna Karan top, worried that the vee-neck might be too low for church.

Although I'm not sure exactly what I was expecting, I'm happy to report that lightning didn't strike me down as I entered Georgia's church. In fact, the pianist kept on playing as a smiling man greeted me at the door, handed me a bulletin and pointed to a half-empty pew.

Well, that was easy.

As the pianist played "What Child Is This?" Georgia and Daniel scooted into my row.

"Good morning," Daniel said with a lazy smile. "Cold morning."

Georgia shivered. "I can't believe you're up this early," she told me, nudging me to move down the pew. "After last night, I figured you'd sleep for a week."

"For some reason, I was up, sort of energized," I said.

"That's from us," Georgia said. "Too much fun yesterday. We've got you all wired up."

"It's a good thing, since I have to open up again at noon, and I'll probably go in early since there are new orders to fill."

Georgia nodded, tucking a strand of golden hair behind her pink ear. "We're going to brunch at Daniel's parents," she said, "but I'll stop by this afternoon to see if you need me."

"Thanks," I said as the pianist hit a new note and the opening hymn began, the choir streaming in up the aisles, filling the church with vibrant sound. At the front of the church, musicians played a cello, a violin, a trumpet and a flute, their music completing the colorful spirit. I closed my eyes, savoring the sweet blend of voices and instruments, wondering if it sounded so good because I was culture starved down here in the Outer Banks or simply because it was heartfelt and inspired.

"They sound so good," I whispered. The choir had done a fine performance yesterday outside the store, but somehow, backed by the ensemble, everything came together.

Georgia gave me a strange look, as if I shouldn't be surprised. "Well, sure."

Oh, God, was I a snob? I'd worked hard to shed the reputation of Yankee snoot when I'd first arrived here, but some vestiges still clung to me.

As the congregation sat and the minister led the group in prayer, asking for God's blessing, I bowed my head and wondered what had drawn me here today.

Remember me, God? I'm back. Probably don't deserve to be, but here I am.

I hadn't been in a church since last year, last Christmas when I'd sneaked into St. Patrick's Cathedral to light a candle and say a prayer for my sister. I don't completely subscribe to the notion that God is only present in churches, but when your heel scrapes along the stone floor of a cathedral, the air thick with incense and watery light sifted through stained glass, it's clear that God is there. At the time my sister had been diagnosed with cancer— a curable kind—but the very word had struck terror in our hearts, especially since we'd lost our mother so quickly to cancer. So I'd knelt down and prayed to the God who is bigger than any cathedral to spare my sister. And, to my relief, He did. She'd made it through the surgery and treatment in a matter of months, with barely a chink in her sardonic armor. How's that for a miracle?

When Georgia had first invited me to her church, she seemed startled by my resistance. "Don't you believe in God?" she'd asked me in a sad voice.

"Well, sure I do," I'd told her, not sure how to explain my reticence. Sometimes I feel dwarfed by conventional religion, frightened by the dogmatic Bible thumpers who insist that doctrine and faith must be one way and one way only.

I imagined the Lord—a fantastic, huge and yet infinitely compact being—watching with awe and amusement as we earthlings grapple with religion, churches and customs. Truly, such a magnificent spirit would have no limitation or delineation, and yet that's exactly what we sought to give Him/Her. A face. A definition. A profile we could wrap our puny minds around.

Yes, I believed in God, but maybe not the same God as Georgia and Daniel's. Maybe my God was funkier than the Lord imagined by the family across the aisle, more colorful than the God in the minds of the mom and two children sitting in the front pew, but hadn't our Creator given each of us our unique capacities to envision God? And certainly, that common belief was what had brought us all here today.

As we sang "Oh, Come, All Ye Faithful," I noticed a familiar face in one of the pews behind me. Turning, I caught the bright smile of Joey, who waved at me by dangling the tassel of his new scarf. I had to crane my neck some more to see his sister, Lila, and a woman with short blond hair, her eyes intent on the hymnal. I smiled at the kids and turned back around in my seat before I got all of us in trouble with the ushers.

The minister, Forest Herman, invited the congregation to sit, then stepped out from behind the pulpit and started his sermon by pointing out the bright lights and sparkling tinsel around town. "The ribbons and bows, Santa caps on the checkers at the

Food Lion," Forest said as he walked among the congregation, gently making eye contact. "The special pies and cookies at Bitsy's Bakery. Christmas trees glimmering in the picture windows of homes we pass. All the trimmings of the holiday season. It's Christmastime, but is this what it's really about? Gift wrap and strings of lights? What does this all mean?"

The meaning of Christmas . . .

With a deep breath, I looked up toward the cathedral ceiling of the church. *Okay, God, now I know why I'm here today.* The Reverend's sermon couldn't have been more tailored to me if I'd ordered it on Amazon.com.

Here was God's message for my indulgence in pine cones and Styrofoam balls when I should be focused on his Son's birthday. I expected now to hear the story of the birth of Jesus—another account of the Nativity Scene—and a reminder that this holiday is to be focused on the birth of the Savior and that the surrounding hoopla distracts from the Christmas message.

"This being the first Sunday in December, I'd like for us to take a moment to visualize ourselves on Christmas Day. Where will you be?" Forest asked. "Who will you be celebrating with?"

Although I'd sluiced Mr. Unmentionable from my mind, I followed the minister's instructions and allowed myself a tiny glimmer of the two of us ensconced in that suite at the Waldorf-Astoria. Maybe brunch with Jane at Tavern on the Green. A carriage ride through snow-covered Central Park . . . then a luxurious soak in our big Jacuzzi tub back at the hotel. . . .

Perhaps not the most pristine thoughts to be having in church, but hey, God created Jacuzzis, didn't he?

Forest opened the Bible, "This from the book of Isaiah. 'The people who walked in darkness have seen a great light; upon those who dwelt in the land of gloom a light has shone. You have brought them abundant joy and great rejoicing. For a child is born to us, a son is given us; and upon his shoulder dominion rests. They name him Wonder-Counselor, God-Hero, Father-Forever, Prince of Peace.' "

Forest paused at the end of the pew where Joey and Lila were sitting. "How about that, Joey? A Wonder-Counselor and God-

Hero. I know my children loved that description. It sounds like a new Saturday morning cartoon on TV, doesn't it?"

Joey nodded happily as people chuckled and his mother hugged him close against her fleece jacket.

"Isaiah's account of this light in a land of gloom and darkness gives us hope," Forest said. "If our lives are darker than we'd like, we need to leave them open for God's light, open to wonder and surprise."

I thought of that blazing star, the shooting star I'd wished on. I was open to hope, wasn't I? Hope that N—*no*—Mr. Unmentionable would straighten out his life, once and for all. Hope that we would have a family together.

"And as we wait expectantly for God's surprises and good news, let's consider the trappings with which we surround ourselves—the ribbons and bows and glimmering lights. Now there's nothing wrong with these small enjoyments. Many decorations and customs are symbols that lead us back to our faith—the star atop our tree symbolizing the star that lit the three Wise Men's path to the Christ child. The Nativity Scene outside Slim's Hardware Store. Bitsy's delicious bell-shaped butter cookies that remind us of our own church bell ringing on Christmas morning." Forest sighed. "I do love those cookies. And the many strings of lights that brighten this season. Nothing wrong with that. But as we enjoy them, let's remember the great light that God cast over a land of gloom. Not only the joyous birth of our Savior, but also God's love for us, the light that chases away our darkness. The key to savoring this season is to remember what it's really about: Love."

I bit my lower lip, realizing that he wasn't talking about my love for Nate. This was about more than romance. Forest was referring to the support in this community, the cheerful bond among neighbors and friends, the energy that had kept my shop alive and kicking amid yesterday's crunch of deadlines and demanding customers.

"Share God's love with others during this season. Open your home to people who have nowhere to go for Christmas dinner. When the demands of the season press upon you, simplify your shopping and focus on being generous to those in need. Be a 'Secret Santa.' And while you celebrate the customs of the season, remember that these symbols lead us back here." He pressed a fist to his chest. "To hearts brimming with God's love. In two years, Aunt Norma isn't going to remember what you gave her for Christmas, but she will remember that you made her feel loved. That's the gift we all want to give this Christmas."

To feel loved.

It made perfect sense, and I realized, lucky girl that I am, I had all that. I felt shored up by the love of my friends; yesterday had been a supreme demonstration of their support. Lola and Ben, Georgia and Cracker . . . they were there for me when I needed them.

But oddly, one name was missing from that list . . . a name I had promised myself not to utter. Damn him, Mr. Unmentionable.

22

Once again, I pushed Mr. Unmentionable to the edge of my thoughts as the service ended and the people of the congregation filed out, shaking hands with Forest.

Outside, just below the steps, someone touched my shoulder and I turned to see Joey's mother zipping her fleece jacket, shuddering against the cold. "I'm Amy Salem," she said, extending a hand. "I wanted to thank you for the scarf. Joey's so proud of it."

"My pleasure," I said, shaking her hand as I looked down at Joey, dancing from foot to foot in the cold. He was wearing that thin sweat jacket again. "I just wish he—" I cut myself off before I could say that the kid should wear a real winter coat. What an idiot I was! The kid lived in a deserted trailer; he probably didn't own a winter coat. "I wish he would come by the shop some weekend," I said, trying to recover. "We've been giving out eggnog. My friend's secret recipe, and it's delicious."

"The Christmas Elf?" Amy squinted at me. "That's a cute place. I pass it on my way to work, but I usually pull the weekend shift."

"You work in Nag's Head?" I asked.

"At the hospital."

Joey tugged on her sleeve, anxious to get out of the cold. "C'mon, Mom."

"I'll let you go," I said. "Nice meeting you, Amy."

Watching them head across the parking lot, I thought of the times Joey's day care class had visited my shop, of the crafts they'd made. Decorative door handles? Tissue-box covers? Felt Santa bookmarks? Somehow, those crafts seemed useless to a family who couldn't afford coats and scarves.

"Coming to brunch with us?" Georgia asked. "You're surely welcome. Daniel's mom is always happy to have another mouth to feed."

Checking my watch, I saw that I had nearly two hours before I had to open the shop. "No," I said, "no, thanks. I have a few errands to do."

"Have a holly jolly Christmas," Burl sang through the store. I swayed merrily as I checked the lining of a coat—a blue, hooded jacket with white and gray stripes. Would it be warm enough? Gortex shell, water resistant. And when the weather warmed up, he could unzip and remove the lining, and wear it in the spring rain. Sliding one arm into the sleeve, I imagined Joey wearing the jacket to school, flipping up the hood, zipping it against the cold. The prospect made me giddy with joy.

Looking over my basketful of goodies, I laughed. Who knew Big K-Mart could be so much fun? I hadn't been in here since my hair dryer broke, but when I'd thought of playing Secret Santa to Joey's family, I knew this was the perfect place. It's probably the biggest merchandiser here in Nag's Head, and they were open on Sunday, even in the off-season.

Yes, it would be perfect for Joey, but what size? I held up a five, wondering if the sleeves would be too long. "What do you think of this for a five-year-old?" I asked one of the nearby clerks.

She nodded. "If he's a normal size. But we'll give you a gift receipt in case he wants to exchange it."

I thanked her, then sidled over to the mittens and hats to find a good match for the jacket. Already I'd found a white quilted jacket with a fake fur collar for Amy. For Lila, a red down coat with a sharp velvet trim that reminded me of the soldiers in the Nutcracker.

As I sorted through fleece scarves and knitted caps, I thought of the useless hats and gloves I'd bought for Mr. Unmentionable over the years. Coach gloves in buttery leather. Monogrammed caps from designer catalogues. Fine quality merchandise that had been tossed into the trunk of his car or the back of the closet because Mr. Unmentionable didn't accessorize. Shame on me for wasting my money.

But not this year. This year, I was buying coats and hats and gloves that would be worn and appreciated. As I lined my good-ies up on the counter, a tall stack of remote-control trucks caught my eye.

Toys. Could I buy the kids toys, too?

Ooh . . .

Better wait and see how the coats were received. I planned to wrap them this week and drop them off with Reverend Herman; let him pass them on anonymously.

"Good morning," the checkout clerk said, adjusting her Santa cap. Her name tag read: Doris. "And how are you today?"

"I'm great, Doris. Fantastic. Better than I've been in a long, long time," I said, running my hand over the velvet trim of Lila's coat.

"Well, I am glad to hear that," Doris said as she began to scan my purchases. "Looks like you're planning to keep a few people warm this winter." She held up Amy's coat and folded it gently.

"I hope so," I said. "I really hope so."

After the spike of weekend traffic in The Christmas Elf, Monday and Tuesday were the lull after the storm, quiet morn-ings of Ben and Cracker rocking by the fire while I assembled custom-ordered wreaths and restocked shelves for the afternoon shoppers. With the shipping deadline approaching, I spent most of my days and nights in the shop, which was fine by me since Mr. Unmentionable hadn't returned on schedule or even called to explain why.

Hmph. I was annoyed but not worried, knowing his level of self-absorption had been high lately. And honestly, I was too immersed in my work and my friends to miss him much.

I was frosting fake berries with white glitter when Cracker jumped up from the rocker and turned off the CD player.

"Excuse me, but it's that time of the day. Dr. Phil's on, and I need to find out all the things I'm doing wrong in my life."

I stepped back as he reached under the counter for the portable TV and propped it on the shelf. "Dr. Phil." I rolled my eyes. "My sister loves him, too. Probably because he's the only man in the world with the guts to stand up to her and tell her to get real."

Cracker clapped his hands together when the announcer revealed that today's show would cover "Life Strategies for Choosing a Mate."

Ben tilted his head thoughtfully. "Sounds serious."

"Jimminy Cricket!" Cracker exclaimed. "This will be advice all three of us can use."

"Right," I said, all the while thinking what I really needed was some tips on how to restrain one's self from killing one's mate after he's been gone for five days without a phone call. As I frosted the berries, Dr. Phil talked about having high expectations for a mate. He wasn't into the chick magazine "checklist" of requirements in a male. However, he did agree that we all have certain requirements, which Dr. Phil considered "deal breakers."

As I set the wreath aside to dry, I wondered what my deal breakers were. I flopped down on my stool and started straightening out sections of garland, unable to think of a single requirement. Was I that easy? A total pushover?

"All I want is to get married," claimed a young woman in the studio. "Really. It's my only deal breaker, but he won't give me that. I thought he was waiting until my birthday to propose, but it came and went without a ring. I don't know what's wrong with him, Dr. Phil."

"What's wrong?" Dr. Phil's arms shot out in horror. "He smells your desperation!"

Just then the phone rang. "The Christmas Elf," I answered.

"Have I got a loser for you." My sister Jane was not big on formality over the phone. Introductions like, "Hi, how are you?" were a waste of time for Jane. "You gotta see this buffalo on Dr. Phil. Serious failure to commit. Made me think of you and Nate."

"So nice of you to call," I teased.

"Really, turn on the TV. You've got to see this big lug."

"Already got it on," I admitted, "though I'm not too impressed with the girlfriend. Don't you find her a little whiny and desperate?"

"And who's calling the kettle black?"

I felt stung. "I am not whiny," I whined, turning away from Cracker and Ben.

"Are too, are too. A million times, are too," Jane said, bringing me back to days when the kid who said it most won.

"If I whine, it's because I'm a pushover. I'm way too easy," I admitted.

"Little Ricki, when you're waiting on a guy like Nate, you don't have a lot of choice. I've always told you, Nate has commitment issues."

"He's committed, all right, just to the wrong woman at the moment. Ouch!" A wire from the garland stuck me under one thumbnail. "But all that's changing, and fast. He might be divorced by Christmas."

"Ach! That's worse than getting coal in your stocking. Worse than Christmas in the tropics. Worse than having to eat fruitcake and—"

"Okay, okay, I get the point."

"Listen to Dr. Phil, Little Ricki. That man is never going to give you what you want . . . what you need. It's time for you to move on. Poop or—"

"I hate that expression," I interrupted her. "And Dr. Phil never said that." I shot a look at the TV screen. "At least, not today."

"I'm using tough love, honey. I'm worried about you wasting your life while Nate strings you along."

"Don't you worry about me," I said as I looped the end of the garland wire around the wreath ring. "How are you feeling? What's the latest on your thyroid?"

"Or my lack, thereof," Jane said irreverently. I was glad she was able to joke about the disease that had rocked her life just a year ago. "Nothing new. My thyrogen levels are excellent. My last radio-active scan was squeaky clean. I'm totally cured, which gives me tons of time to obsess over you, bubby. Exactly when are you coming to town? Not that I don't love you dearly, but since I've got my own beau this year my social calendar is filling up rapidly. Emma's, too. In fact, her new guy is ditching his family in Oregon to spend Christmas here in New York."

"Sounds serious," I said. "And how is Marty? Have you moved into his apartment?"

"Well, not really moved. We do spend most nights together, but right now I think we're both happy with the status quo."

"I was just wondering. Whenever I call you're not home."

"Have you been trying to reach me?" Her big sister instinct kicked in. "I knew it. Did you and Nate break up? Are you okay?"

"Nate took off for Rhode Island on Friday and I haven't heard from him since."

Jane grunted. "So he ran back to her? After all this time? What a bastard."

"Actually, he went back to finalize the divorce, sign some papers. And see his kids."

"And no phone calls? What's that about?"

I shot a look at Ben and Cracker, who were commenting on one of Dr. Phil's guests. "He's mad at me because I didn't go along, but I couldn't drop everything here."

"Of course you couldn't. You shouldn't!"

"This is my busy season."

"Oh, please, does he need you to dry his tears and guide his signature on the page? Really, he's asking too much," Jane said.

Although I had blocked Mr. Unmentionable from most of my thoughts, I felt a new sense of empowerment as I soaked up Jane's righteous indignation. Really! It was one thing to support the man, quite another to escort him to divorce court.

"Are you okay?" Jane went on. "Christ! That is so like Nate. Hit and run. He wounds you, then runs from the scene of the crime."

Wounded? With the phone pressed to my shoulder I snipped the loose end of wire from the wreath and held it back for assessment. The teal and emerald leaves curled around the frosted white berries in a cool combination—cool colors, soothing textures. It reflected my mood today: cool and content. Hardly wounded.

"I'm really okay about this," I told Jane. "Better than you'd think."

"I can barely believe that. I mean, you sound okay, but if I were you I'd be next in line for a personal consult with Dr. Phil."

"No, I can handle this," I said, not completely sure of the outcome, but confident that things between Mr. Unmentionable and me would turn out fine. "I've come to see it's just one small part of the big picture, and there's so much to do here."

"I know you must be crazed with the Christmas rush."

"It's been busy," I admitted. "But not too hectic to prioritize." I'd found time to call Forest Herman and tell him about my shopping trip for Joey's family. He seemed pleased by my Secret Santa plan, and I asked him if he knew about the family's housing circumstances. He told me that he'd recently been apprised of the situation and was looking into a way for the church community to assist, but in the meantime, my Secret Santa idea was a good one, and he promised to approach Joey's mom.

At the moment, the coats were hung on doors around the house, polar soldiers that greeted me each night, but I promised to wrap and deliver them by Sunday. I had spoken to Georgia about the family's trailer home, and she had learned through Daniel that their cottage had been destroyed in the last hurricane. The property was still there, but Daniel wasn't sure about the prospect of rebuilding, didn't know if they'd had insurance. This had brought the regulars in the shop to a discussion of hurricane damage—which in the Outer Banks is always good for hours worth of amazing tales.

"So I guess this is a bad time to ask about Christmas," Jane said, interrupting my thoughts.

Right now, everything involving Nate seemed like bad news. Although he had agreed to go to New York, somehow that seemed shaky right now. "He said he would go with me," I told her. "But now I'm not so sure."

"But honey, you've *got* to come," Jane went on.

"I'll be there, definitely. And maybe Nate will come along, too."

"Make sure he brings a warm jacket, the way he complains about the cold. That nonsense about feeling the cold now that he's lived down south. You'd think the man grew up in a rainforest."

"I think he'll survive."

"Oh, I'm not worried about him, I just like to complain. Really, honey, don't let this mongrel ruin the holidays for you."

I thought of Joey's family wrapped in warm coats and mittens. I let myself imagine Lila's smile on Christmas morning when she opened a package to find a gift she wanted. "Don't worry about Christmas," I said. "No one can ruin that for me." This year, Christmas wouldn't revolve around buying Nate's favorite aftershave or ice-skating at Rockefeller Center or slicing into the turkey Emma roasted.

And as I tucked the teal wreath into a box and checked my list for the next order, I felt the shop swirl around me with new meaning. The trees glowed with fiery spirit. My friends' voices warmed the hearth with the same old jokes and stories. The Christmas cuckoos chimed and chirped a new song as Sally Painter, one of the women from Georgia's quilting bee, hung a new Christmas quilt in the frame near the window, another detailed journey encoded with snowy scenes of country churches, ice-skaters, and carolers, and stained-glass windows.

"Are you okay?" Jane asked.

"I'm fine," I said, and for the first time in years, it was true.

23

Clarity of vision.

As customers came in that afternoon, windows opened all around me and I began to see my shop, my friends, and my own designs in a new light. My work wasn't a negative thing; there was no shame in trying to capture and share the mirth and beauty of the Christmas season. I was elbow-deep in garland, wiry wisps of hot glue strands clinging to my clothes, glitter in my hair, but I was immersed in a labor of love along with a crew of friends whose support made the hours whiz by like pages flying off a calendar.

When I got the call on Thursday, I clung to that clarity of vision, determined not to buckle under the usual pressure. I would forge ahead with Nate, but some things would change around here—starting with my usual blind forgiveness.

"I'm on my way home," he said. "Should be there in time for dinner tonight."

"Oh, really?" I turned away from some customers and lowered my voice. "I'm not sure if I'll be available tonight. This is my busy season, and wait a second, who are you again? Is this the boyfriend who lammed out of here on Friday and hasn't called to check in? Not even once?"

"Babe . . . it was so hectic at home."

"Uh-huh." I untangled a strand of lights. "I know hectic. Been there, done that." And what did he mean by calling Rhode Island home after we'd been living in the Outer Banks for almost three years?

"You're mad, right?"

"Not really." I didn't want my moral indignation reduced to a childish snit. "Let's just say I'm concerned about your lack of accountability, and a little alarmed at the total disconnection. I mean, not one call."

"Well, my cell wasn't ringing off the hook. You didn't call once," he whined. I pressed my eyes closed, sure he was going to launch into a big "Nanny-nanny-foo-foo!"

"You felt compelled to run away, and I wasn't going to chase you down," I told him, wondering at the truth in those words. Wasn't this really about more than Nate seeking a divorce? It was about the tug-of-war between us, the struggle to bring our relationship to a place that was comfortable and rewarding for both of us.

"You're developing a thick skin," Nate said, "and I'm not sure I like it. I guess I have those shiftless friends of yours to thank, right?"

I shot a look over at Ben and Lola, who were helping customers. Ben had climbed on the step stool to reach a snow globe for someone, and Lola was explaining the history of one of the Christmas-carol-chiming clocks for a woman from Hatteras. "Is that a joke?" I asked. "Or have you lost your mind?"

He laughed . . . a cold, brittle sound. I felt an unsettling distance between us, and I wished he would somehow just hang up and appear in the doorway so we could really work things out, face to face.

"You take things so personally," he said. "Look, I'm getting back on the road, but I should be pulling up to the cottage around six or so. We'll talk over dinner, okay?"

"Okay." Hanging up, I felt a mixture of disappointment and relief as Lola carried a clock to my worktable. "Mrs. Landy would like to have this shipped," she said.

"No problem," I told Mrs. Landy and started unrolling bubble wrap. I leaned close to Lola and said, "That was Nate. The cold snap is over."

She nodded. "Sounds like progress. Maybe you've reached your crossroad."

I smiled, thinking that would be a good thing, though there was so much going on around me that I wasn't able to absorb the implications. I just knew that Nate was on his way, which meant I needed to see if Adena could cover the shop for the evening hours while I ran home and tidied up. And I would need to get some groceries. And while I was at it, I might as well put together a nice meal, since it's so nice to have real food after you've been living on diet soda and rest-stop burgers for a few hundred miles.

Dinner was a labor of love, and the work was shared by my Nag's Head family, who seemed more jubilant than I felt when they learned that Nate was returning. Lola brought me some clam chowder that her husband made, Cracker donated some breadsticks from the Crusty Captain, one of Nate's favorites, and Ben gave me some fresh flounder that one of his fisherman buddies had caught. And just before I left the store, Cracker had rushed out of the bar with a list of ingredients—his secret recipe for eggnog. "It's all in the vanilla pudding mix and ice cream, but don't tell Nate that. Oh, and you'll need this," he said, handing me a bottle of brandy. "You can get Nate good and drunk and take advantage of him."

That had made me laugh. "Nate will probably want the brandy straight up, but thanks," I said. "Divulging your secret recipe. Wow. I must rate as a friend."

"Oh, don't get yourself all carried away," he'd teased, hurrying back inside from the cold.

Now, as I dipped the fish in egg and coated it in flour, I felt a rush of gratitude. My friends had been so supportive, so helpful during this difficult week . . . which, actually, hadn't been that difficult at all once I stopped worrying about Nate. Okay, I'd had some fun . . . but it was after six, and I needed to prepare the

salad greens and saute the fish and get the chowder heated before Nate pulled up.

I worked briskly, knowing I was running late. Fortunately,
Nate was behind schedule, too, so I had time to pop the fish in
the oven, fix my lipstick and open a bottle of wine before he
plodded in. I flaked on the couch and relaxed for a moment,
taking in the coats that still hung over the French doors. I had
straightened up around them, and now it occurred to me that I
had better get those things boxed and wrapped before Nate saw
them. He wouldn't understand my desire to help someone I didn't
know. He would think that I was being nosy, overstepping the
boundaries between strangers. I took down Lila's jacket, then
paused as my hand touched the velvet trim. Why was I worried
about Nate's perception of this act of goodwill? Had I dwindled
into a mouse?

I plunked the coat back up onto the door and called Nate's
cell. Pacing the cottage as it rang, I padded over the thick turquoise and navy rugs that covered the pale wood floor to warm
my feet by the fire. I paused at the shelf of blue glass objects I'd
collected and carefully arranged, the wall of glass brick that cast
interesting prisms across the room on a summer morning, the
gold wreath over the fireplace, the small ceramic tree I'd brought
home to take the place of a fresh tree this year. This cottage had
been decorated with so much love, but now it seemed trite, like
an adolescent's dream room, over-decorated and well-equipped,
yet still waiting for its use to be fully discovered.

And why wasn't Nate answering, damn him?

I checked the fish and the clock. Seven-fifteen and the fish
was still tender. Seven-thirty, fish drying fast. Seven-forty-five, fish
on verge of flopping.

At eight I served myself fish and salad, imagining that Nate
could eat while I brought him up to date on the Christmas rush
at the store. The flounder was sweet and meaty, reminding me of
the first time I'd had fresh fish as a kid, one evening after my
grandad had a good catch on Lake Michigan. The perch he
boned and fried up had been so unlike the planks of swordfish
I'd watched my mother bake for herself and Dad, so alien to the

tubular fish sticks Jane and I dined on with macaroni and cheese on the side. There was nothing like a fresh catch.

I pushed the salad away and called Nate again. Had he turned his cell phone off? Or . . . possibly an accident. Sucking in my breath, I imagined the cell phone ringing in his pants pocket as emergency room doctors worked on him. One of the nurses would remove the phone and turn it off so that it didn't disrupt the equipment, and how long would it take them to notify me? Was there any documentation to indicate that I was his unofficial next of kin?

"Stop it," I said aloud. This wasn't the first time Nate had left me in the lurch, not the first time I wandered through the desperate ER scenario. And really, what was the big deal if Nate ate the dinner I made? So what if he missed it? He'd probably make some crack about how he had fish already this week.

The teal candles on the table had burned down dangerously low, beads of hot wax creeping down over the brass ridge. I blew them out, turned off the oven, yanked the fish from the oven. Oh, well, nobody likes leftover fish. Still, my eyes teared at the way I'd artistically splayed lemon wedges around the platter. Vivid yellow, juicy lemon wedges, now warped and puckered. As I scraped the fish into the trash, I saw my feelings for Nate tumble along. Another delicately breaded fish fillet—whomp! The little cup of capers on the side—ping, ping, pong.

I tossed in the salad greens for good measure, then kicked the can closed, sank down at the kitchen table, and sobbed.

How did I let this happen? My hopes and dreams, now in the can.

And with my inevitably bad timing, that was when the lights of a car illuminated the glass brick. Still, I couldn't stop sobbing into my hands as Nate banged on the door, then keyed his way in.

"Ricki?" He tromped in, dropped his duffel bag in the hallway, looked around curiously then frowned when he caught me crying. "What's your deal? What, is it that time of the month?"

I pressed my face into my hands, reminding myself not to kill him because he'd stepped into the middle of my meltdown. He had some catching up to do. "You're late," I said, swallowing over the lump in my throat. "I cooked dinner, but now it's too late."

"Really? You cooked?" He tossed his coat on the back of the couch and opened the fridge behind me. "I hit the worst traffic on 64. I mean, no reason. Just wall-to-wall cars. I was steamed."

"I called you," I said tightly.

"What are you so upset about? I'm the one who was sitting in murderous traffic. My cell phone was low on juice, and I had the charger in the trunk. Didn't want to stop and get it."

"You couldn't hop out and grab it while you were waiting in all that *murderous* traffic?"

"Ricki, really, listen to yourself," he said. "Is this any way to welcome me home?"

That hurt—that he would criticize the grand welcome I'd planned, my big effort that had failed dreadfully.

Or had it? I'd had everything in place—a lovely dinner, a warm cottage—I'd done my part, but Nate hadn't arrived on cue.

I lifted my head, tears blurring my vision. My blue glass collection, the wreath shimmering over the mantel, Nate's duffel bag—all were just blurs of blue and gold and black. I swiped at my eyes, desperate to see the true details, longing for the clarity of vision I'd achieved earlier in the day.

Nate cracked open a can of soda, then held out the plastic pitcher. "What the hell is this?"

"Eggnog," I said. "Cracker's secret recipe."

He held it to his nose and winced. "You won't catch me drinking it." Nate hung on the fridge door, facing away from me.

"Well," I began, "was your trip successful?"

"It was great," he said. "Great to see the kids, nice to spend some time with them. I'm really tempted to go back, maybe after the divorce is final. Pack up and just go. We could stay in a hotel till we find a place. And you know who I ran into? Ted McGreavy. Can you believe it? He said he'd be willing to bring me back into the agency if I'm ever interested."

"What? Whoa." I held my hands up, fingers splayed like a traffic cop. "Did you just drop two little bombs there? That your divorce still isn't final . . . and that you want to move back to Providence?"

"What's the big deal? Would you put your hands down? When did you become so reactionary?"

"When you started charting a course without me," I said. "Keep making decisions without talking them over with me, and I have no choice but to react. What happened with the divorce?"

"It's ongoing. These things take time."

"Three years, Nate? Four? Five?"

He slammed the soda down on the counter. "Excuse me, but am I under attack?"

"Maybe it's time for you to answer some questions, Nate. Are you serious about moving to Providence?"

"Sure. You know I miss the girls, and I've always felt bad about dragging you down here."

"You didn't drag me, Nate. It was something we were doing together. A joint effort." Or at least, that was how I'd once envisioned it.

"Anyway, don't you want to go back?" He started routing around in a cupboard. "Get away from this deserted wasteland. I can't tell you how good it felt to be back in civilization for a while. I really miss it. The sports events. Concerts and museums. Four-star restaurants."

"The traffic," I said, "and the crime. Remember how our Honda kept getting stolen? How we'd have to circle for hours to get a parking space? Remember parking tickets, Nate? And your Visa bill. Some of those four-star restaurants put you over your credit limit, or did you forget about that?"

"You're missing the point!" He found a can of cashews and cracked open the aluminum lid. "Don't you want to blaze a trail out of here, babe? Let's hit the road and never look back—at least, not until we're eating lobster in the posh back room of Agora's." He popped a cashew in his mouth. "Remember how you loved that place?"

"That was a hundred years ago." I shook my head. "Now I'm happy with a cup of chowder at the Crusty Captain. Or a dinner at Calico Jack's. Or even frozen drinks at Kokomo Joe's Tiki Bar. I don't need fancy restaurants and city life. I'm happy here."

"Oh, really? You really like living in a place where surfboards, kites, and hammocks are big business?"

When I just stared at him, he rolled his eyes. "You really have sunk low. And while we're on trailer trash, this place is a mess. What's with the merchandise hanging on the doors?" He nodded toward the French doors.

"The coats are a gift." I turned to look him in the eye. "For a needy family. I just need to wrap them."

Nate shook his head. "You got sucked into that? You actually think that family can't afford their own coats?"

"Actually, Nate, I know they can't." I took the coats down, one by one, and started folding them neatly into the gift boxes I'd bought.

"And what about welfare or food stamps? They're probably loaded up with government subsidies. Raking in our honest tax dollars, while you're encouraging them with free handouts."

A vein pulsed in my eyelid as I stopped folding and stared across the room at him. His intense brown eyes, that dark beard stubble over his square chin. What had once seemed so attractive was now repulsive and raw, as if his moral malignancy brimmed over and showered ugliness over his skin and hair and eyes like a fountain. "You're wrong this time, Nate. I know the family, so you can put your Republican paranoia aside."

"How much did you spend on all that stuff? What'd they take you for?"

Ignoring him, I folded tissue over Joey's coat and closed the box securely.

"God, I'm hungry," he said. "What's that smell? Did you cook fish?"

"I did, and it was delicious."

He routed through the fridge. "Well, where's mine?"

With the boxes stacked in my arms, I tromped into the kitchen and pressed my foot on the pedal of the garbage can. The lid flopped open to the aroma of fish and lemon with a hint of capers. "There's your portion," I said with a smile. It would have given me great satisfaction to grab a handful and slap it onto a plate for him, but my arms were full of packages.

"That's disgusting," he moaned, but I was already headed out the door. I could tell Nate was shocked, off his game. "Where are you going?" he asked.

"Just getting these out of the way." I had decided to stow the merchandise in my trunk. Not that Nate would hurt anything, but I didn't want him tarnishing my act of goodwill.

"When are you coming back?" he called after me. "Your coat . . ."

Actually, I hadn't planned to *go* anywhere, but now that Nate mentioned it, escape seemed like a far better evening activity than sitting around while he moped over food and made plans that probably did not include me.

And as I slammed the trunk shut and went back inside for my coat, I realized that was the real issue between us. Nate's plans had never included me. Never, never. And me, fool in love that I was . . . I thought it was all about *us,* about our adventure together. I thought we had a shot at falling in love.

But Nate was not a candidate for love. Not now, and not before, when he'd been with Gina. I actually felt sorry for her as I slipped on my down jacket and zipped up. She and I had more in common than I'd thought—we shared an attachment for a dark-eyed, attractive man with a mercurial temper and a penchant for self-indulgence, a man we thought we could reform and refine into a reasonable human being worthy of sharing our lives. On that point, Gina and I had both been mistaken.

I got in my car and drove, heading toward the center of town. At the turnoff for the Crusty Captain I kept going, not really wanting to see anyone, not wanting anyone to see me in turmoil. I parked in the empty lot by City Hall and walked to the beach. The wind, such a constant at the ocean, was surprisingly mild, though it tossed my hair around my face, making it difficult to see. I scraped it back and tied it off with a scrunchee from my pocket. There.

And suddenly, I could see again. That clarity of vision had returned, and the velvet darkness revealed variegated lines of seaweed over the hard-packed sand just above the break where waves crashed and foamed violently. Dots of lights stretched up the coast, each one a home that stood occupied—quiet sentinels along the beach, unlike the days Ben had described when nags pulled lanterns along the shore to confuse merchant ships.

Strange that such a desolate scene could bring me any peace, but I could see myself in those banging waves, I could see my relentless search for symbols and meanings. It hadn't really been an open-eyed search so much as a quest to find the symbols I wanted: the path to love, to happiness which, as defined by me, would be marriage and motherhood. As my sneakers slid over sand I thought of the fluctuating temperature of my moods over the past year . . . so tied to Nate's progress with his divorce, so tied into Nate's shifting temperament. Nate's desires, Nate's sense of humor, Nate's demands. My life was wrapped around Nate's; I was emotionally reliant on a man who had disappeared for six days and returned without a phone call, without a kiss, without a welcoming embrace.

And now he wanted to move north, go back, after I'd built a business here, made friends here, found a family here—none of those things were considerations for him. When had he lost track of me?

I stopped walking and planted my sneakers firmly in the sand, lifting my face to the sky to search for the constellations Ben had shown me. Was that the Big Dipper—or just a blinking satellite? I considered wishing on a star, but felt way too sober to muster the enthusiasm. Besides, what did I want, anyway? What were my desires? As Lola had said, where did I want to be in five years?

I wanted to stay in the Outer Banks, of course, running my little shop. I'd pictured myself married to Nate, with a baby. But how would that be?

Well, honestly? Awful.

I shoved my hands in the pockets of my jacket and shivered at the image of a little crying baby, me pacing the cottage with baby on shoulder, Nate pestering me about his dinner. Nate's patience was thin now, but a baby was not going to improve his self-centered, sour disposition.

Nothing good would come of it.

I shot ahead and started running, my feet pounding the sand, my arms pumping at the air. At first I was just trying to channel my anger, then I realized I had a place to go. Lola's one-story house stood in a cluster about a mile ahead, and a light was on.

My torch in the darkness.

24

"Honey, look what the wind blew in from the beach," Tito said with his usual deadpan expression.

Her hands curled around the control stick, Lola was so intent on the video game that she could only spare a quick glance. "Ricki . . . hi, honey. I just got to this level and Gollum is killing me."

"It's The Hobbit," Tito explained. "The boys just got the game."

Rusty and Taylor sat on either side of Lola, their arms crossed, their dark eyes intent on the screen.

"No—Mom! You can't get there from here," said Rusty.

"It doesn't hurt to try," Lola said as a thundering crash sounded from the TV and the occupants of the couch relaxed.

"You're toast, Mom!" Taylor grinned.

"Don't call your mother names," Lola said in a half-serious voice as she handed the control stick to Rusty and stood up. "I'll try again later." She went over to a small wooden box on top of the mantel, then motioned to me. "Let's go on the porch. It's more quiet there."

The porch was a glassed-in room that overlooked the ocean, furnished with a couch, table, and chairs covered in tropical-print cushions. Lola took a seat at the table, lit a votive candle, opened the box, and started shuffling her tarot cards.

"How did you know I needed a reading?" I asked as I sat across from her. Not that I stopped by all that often, but I had been here a few times just to visit.

Lola shrugged, her purple velour robe shimmering in the dim candlelight. "Let's put it this way, I had a feeling you weren't here for more clam chowder. How was it, anyway? Did Nate like it?"

"We didn't get that far," I said.

She stopped shuffling, her eyes catching mine, as if the room had grown suddenly darker. "And now you're at that crossroad."

"I think I'm beyond that point." I pulled the scrunchee out and finger-combed my hair. "Lola, I think it's over for Nate and me. And that makes me feel like a failure. It just seems so wrong, that somehow, I just need to know I'm doing the right thing. A sign."

"You and your signs." She bit her lower lip and tapped the cards with a coral fingernail. "Cut the cards. I'd like to give you a longer reading—maybe the Celtic Cross—but we don't have much time. *CSI: Miami* is on at ten." Lola had her chosen shows; just a handful, but she never missed them.

"Can you take the Fool out of the deck?" I asked. "I don't want to be a fool, not anymore."

Lola splayed her fingers over the cards, as if performing a spell over them. "I cannot remove that card, but I can tell you that if it does not apply, it will not appear."

I rested my hand on my chin, sulking. "Promise?"

The corner of her mouth lifted in a lopsided grin. "Something tells me you are now enlightened?"

I swallowed back my lingering reservations. "I've taken a hard look at myself. Picked up on some of the not-so-subtle signs from Nate. All the signs I've ignored and denied for so long." I twisted a strand of hair over one shoulder. "I used to be so good at understanding things, reading between the lines. What happened to my ability to interpret the world?"

"You've been trying too hard. Not every sign is an omen. Sometimes the stop sign simply means that you stop your car while someone else goes by. It's not always a message to stop your entire life."

"Well . . . duh. What can I say? As the cards know, I've been a fool." I cut the cards, not even trying to put a whammy on them this time. Maybe I was moving up in the learning chain.

Lola lifted the cards and turned over the top three. "The Death card, the Two of Wands, the Prince of Cups. And for your significator . . ." She turned over a card with a trill of delight. "Ah! The Magician! It's textbook tarot."

I blinked, relieved that it wasn't the Fool. "What does that card say about me?"

"That you've embarked on a journey. What's intriguing is that this card follows the Fool in the deck, so it looks as if you yourself have embarked on the journey through the secrets of tarot."

"At least I'm moving on," I said.

"The Magician is often connected to the god Hermes, who was a good shepherd to souls. Hermes was the god of journeys. In pre-Christian times, Hermes pillars stood at main crossroads in the Greco-Roman world. Do you see the symbols here? Journeys, crossroads—many of the things we've been speaking of."

"As long as it's just a spiritual journey, I'm in," I said. "Nate wants to move back to Rhode Island, and I'm *so* not ready for that."

Lola shook her head over the cards. "No, I don't see that type of movement. Maybe a visit, but you're not going back there." She reached across the table and pressed my hand. "We won't let you go."

I squeezed back. "I'll hold you to that, though you may find me sacked out on your living room sofa."

"You're always welcome, though, as you can see, it gets crowded in there." She stared intently at the other cards. "The Death card—transformation. This is the end of an era, the beginning of something new. Could signify the end of your relationship with Nate, but with that card in the past position, it looks like that already ended. Then you have the Prince of Cups in the current position. This man is a visionary messenger," Lola went on, barely able to contain her enthusiasm for this card. "This is a complex hero who inspires. He is gentle. Sensitive. Courteous."

I laughed. "Sounds great! When do I get to meet him?"

Lola smiled. "This man is already in your life. Someone you know."

I shook my head. "Definitely not Nate."

"Definitely not. But Ricki, you are surrounded by people who love you. Sometimes I think you don't see that; with your eyes focused on the big symbols, your sights are set on such a distant destiny that you don't see what's around you."

Clarity of vision. "I think I know what you mean," I said.

Next Lola tapped the card in the future spot: the Two of Wands. "This indicates that you are in the process of building an alliance. A partnership of two powers. Yin meets yang."

I shook my head, confused. "Romantic? Or in business?"

"It could be either, though coming with the Prince"—she touched the two cards—"I would suspect romantic. Do you see the two figures on the Two of Wands? One is like the reflection of the other, and yet they are polar opposites. Lunar and solar, male and female. The basic idea of this card is that alliance is necessary if anything is to be accomplished, and each partner must be reconciled to the different qualities of the other."

"Well, I've always been big on teamwork," I admitted, "though I don't see where this card fits."

"Let's say there's an alliance in your future, and that is a good thing." Lola checked her watch. "Do you want to stay and watch *CSI?*"

I sighed. "I think I'd like to stay the night, if that's okay. I'm not really up for facing Nate right now." It occurred to me that he might not realize that it was over, which would entail another huge argument in which he would outline his achievements and finer points in much the same fashion that he profiled a vacation rental home.

She frowned. "What will you do? Do you have a plan?"

"I'm working on it," I said, hoping that Nate would move north sooner rather than later and let me keep the rental cottage. Fortunately, money was not an issue and I could easily pay the rent on my own. But what if Nate didn't leave? "I'll figure it out tomorrow," I said as I followed Lola into the living room, glad to be in the comforting home of a friend.

The next morning, I awoke to the smell of freshly brewed coffee—Tito's favorite blend, which he ordered online from Hawaii. Sipping it in the quiet of the kitchen was heaven. Tito insisted on giving me a ride to my car on his way to work, and by the time I pulled into the drive of the cottage, it wasn't even seven. Nate was asleep, which was fine by me as I'm a huge advocate of delayed confrontation.

I showered and pulled on fresh jeans with a winter-white sweater set and wondered if I should risk waking Nate with the noise of the blow dryer. My question was answered when I cracked open the bathroom door and saw the empty bed. Uh-oh.

"What happened to you last night?" he called from the kitchen. "You didn't even call."

He'd been away for how long without calling, but now I was in trouble after one night? "Look, Nate, let's not nit-pick here. It's clear that things between us are not going to work out, at least, not in the long run, and I think it's best for us to just separate now and cut our losses."

"What?" he snapped. "What's this about? Did you meet someone while I was gone?"

I thought of the conventional wisdom about how it's always easier to break up when you can claim that there's "someone else," but I couldn't lie just to get myself off the hook. "It's not about someone else, Nate. You and I have different priorities, different goals. I want a family and, well, you've already got one, and it sounds like you're ready to head back to them, and honestly, I don't want to stop you. Maybe I've been too indecisive before, but recently I realized that you've always made the decisions in our relationship; you charted our course with no input from me. Well, I want to make my own plans now, and to be blunt, they don't involve you."

"So dramatic." He cracked open a soda and sat at the table. I have always hated it when he drinks soda in the morning, but I wasn't about to harp on that now. Drink away, Nate! Come tomorrow, you drink alone! "You know, Gina told me you would do this."

"Did she?"

"She said you wouldn't wait for the divorce to be final."

"Smart woman," I shot back, resenting the image of me as a gold digger. "She must have realized that most women don't hang around for ten or twelve years." I stewed over Gina's last stab as I ducked back into the bedroom to dry my hair. Annoying, but I was leaving all this aggravation behind. Though I admit to being surprised at the way Nate was taking this. So far, no broken glass.

As I coiled the wire on the blow dryer, I tried to broach the subject of territory with some delicacy. "So . . . since we can't live together, when do you think you'll be heading up north?"

"What's it to you?" he groused. "I expect you to have your things out of here by the end of the week."

"But Nate . . . since you're leaving, I figured I'd keep the cottage. I can pay the rent, and—"

"My name is on the lease," he said. "It's mine."

"But you're leaving!"

"So I'll sublet. But not to you."

"You've got to be kidding."

He tossed back a swig of soda, his eyes glittering dangerously.

"You're not? That is so low."

He shrugged. "I'll need your key by Monday."

At that I slammed the bedroom door in his face. My hand quivered in fury as I took out two suitcases and started piling in my clothes, shoes, cosmetics. I wanted to take as many things as possible right now to avoid small trips back. With productive anger I slapped in pairs of jeans, tucking in bulky sweatshirts and sweaters and zipped-up cases of shampoo and lotion and conditioner.

Somehow I hadn't expected Nate to be mean about this break, but his cruelty underlined my resolve in bold, red strokes.

It was over with Nate. Time to move on.

25

I was over the loss of the cottage in about ten minutes. If that was the price I had to pay to scrape Nate out of my life, I figured I could well afford it.

I marched past Nate, who was flipping through channels, flaked out on the sofa with a major case of bed head. "You'll get my key in a few days." You worm. With a carload of suitcases and duffel bags, I sped away from the cottage, gravel flying under my tires. Ha! I'd always wanted to make an exit like that.

When I pulled up outside The Christmas Elf, Ben was coming out of Miller's with a cardboard tray of coffee and a paper bag. "Lola sent us bagels this morning," he called, nodding toward the bag. "She said you two had a late night. Something about a sleepover party?"

"Something like that." I unlocked the door, pulled off my coat, and went through my morning routine of turning on lights, checking the thermostat, winding clocks, and setting up a series of Christmas CDs for the day. This shop had been a great escape for me—my real home—and for a moment I wished I could move in here, though that would never work. I sighed.

"What's up?" Ben asked, handing me a cup of coffee. "You look like Santa cancelled Christmas."

"I'm going to need a place to stay," I said, curling my fingers around the warm paper cup. "Wow. I guess I'd better call a realtor."

"What about Nate? And Munchin Realty?"

"I won't be calling Munchin," I said. "Nate and I split up, and he's not going to want to help me."

Ben nodded, untucking the navy blue scarf at his neck. He slid his rawhide jacket off and sat on a stool beside my worktable. "Are you okay?"

"I'm fine. Actually, better than fine. I feel lighter. Liberated." I shrugged. "Hey, I just got rid of some excess baggage and it feels great."

Ben's smile lit his eyes and made the corners crinkle in sort of a cowboy way, and I knew he understood it all—the feelings of hurt and failure and liberation, the chance for a "do over." "Good for you," he said.

As we sipped our coffee together, I sat down on the stool beside Ben and thanked God for this colorful scene that was my life; this was just a shared moment with Ben in the shop, but it reminded me that I did have a life. It might seem silly, but I was grateful that I branched out here with the shop and my friends and the folks at the senior center and the kids from Diane's day care center. All this time, in the years that I'd been here with Nate, I thought I was biding my time—waiting for his divorce, waiting for a proposal, waiting for our lives to begin—when all along, I was weaving my own dreams in the fabric of this community. I was one of the small squares in the quilts from Georgia's quilting bee: a compact image, and yet an integral part of the exquisite grid of signs and symbols.

A second later the quiet moment was gone when the door bells jingled and Cracker popped in. "I just spoke to Serge and he's coming next week—the eighteenth. Will you still be here, Ricki?"

I nodded. "That's the last weekend that the shop is open, so I'll get to see him."

"I'll still be here," Ben added as he moved over to one of the chairs by the fire.

"You're always here," Cracker said, turning to me. "Is it true about Nate? You two are . . ." He made a chopping gesture at his neck.

"Something like that. He's heading back to Providence this weekend."

Cracker pursed his lip. "Mm-hmm. The worm turns."

"How's Serge doing?" I asked, trying to change the subject. "Did you tell him we miss him around here?"

"He's fine. He got some more information on the history of eggnog. Says I should change the name of the bar to 'Grog and Fog,' but I think that's taking it a little bit too far."

"So what's the new nog source?" I asked, always up for Christmas trivia.

"Well, some people think the 'nog' in eggnog comes from the word 'noggin,' which was an old European term for a small wooden mug used to serve milk and egg punches."

"That would be a cute item to sell," I said. "Little carved noggins to serve your eggnog in? It could come in sets of—"

"Wait, there's more," Cracker interrupted. "You see, Colonial Americans called rum 'grog,' and when they made this egg beverage in the colonies they added rum instead of wine, which is what the Europeans used. Hence, people began to call the drink 'egg and grog,' which might have simply been shortened to eggnog."

"Serge is a wealth of information," Ben said.

Cracker rubbed his hands together deviously. "Yes, but he has yet to come upon any reference to Voodoo Eggnog, so I must believe that my drink is an original. If I were a man of ego, I'd submit it to some contest or bartender's journal, but I prefer to maintain the secret recipe in relative obscurity here in these Outer Banks."

"Well, Voodoo Eggnog is certainly delicious, but it didn't work on Nate," I said. "In fact, it sent him running."

"Um-hmm." Cracker folded his arms. "I rest my case."

* * *

Later that day, I left Adena in charge of the shop and I headed over to the church to meet with Reverend Forest. He'd called to say that things were developing with the Salems' housing situation, perhaps I would like to join an informal meeting there? Although I wasn't sure that I could contribute, I figured it was worth a shot.

In the church parking lot I unloaded the gift boxes that Adena and I had wrapped in cheerful Christmas prints and tied off with bows containing tiny ornaments. I went to the door that Reverend Forest had directed me to, the building behind the church where Sunday school classes were usually held. I heard a woman's voice floating down the hall—a familiar voice, so I followed the voice and the light spilling out from a classroom. Inside, Diane—Joey's teacher—was speaking with two men. The reverend stood up and welcomed me, and as I went to put my packages down I caught a look at the other man . . . Ben.

"What are you doing here?" I asked.

"Now that's a fine welcome. I might act as the general contractor on this project."

"Ben used to work with Habitats, and we figured his engineering experience might be helpful," Reverend Forest added with a smile. "But honestly, Ricki, we will take any volunteers we can get. We're always in need of helpers."

I sat in one of the desk chairs. "Is there anything that can be done? I mean, about their home?"

"I've been in touch with Amy Salem, and I think there's a great deal we can do," George said. "Right now we're trying to get financing for Mrs. Salem, so that we can purchase the materials to complete the renovations on their home. I think the outlook is excellent, but I do worry about their living conditions in the interim."

Diane shook her head. "I had no idea Joey was living in such poor conditions, but it does explain a few things, some of his behavior."

"I wasn't invited inside their trailer," I said, "but it looks rustic. They're roughing it."

"No water or electrical hookup?" Ben winced. "We've got to change that."

"Perhaps there's a member of our congregation who would take them in for the next six months or so," Reverend Forest suggested. "Just until the renovation is completed."

I would have liked to offer, but I had to remember my new homeless status. As the others talked about possibilities, an idea formed. The cottage would be empty. Nate held the lease through June.

"You know," I interrupted Forest, "there's a furnished cottage opening up for a sublet and it just might be perfect."

Diane shook her head skeptically. "This time of year?"

"Trust me, it's perfect." Already I was picturing Joey and Lila opening Christmas gifts by the fireplace, the winter sun shining through the glass bricks and illuminating the blue glass collection. "And I'll be happy to contribute toward the rent, as long as someone else deals with the realtor."

Ben's eyes connected with mine as he caught my idea. "Not bad," he said, nodding. "I think it might work."

26

The bells jingled as Ben cracked the door open and shouldered his way in, his hands full with a tray of coffee and a bag of pastries. "What, no customers yet?"

I laughed, tying an apron behind my waist. "It might even be a quiet week, with the regular shipping deadlines over. At this point, most people will just be shopping for small gifts and ornaments to add to their collections."

"Well, thank God for that," Ben said as he handed me a cup of coffee.

I nodded at the full tray. "You feeling extra thirsty this morning?"

"I ran into Cracker at Miller's. He said he's coming over. And then there's Georgia."

"Oh, right!" I'd nearly forgotten that Georgia was coming in early to talk about possible employment. Although the rush had slacked off, The Christmas Elf now had more than enough year-round business to warrant a full-time employee, and with her creative ideas and personal charm, Georgia would be perfect. I tucked holly-printed tissue around a large wreath, then put the gold lid on the gift box. "I could use Georgia's help right now.

This is going out by FedEx, along with five other special orders. And this one's going to Chicago." I tucked a fat stream of brocade red ribbon under the box and started to assemble a bow.

"I'll help you with that," Ben said, pressing down the ribbon with one thumb. "You tie, I'll hold."

"Thanks. And thanks for all your help this weekend. It was great of you to play Santa again."

"As I said, I've got the hair."

I snipped the end of ribbon and shook my head. "Santa has snow white hair. Yours is more silver."

"Premature gray. I worried too much in my younger days."

"And do you worry now?" I asked.

"Only about things that matter. About making sure children are warm and well-fed."

"You really *are* Santa Claus."

"About a certain girl who found herself stranded on an island."

That gave me pause. Partly because most people were too politically correct to use the term "girl," partly because it took a moment to realize he meant me. "You worry about me? That's so sweet." My heart was beating a little faster than usual, and the potpourri spices seemed sharp and heady in the air. "I'm not stranded. Not really. I'm happy to be here, and Roxanne thinks she'll be able to find me a condo in January. 'Til then, Lola's stuck with me. Except when I'm in New York." I shot a look at the calendar. "Holy Christmas! I have to make plane reservations. Or maybe I should drive. I don't know."

"You could stay here," Ben said, picking up a cluster of berries from my worktable. "We could have a small party. Cracker and Serge will be here. Georgia and Daniel."

I looked up at him, my heart beating painfully in my ribs. More than anything, I wanted to spend Christmas with Ben, and it wasn't until this precise moment that I put that together in my mind. Mysterious, quiet Ben. Benjamin Slater, who sat by the fire and read his newspapers and brought me coffee and helped to entertain the customers. Ben whose deep, soft voice soothed everyone's worries.

"Ben . . ." I reached out and put my hand over his. "I can't spend Christmas with you." He glanced away, disappointed. "Even though I'd love to! There's nothing I'd love more, but I promised my sister I'd go to New York, and she had this major health scare last year so I can't really get out of it. But . . . I've got a suite booked at the Waldorf and. . . ."

What was I suggesting? Here Ben was holding out an olive branch and I was snatching it up and jumping his bones.

"I mean . . . you can have it. The suite. I mean, if you want to come to New York." His fingers curled under mine, his touch warm and soothing, maybe a little arousing, unless that was just wishful thinking.

"Why would I take it?" he said softly, lifting my hand and stepping around my work table to close the distance between us. "A suite at the Waldorf would be no fun without you in it."

I was worried that he'd feel my heart thumping as he pulled me against him, but then it didn't seem to matter. Because we were kissing and his breathing was heavy, too, and the way his hands moved over my shoulders and back, massaging and melting, and our lips pressed together, the soft texture of his mouth with sweet coffee taste, the soapy smell of his skin, the thick, silky feel of his hair. . . .

We kissed and cuddled, and I wanted to cry over my own idiocy, over the way that time unravels certain mysteries that simply cannot be revealed until destiny allows. Ben had been here all along, right before my eyes, but then, I'd been suffering from cloudy vision.

The bell at the door jingled, and Ben ended the series of kisses with a sigh. "Jingle bells. Sounds like an angel just got her wings."

I smiled and pressed my head against his chest, unable to let go just yet. "That's a beautiful symbol," I said.

He touched my chin and lifted my head. "To hell with symbols; I think it's true."

And he let me go with a squeeze of my hand, then went to his chair by the fire as Cracker sauntered up to my work table, grabbed a coffee and mouthed: YOU AND BEN?

I nodded, then laughed as I fell back on a stool, pretending to start a new wreath, though mostly I was just fingering beads and sorting out tiny ornaments, my mind consumed by overwhelming joy.

"Well, sugar," Cracker drawled, cocking an eyebrow, "score one for Voodoo Eggnog."

A Christmas Sky

December, 2004

Emma

27

My timing is way off; I know that.

Right now my apartment is full of people—friends and coworkers, sipping champagne and spiked eggnog and talking about their Christmas plans—while the hostess of the party is holed up in the master bathroom. Not the most hostessy thing to do, but I can't wait any longer. I bought the pregnancy test this morning and planned to take it right away, but then Randy surprised me by taking me out to brunch. And then our afternoon was cluttered with party errands: chilling the champagne, mixing the eggnog, picking up the salads from Dean & Deluca and the bagels from Zabar's. The only window of time would have been while I was taking a shower, but then Randy suggested that we soap up together and I didn't want to set the pee test up in front of him since I wasn't ready to tell him that I might be pregnant with someone else's baby.

Yes, my timing is totally off.

So I'm sitting here on the edge of the tub in the master bathroom, watching the little stick that I peed on to see if a cross appears. A cross—that would mean I'm pregnant. Funny that the laboratory people would choose a cross: the symbol of crucifixion. Which is what I'll do to my little brain if I am, in fact, pregnant right now. How ironic that would be: the Christmas gift I'd always dreamed of, the ultimate gift of a baby, a new life. I have always dreamed of becoming a mother, and over the past few months with Randy I've been able to visualize that dream clearly.

But under very different circumstances.

In the scenario of my dreams, my baby has a loving father: a capable, kind man who fills out the perfect triangle of my loving, nuclear family.

That man is not Jonathan Thompson.

Randy, however, would be the perfect father. He wants to be a father, and I want to be the mother of his child. In fact, we've been trying to get pregnant for the past six months. The bitter irony: if I'm pregnant right now, it's not Randy's baby.

I turn to the towel rack beside me and bury my face in a fluffy maroon towel. It smells of fabric softener and freshly bathed baby. Sweet. If I'm pregnant I'm going to need special baby soaps, along with Vaseline for diaper rash and a truckload of Pampers. I know my fair share about babies from my nieces and nephews—seven of them, two in New Jersey and five in Maryland. They won't believe their Aunt Emma is pregnant. That is, if I am. At the moment the little stick isn't forming any color patterns at all, which throws me into a bit of panic. What if I did it wrong? Fifteen bucks for this kit, what if I didn't hit the right spot? And how stupid would that be?

Through the wall I hear laughter; I withdraw from the towel and listen carefully. It must be coming from the main bathroom, which butts up against this room. I recognize Jane's voice.

"Well, hurry up and get your ass in here before everyone at the party sees."

The thump of a shutting door.

"Are you planning to take advantage of me, young lady?" That's Marty, Jane's guy. "Here and now? I have to question the wisdom of—"

"Just shut up and kiss me," Jane tells him, and I go back to the fluffy towel and press my face into the sweet scent and shudder.

And then there's excruciating silence during which I have to wonder and worry what might be transpiring next door. I flush the toilet then run the cold water to create a shield of noise. I know it's a crime to waste clean water that way, but Jane's my best friend in the world and I can't stand feeling like I'm hiding in her pocket while she makes love to Marty.

Jane and Marty are a great couple. I think Randy and I make a good couple, too, which is why I don't understand how I could have botched things up like this.

I press my face against the cool tile and look over to the shower stall where Randy and I made love this afternoon. When I'm with Randy, it's as if we belong together. The feeling is diametrically opposed to the tangled, angry passion that used to burn between Jonathan and me. Damn him.

I flash back to that night nearly a month ago: Thanksgiving weekend. Randy flew out on Wednesday morning, heading off to Oregon to spend the holiday with his mother and siblings, nieces and nephews. It was early—before work—but I cried when he said good-bye, not wanting to see him go. I had spent the past few months trying to pinpoint when I was ovulating, and as luck would have it I was going to be ripe that weekend while Randy was gone, so add hormonal anguish to the whole separation thing. I walked him down to the lobby and told him I was worried about him flying during the holidays. He seemed moved by my rush of emotion, and down in the lobby, in front of the window leading out to Amsterdam Avenue, he pulled me close and whispered: "This is the last Thanksgiving we'll spend apart." Watching his yellow cab head off toward LaGuardia, I worried that he would never come back—a prescient flash of doom. At the time I didn't realize that the bad luck would fall in my path, not his.

That was the weekend Jonathan stopped by. It was Friday night, and I'd just gotten off the phone with Jane to beg off dinner, having been at work since eight o'clock that morning trying to learn the mechanics of a large Manhattan branch of Mainline Bank; trying to hold my ground as a supervisor though I was mostly feeling lost; trying to adhere to corporate policy among employees who despised the corporation; trying to stave off a headache . . . without success on any of these fronts. Stretched out on the sofa with a bowl of cold edamame beside me and a Lean Cuisine Mac 'n' Cheese under my chin, I groaned when the intercom buzzed.

"There's a Mr. Jonathan Thompson here to see you, Ms. Dombrowski," Steve the Doorman said.

Ugh! The last person I wanted to see.

"I'm sorry," Steve corrected himself. "That's *Officer* Thompson."

"Like that makes him any better than the rest of us," I said with the intercom off. Jonathan had always been quick to use his police ID for preferential treatment: to get us into clubs, to get a reduced bill at a restaurant, to summon instant respect. Well, it wasn't going to work on me anymore. "Tell him I'm on my way out," I said into the intercom, then went into the kitchen to rummage for a bottle of wine. As I popped the cork, I wondered how I could have thought I was in love with Jonathan Thompson. Maybe part of the allure was his last name. Marriage would have made me Emma Thompson, like the actress who could do no wrong in my book. Last-name fantasies are the big hazard of being born with a name like Emma Dombrowski. Nothing against my Polish grandparents, but couldn't someone along the line have shortened the name to Donner or something? Instead, I get saddled with this wonker of a last name, which puts me on the perennial husband hunt for something better. Randy's last name is Walker. Could the man be more perfectly suited to me? Emma Walker . . . I loved the sound of my future self.

I was pouring chardonnay into a glass when the doorbell chimed. That bastard! I thought, slamming the bottle on the counter.

I threw open the door, annoyed by the irreverent gleam in his pale blue eyes. I said: "You're not supposed to be up here."

"I came to pick up my stuff. Stuff that's rightfully mine. How come that guy doesn't know me? I used to live here."

"That was more than a year ago, Jonathan. Now you have no right to be here."

"Oh, I have rights." He stepped inside, walked right past me, surveyed the living room. "I've got MasterShield," he said, flipping his badge at me with a flourish.

I folded my arms across my chest. "Did you pull a gun on Steve? Or just tell him that you're 'on the job,' that big insider code."

"You gotta know how to talk to people," Jonathan said. "Put your time in the NYPD, you learn how to talk to people."

"How long's it been now, four years?"

"Five." He grinned, pausing to look me up and down. "You're still looking hot, Emma." He held out his arms. "And I haven't put on the pork yet. Actually, I've been working out." He flexed an arm and moved closer to show me a blip of biceps. "Feel that."

"No, thanks."

"I joined a gym. After I appeared on *Guiding Light* I realized that maybe modeling was the thing. I mean, acting is the ultimate prize, but modeling is a good start. You know the guy who plays Ryan on *All My Children?* He got his start as an underwear model." He pressed a hand to the crotch of his jeans. "You've seen the package, Em. What do you think?"

"I wish you and your package luck," I said. The last five minutes were an instant reminder of the many reasons Jonathan and I had broken up, and I figured the best way to get rid of him was a quick pat on the back, then a boot in the butt.

But Jonathan had other ideas, as he sank down into Randy's leather chair and stared up at the ceiling. "You painted the ceiling blue? Ceilings are supposed to be white."

"It's cerulean," I said, glad that I no longer had to take decorating advice from a cop. It had been Randy's idea to bring color to the room through the cathedral ceiling, and we'd both been enchanted by the result, sometimes snuggling on the couch and staring up hopefully, as if gazing into our future. "The color of the sky."

He surveyed the room. "What is all this crap? That painting . . . Is that a bunch of stars or alien eyeballs?"

It was Randy's work, entitled "Country Sky."

"And that mess in the corner?"

Randy's paintbox.

"And what, you got a bike up here?" He eyed me suspiciously. "Don't tell me you ride a bike now, Em."

"It's my boyfriend's stuff. He lives here now."

Jonathan's jaw dropped. "I'm crushed!"

"Yeah, right. Will you leave now?"

As he took a deep breath and glanced back at the painting, I could see that my words had hit him like a physical blow. "Christ . . . I can't believe you hooked up with someone else."

"Jonathan, it's been more than a year, and you moved in with Lindsay." That would be *the* Lindsay Green, "Weather Watcher" on *Eyewitness News 6.* I'd been devastated when Jonathan took up with her. Inside, I knew he was pursuing her partly because of her showbiz connections—the limo ride to fame—but it hurt to be replaced by someone so perky, so blond. A gentle, mild weatherfront. "You moved on," I said. "So did I."

He sighed. "And where's the boyfriend now?"

"Not here at the moment," I said cautiously. "If you'll give me a minute, I'll find the key to the basement locker. We moved your things down there."

"Had to get me out of sight, huh? Does he feel threatened by me?"

Not in the least, I thought.

Jonathan looked back at Randy's painting, sucked in a breath, then let out a sob. "Oh, shit, Emma! My life is shit!" Much to my amazement, he pressed his face into his hands and began to cry. Wail. A major meltdown.

I suspected forced drama until he brushed away his tears and I saw that his face was a red, puffy mess. Tentatively, I stepped toward him.

"It can't be that bad. You always weather the storm, or at least that's what Lindsay would say."

"She broke up with me. And I really loved her."

Oh, just drive needles in my eyes, why don't you? "There, there," I muttered. "At least you've got your acting career, right?

And the modeling? People love that you're a cop in your spare time." Which was sort of the way Jonathan perceived his life.

"I don't know what to do. I didn't know where to turn. Lindsay's gone and so is *Guiding Light.* I made a pass at the casting director, and she didn't take it well. If I even get close to the set, they're threatening to slap me with a restraining order."

I felt my eyes bug out wider. "Whoa! You've been busy."

"Busy fucking myself!" he said in a fit of anger. "I've fucked everything up."

I wholeheartedly agreed, but wasn't going to kick him when he was down.

"I've screwed myself over, and hurt the people I care about." He lifted his chin, his wet eyes meeting mine. "I've hurt you, Emma. I'm sorry for that."

Despite his flaws, Jonathan did have a gift for sincerity. In that moment I felt his pain, accepted his apology.

"Look. . . ." I stepped closer, leaning on the arm of the big leather chair. "You followed your heart. I've always admired your ambition. This time it didn't work out, but that's no reason to stop. I'm sure there are bigger and better opportunities in your future."

He gulped. "Do you know anyone at the Ford Agency? I need an 'in' there."

"Nope." I rubbed his back. "I got nothing for you, Jonathan. But I'm sure you'll work things out."

He pulled me down into the broad chair so that I was half on his lap, and I gave him a warm, supportive hug. Shades of the old Jonathan emerged—a snuggly bear, a vulnerable spirit. I'd been mistaken to think that I'd loved him, for our relationship had never been a partnership; it was more like an adoption of a wayward bad boy. I hugged him hard, willing to help him out one more time.

He pressed his face into my shoulder and for a moment I thought I felt his warm mouth opening against my skin. No . . . it couldn't be. I rubbed his back again, and he burrowed in against me like a child. He pressed his face into my chest.

"I've missed you so much," he whispered against my breast.

I touched the dark curls on his head. "You're going to be okay, honey."

"I know." He ran his hands along my waist, burrowing close. The slightest movement sent a twinge of longing through me. I held him sedately, rocked him, as the feeling began to grow. Then I realized its source: he was nuzzling my breast, working it with his tongue through the thin material of my nightgown.

I gasped and pushed him away. "Jonathan! Stop it."

"I'm sorry. It just seemed right. You're so nurturing, Emma. And you taste good."

I moved over to the couch, closing my robe around me. "Listen, I've moved on to a healthy relationship. I'm not going to jeopardize that, Jonathan."

"I understand." He held up his hands. "I totally get that." He took a deep breath, trying to steady himself. "Do you mind if I hang out here awhile? Just 'til I pull myself together."

I really did mind, but what were the options? Ask him to leave, then endure his tirade on the cold brutality in my soul? Because that was the way Jonathan snapped, the level of his self-absorption. Weighing the trade-offs, I thought it best to let him ride it out here. "You can hang here, but just for a little while," I said, tacking on a lie for security. "Randy's going to be home later, and you're probably not in the mood to meet him." I picked up the remote and clicked on the TV. "Right?"

He shook his head, his eyes red from crying. "That lucky bastard."

A rebuttal formed in my brain, and I longed to blast Jonathan with every point. *You could have been that lucky bastard! You could have had me if you hadn't chased every skirt that walked by when you were on patrol. You and I would be a couple if you hadn't dumped Emma the Banker for Lindsay the Weather Girl.*

I looked at my fingernails, ticking off each point to myself, knowing that in the end it was a waste of time to voice my argument. Jonathan had moved on, and so had I. And in the end, I was much better off without him.

28

That night, after another hour or two spent describing the unfair hand he'd been dealt in the deck of romance and career, Jonathan dozed off on the couch. I plodded off to bed, mildly cursing myself for being such a softy. Fine, let him flake on the couch. I would duck out to the gym in the morning, then bring the doorman up to help me escort Jonathan out and on his way—though I doubted he'd be here that long. If there were females to be sniffed and celebrities to hound, Jonathan would not rest long.

I took a tiny sleeping pill, crawled into bed, and called Randy on his cell. As it rang I debated whether or not to tell him about Jonathan, then decided against it. If I were the one thousands of miles away, I'd freak to hear that my guy's ex was staying over. On the other hand, a casual mention once he was back would seem totally innocuous. I decided that a simple "Oh, by the way, the idiotic ex stopped by to pick up his stuff," would cover it. After a few minutes of yawning into the phone, I wished Randy goodnight and shut off the light. It was at some time during the hours of darkness, in the haze of sleep, that I felt a body beside me. Accustomed to having Randy there, I rolled over and backed against him, glad for the warmth. His hand slid over my hip, caressing my butt, and I sighed and moved deeper into sleep.

Sleep was seductive, so much so that when I felt his hand cup my breast, I wanted to resist him. Sleep was better now.

Then his fingers moved over my nipple, teasing and caressing until it tightened. I felt my body begin to coil as his hand moved to my other breast, then down my belly, smoothing a path down over the ridge of my hip bone to the sensitive crease at the top of my thigh. My nightgown pushed aside, his fingers teased the folds between my legs, dipping into the hollow there, causing me to moan against my will.

Okay, then, sleep could wait. I opened my eyes to shapes and colors I didn't expect: dark curls on the white pillow, angular face.

Jonathan.

"Huh?"

"It's okay, baby," he whispered.

"No . . ." I stopped his hand, tried to push away but felt weighed down by the blankets. "It's not okay."

"Emma, Emma . . ." He caught my hand and caressed my arm, kissed my knuckles. "Don't freak. It's just me. You're fine." His hand spread sensual warmth up my arm, over my shoulder then down to one breast.

I wanted to get away, knew I had to escape, but something held me there. A primal need. Sheer enticement. Sexual desire.

He pressed his lips to mine and I succumbed to his kissing, remembering his technique of the plundering tongue and his taste, the odd tang of that clove-flavored chewing gum he loved. As we kissed and caressed each other, I remembered the way his body fit so well against mine. A simple law of physics. Randy was my mate in all ways, but Jonathan's body fit mine like a plug in an outlet, a clean match. Boy fits girl.

"I can't do this," I told him.

"You can." He pushed my nightgown aside to suck on one nipple. "And you will. We were always good together, Emma." He nudged his hips against me, pressed his naked erection to my thigh, turning my resistance to smoke. "We fit together, you and I."

"In bed," I said, turning my head away as he grabbed my hips and pulled me down off the pillows. "We were good in bed, but sex is no mystery. Any two people can engage. Oh!"

Already he was between my thighs, his taut groin pressing into me. God help me, I loved the way he felt. I wanted the sex. My body was on fire, just not for this particular man.

"You like that?" He teased, his face inches from mine, his blue eyes shiny and stern. "You want it, don't you?"

"Yes!" I hissed. "But we can't."

"I think we can," he said, pushing my legs onto his shoulders to take me with his mouth.

As he nudged me toward orgasm I gave in. Just this once. One short visit to the past. Quick ex-sex.

Once, and then I'd be rid of him forever.

In so many ways, Jonathan was a masterful manipulator, an above-average technician. He worked my body into a frenzy, then rose up to plant his lips on mine.

"I knew you missed me," he said with a jab of his hips between my legs.

I gasped at the hard stab. "A condom," I breathed. "You need a condom."

"Don't have any."

"Of course," I said, wanting to stop but unable to slow the rhythm thrumming through us. Jonathan never carried condoms, never took responsibility. Why should that change?

"Don't worry," he said in a strained voice. "I'll pull out."

Pull out? Hadn't heard that one since I was sixteen! That was total nonsense, utterly ineffective and I knew it. But at the moment I couldn't let myself care, and I certainly didn't think anything would come of this. Six months of unprotected passion with Randy and I wasn't pregnant yet. What were the chances of that happening in a five-minute fling with Jonathan? Really, I had a high math aptitude, had majored in statistics in college and worked with numbers every day. I knew a thing or two about probability, and what were the odds?

I glance over at the pregnancy test stick and my jaw drops. Apparently, I've hit my one in a million.

I move closer, to the closed toilet seat, and stare at the little pink cross. Oh, yes, there are definitely two lines. Definitely a cross, God help me.

I curse softly. There is my answer, my ticking time bomb. I hold the hot potato with no clue where to toss it.

With a frantic feeling, I snatch up the pregnancy kit, shove it in the plastic bag from the pharmacy, and twist the ends around twenty-five times before throwing it into my side of the vanity.

Okay, then. Time to face the music.

29

I move quickly through the hall of the apartment, to the dimly lit room that is now alight with silvery stars of various shapes and sizes glistening over our cerulean ceiling—Randy's rendition of a Christmas sky after some teasing from me. The subdued lighting and vaulting panoramic sky have the desired effect, casting an aura of calm over our supercharged Manhattanite friends. People seem relaxed, their laughter bubbling gently, their conversations various pools of enchantment.

I take a deep breath, catching a wave of cinnamon and orange from the wassail Randy left heating in the kitchen. Such a perfect party . . . all that's lacking is the hostess with the most-ess news. *Don't you look great! So glad you could make it. Have a glass of eggnog, and, by the way, did you hear I got knocked up by my ex? Isn't it ironic how whatever can go wrong, will?*

"It's about time you made an appearance," Jane says, stealing up beside me in her smartly tailored striped silk shirt adorned with a fake fur shawl. "Randy's been giving you credit all over the place for the Starry Night decor. You've really got that man hoodwinked."

"You think so?" The words stick in my throat as I think of the ultimate and obvious deception: passing this baby off as his.

Jane squeezes my arm. "Emma Dee, you look like you just saw a ghost."

I take a deep breath, remind myself that this room is full of people I like, people Randy and I invited. That alone should calm me, if I can just get the taste of guilt out of my mouth.

"I like the blue ceiling," Jane says. "It reminds me a little of the way Mom decorated the place. She went for the big, bold colors."

My apartment used to belong to the Conners. When it was time to sell, neither Jane nor Ricki wanted the place, but they were happy to pass it into my hands, assuring me that any ghosts from the past had long been laid to rest. It might seem odd to buy your best friend's childhood home, but in a market where the perfect place keeps getting snatched from under your feet by faster, higher bidders, I felt lucky to have secured this apartment.

"Great eggnog," Jane says. "Marty wants to know your recipe, and he considers himself a grog afficionado."

"A drink," I say. "That's what I need." I leave Jane and spin toward the kitchen, already in motion as I realize I shouldn't consume any alcohol now. While no one is looking I mix a fake candy-cane cosmo—just cranberry juice and seltzer in a cosmo glass—then rejoin Jane, who's now mixing it up with Marty and a cluster of workers from the bank branch I'm assigned to. Bank policy shuns administrators like me mingling with nonexecutive track employees, but I figure my private life is my own business, and I can barely tolerate the stuffed shirt executives. So I invited the tellers, including our head teller, Thai Ng.

"There she is! There Miss Emma!" Thai says, wiggling out of the bank group to embrace me. "Air kiss!" she calls cheerfully.

"And sporting a candy-cane cosmo," Jane says wryly. "Brave soul."

I toast the bank crowd. "So glad you could make it."

A handful of tellers have shown up, including our trainee,

Manuel Alvarez. "I love your apartment, Emma," Manuel says politely. "I've never seen such decorations. It's like a museum!"

"Too much!" Thai agrees. "Your boyfriend have talent, for sure. Way over the limit."

"You mean over the top," I suggest, gazing up at the comforting stars.

"Whatever! He golden," Thai says emphatically. I'm not sure how long ago she emigrated from Vietnam, but her English is still choppy and singsongy, and I doubt it will ever improve much. Her voice always strikes me as friendly and chatty, and her banking skills are impeccable. So far Thai has been the only glimmer of life in my entire eighteen-month training program.

"Randy told us he's designing the set for a new show," another teller named Astrid chimes in. Management is down on her for multiple piercings and a fiery red henna dye-job, but since she confided that she plays bass in a rock band at night, I've taken a liking to her and have tried to give her a later schedule whenever possible. "He says it's sort of a downtown *Phantom?*"

"Right," I say, giving the synopsis: "Society's rejected emerge from the underworld to a city of light."

"Is that why I heard him talking about designing sewer caps?" Jane added. "Charming."

Thai throws up her hands. "Beautiful! Dat's beautiful! And Randy say you inspire the stars." She gestures to our ceiling. "A Christmas sky! He really love Emma."

"What did I say?" Jane nudges me. "You've got him wrapped around your little finger."

"It's just that I was telling Randy about a Christmas tradition in our family. My father always had a working telescope, and when we were kids he bundled us up on Christmas night and pointed us up to the sky. There's something magical about a Christmas sky, so dense with stars. Dad used to say that we could still spot the star that guided the Three Wise Men." I glance nervously at Jane, expecting her to jump all over that, but she's just listening. "It probably sounds sentimental."

"Not really," Astrid picks up. "If you know anything about astrology, there's a connection between the alignment of the planets and the birth of Christ. Whether or not you believe he was a savior, there were definitely cosmic forces at work two thousand years ago."

"Really?" Jane squints at Astrid, clearly intrigued. "And do you know much about astrology? I'm an Aries with Pisces rising, but I never knew what the hell that meant . . ."

As the stream of conversation splits into various tangents, I think I might just survive this party, this gathering of good and earnest people. The party, yes. The pregnancy? I'm not so sure.

Jane's sister, Ricki, arrives fashionably late with her new boyfriend, the retired engineer turned surfer dude. Ben is shaggier then I expected, and yet sophisticated in such a kind way, handing me a bottle of wine and telling me he hopes I like reds because this one got high marks in *Wine Spectator.* He gets drinks for my friends from the bank, helps Marty ice down more champagne, and immediately hits it off with Randy as they discuss constellation patterns and trajectories of light.

I pull back from the conversation and wonder about the strange language among men—some men—who speak of cars and sciences and plumbing as if those topics were childhood friends.

Ricki joins me, her cheeks a giddy pink, as she digs a fork into pasta salad, her eyes on Ben. "He's amazing isn't he?"

"Not at all what I was expecting. Not engineery. And his hair is so cute. I like that silver."

"I like him so much, sometimes I think my heart's just gonna up and pop," Ricki says, her mouth crumpling in a silly grin.

"Do you like him?" I tease, "Or do you like-like-like him?"

She sighs. "Don't get me started. You don't know how close I came to making a huge mistake with Nate."

"We all make mistakes," I say, thinking of my predicament but veering off it quickly. "How's the shop coming? Jane says you're having some trouble with the books."

"The shop is great. Business is booming, but my bookkeeper moved to Atlanta and I haven't been able to balance the books ever since."

"Want me to take a look at them?"

"Would you? I hate to pile more work on you."

"Bookkeeping is therapy for me. A far cry from work these days, believe me. Drop the books by some night and I'll take a look."

"And for that you'll have my undying gratitude . . . and my firstborn." Ricki holds her salad aside to hug me. *No, thanks, got my fill of baby right now,* I want to say.

"And I can't wait for Easthampton. Marty's place is supposed to be charming." Jane's boyfriend has invited us to his Hamptons house, a quiet place in a wooded section of eastern Long Island. "You've been there, right?"

"Last summer," I say. "And it's very cozy. Looking forward to it, though Randy and I can't spend the whole week there. We'll both be working until Christmas Eve."

"Isn't it ironic that none of us is single this year? Our sad singles dinner has blossomed into a couples thing."

"Who are you calling 'sad' singles?" I say, patting her back. I always liked Ricki, but I came to adore her when she bolstered her sister during the thyroid crisis last year.

"It's going to be a great Christmas," Ricki says. "We'll figure out who's bringing what. I'm a better cook than Jane, but I'm planning to use her apartment to do some baking. Did she tell you Ben and I are staying at the Waldorf?"

"Nice?"

A wicked grin crosses her face. "Decadent."

Randy summons me from across the room—I feel the electric current between us, his warm eyes loving me from a distance. How will I tell this man I've betrayed him?

"Kerry was admiring your Christmas sky," Randy tells me.

"It's fabulous." Kerry glances up from an open book of photographs—pictures from the last production he worked on with Randy. He cocks one pierced eyebrow. "I've just got tacky red lights up at my place."

"Early bordello," Sheryl tells him. "Fits with the theme of your decor."

"I'm looking for another place," Kerry says defensively.

"You should come to Brooklyn," says Gil, also from the set design crew. "Park Slope is the new center of the universe."

As Randy slips one arm around my waist, I feel relieved to have my two bedroom co-op on the Upper West Side. The second bedroom with the computer and Randy's easels will make a great nursery. I shiver slightly as he kisses my neck.

"You okay?" he asks.

"Just tired. The rush of preparty adrenaline has worn off." *And guilt is very tiring,* I think. It's exhausting.

I am glad when the theater gang heads downstairs, planning to have dinner at Casa Mexicana, two doors down. They are the last guests to go, my bank friends having hurried off to be with family and friends for dinner, and Ricki and Jane having gone to burrow into warm pillows with their mates. Randy tells the crew that we might meet them in a bit, but I know it's just a friendly send-off; better to leave the possibility of the night open.

When the door closes, his eyes encompass me. "Have we paid our social dues for the season?"

I pick up two pillaged platters and bring them into the kitchen. "Did you see Ricki's gift?"

"Why do people feel compelled to bring gifts?" he calls from the living room.

"Tradition." I go to the dining room table and unveil a potted evergreen decorated in tiny gold and blue stars.

"Whoa." He seems startled. "Nice."

"She's a Christmas fiend."

"It shows." He turns the tree, then tugs on my hand. "Saves me from having to go and cut one down in Central Park."

I laugh as he pulls me onto the sofa. "You can't do that."

"But we need a tree. Got to have a tree. It's tradition." He nuzzles my cheek with his nose, then kisses me.

It steals my breath away, and I remember the electric charge between us, so achingly familiar yet brand new. Our hands study the familiar maps of each other's body as we begin to make love. I let my mind tumble into him wholeheartedly, then feel a lash from the whip of guilt.

Is this right? Is it somehow wrong to make love with Randy now that I know I'm pregnant with another man's child? Our relationship has always been honest, and I'm a terrible liar. Should I tell him about Jonathan?

No. The truth would only hurt Randy. He probably wouldn't leave me over it, but it would throw useless muck into our clear, sweet relationship. I won't tell him . . . at least, not now.

I let the dark feelings go as I kiss Randy and rake his hair back and gently hook my fingers into the pale peach shell of his ear, settling onto the fleshy lobe, a sensitive region. He has already found the muscle in the side of my neck, my hot spot, and his lips press a massage there that lifts me into a place beyond this sofa, beyond this planet.

As our clothes drop to the floor and our bare skin melds I am reminded that we complete each other. Soul, skin, and spirit merge in a magical way, far surpassing the mechanical sexual exchange I'd experienced with Jonathan and every other previous boyfriend.

"I love you," he whispers.

I tell him I love him as I open myself to him and vow to guard and protect our sacred love. For now, I must protect him from the harsher truths.

30

On Monday morning I drag myself to work, still tired, slightly queasy, and annoyed that I let my MetroCard expire. I have to buy a pack of tic tacs from the deli to get enough change for the bus, then worry that the minty burning might not be good for the baby. My baby. I have to start rethinking my moves, unless I'm going to do something I never wanted to do . . .

I scoot into a coveted single seat on the bus and look out the window, not wanting to think about the unthinkable. I've always identified myself as pro-choice, but it isn't a decision I imagined myself making. I focus on the giant snowflake strung over Fifth Avenue, the buildings wrapped like packages in giant ribbons, the wreaths around the necks of the lion statues outside the public library. 'Tis the season to be jolly; save your maudlin thoughts for the January freeze.

At the bank, the branch manager has the employees huddled like Christmas elves around a fake tree in the lobby. Astrid mugs and hangs a decoration from one of her baby dreads as if to say "Merry F-ing Christmas."

Thai plucks a red velvet bulb from a box and salutes me with it. "Oooh, Emma, whatsa matter with you? You don't look so good."

"I'm fine," I say, "but what's all this?"

"We're decorating, of course," replies Oliver Pluckett, the manager. He hands me an ornament shaped like a snowflake. "Come help us, Ms. Dombrowski. Show your Christmas spirit!"

Oliver Pluckett is the only person in this entire branch who insists on calling me by my last name. "I love Christmas, Mr. Pluckett," I say, weighing the merit of Oliver's fine intentions against the fact that the people from corporate will have a cow when they see the tree. "But we have to be considerate of all our customers, and some of them don't celebrate Christmas."

"I tell you dat, Ollie," Thai says. "I tell you dat, but you don't listen."

"Northshore Bank has a tree in the lobby," Oliver argues.

I shrug. "A different corporate policy," I say, all the while thinking he should apply for a position at Northshore and make my life a hell of a lot easier. I duck into the break room thinking of hot tea but there's no hot water, only brewing coffee, its odor hanging in the air like heat waves off fresh tar.

"Why am I so nauseous?" I whisper to myself. The back of my neck is damp with perspiration and I no longer want tea or any breakfast at all.

Of course—the pink cross. Thai enters with her big blue bank mug. "Maybe I should go home," I say, looking at the wall calendar and trying to remember how many sick days I have left this year.

"No, Emma," Thai says quietly. "No home." With a furtive glance at the door, she adds: "Big boss coming today. Coming to see you. Surprise review."

"Shit."

"Don't worry, Emma! You good worker! You do fine. If Thai can do it, so can you."

"I'm not so sure anymore." I sink down into a chair with the realization that banking and child-rearing are a horrible combination. I am approaching the end of my executive training, a

probationary period, and if they find out I'm pregnant . . . ugh.
I've heard horror stories of demotions, women passed over for
promotions, career dead ends, all illegal but it transpires nonetheless in the Big Boy world of banking. There was a time when I
actually enjoyed my job, finding satisfaction in the way numbers
always made sense, always added up the same way no matter who
tried to finagle things. But the management training program
took me far away from numbers, thrusting me into telemarketing and information technologies, corporate investment strategies and human resources. My last rotation, in sales and marketing,
had not been a good one. I was off in Aruba with Randy when
my boss, Gilbert Holcum, came to review me. Not my fault, I know,
but he stuck me with inferior scores on that rotation, checking
off "Needs Improvement," right down the line.

"Needs improvement?" I complained to Randy. "Where are
they going to find a more dedicated, more honest employee
than me?"

"In Aruba?" he teased.

"It's so unfair, and it's so far from what I want to be doing. I
should just quit. Leave them high and dry."

"You can, you know," he said. "You're allowed to walk away
from something that isn't working for you."

But we both knew I couldn't. Not Emma Dee. I wasn't a quit-
ter, couldn't stand to walk away and admit defeat. I'd finish the
training program and then quit the damned job. And now, in
the break room, I moaned as a wave of NEEDS IMPROVEMENTS
rolled through my thoughts.

Here I am at the end of the road, finishing the program in the
personal banking division, and the wolf is knocking at my door,
ready to blow down my house of straw.

"Do you think Ollie get in trouble today?" Thai says, interrupting my lamentations. "Over Christmas tree?"

"Yes," I answer. "And so will I." I grab my coat. "I'll be back
soon. Cover for me."

"You golden," Thai calls as my heels click over the marble
floors. I look down at my black Manolo Blahnik power heels—

the one thing in my favor today. At least I picked a pair of kick-butt shoes that cover toe cleavage.

When I return with an electric menorah and a sign that says "Season's Greetings," my executioner awaits me. Gilbert Holcum watches me from his seat in Oliver's cubicle. I don't meet his eyes—not so difficult, since they're hidden behind a shiny wall of spectacles. Instead, I plug in my "All-Purpose" decorations and hope that he finds my attempt at holiday equilibrium acceptable. As I set things up, I hear Thai talking cordially with a customer she calls "Tyler-Mommy." The woman seems charmed, happy to chat about their children, who seem to be in the same day care, but I realize that Thai is not following bank policy and should be using the woman's last name. That damned "You'll Get a Ten-Dollar Deposit If I Don't Smile and Call You by Name" policy tries my patience. I had to sign pay vouchers three times; three little old ladies who did not hear their names because they declined to wear their hearing aids. And since when is a smile a prerequisite in the work place? Now management is telling us how to emote?

I glance at Holcum, wishing I had ten bucks for every time he didn't smile at me. Like now.

"You're late, Ms. Dombrowski." Holcum's glasses show my reflection—flushed face, red hair wild with static electricity.

"I was here earlier," I say, then decide not to take this one on the chin. "Mr. Pluckett insisted on putting up a tree, and I knew we needed to balance it with more culturally diverse decorations."

Oliver's head bobs up from his stance at the greeting desk. Well, what do I care? The man refuses to use my first name.

"Is that true, Ollie?" Holcum asks him, holding a finger in the air as if to stop time.

Oliver excuses himself from a customer and joins us, whispers: "It was the first stage of many things I'd planned." Good old Benedict Ollie.

Holcum's sneering facade is unaltered. "Proceed," he dismisses me, as if I am blocking his view of the show.

In fact, I am, as Thai is now passing out candy canes to customers waiting in line. One elderly customer declines, saying he's diabetic, and Thai touches his arm with a look of understanding.

"Ooh, I know—no sugar. That tough, but you better off. Better to give up yum-yums than nookie-nookie." The customer smiles, but I turn away and head for the break room before Holcum asks for a translation.

With my executioner watching my every move and scratching notes, the day is painfully long. I keep busy waiting on customers, mostly elderly women who insist on visiting the branch to cash in their Christmas Club accounts in the presence of human tellers—two things that most other banks are trying to phase out. I see the vestiges of old banks all over the city—corner streetfront spaces that are now 24/7 pharmacies or Starbucks or Japanese restaurants. The banks themselves have been reduced to tiny closets with a handful of ATMs inside, often with ragged-looking people waiting in the doors for handouts. I hope our bank isn't going in that direction, then kick myself for caring so much as I smile wider at Mr. Apostolides, whose name I butcher.

He points to the guaranteed name-and-smile sign. "So, you say my name all wrong . . . Do I get, maybe, five dollars, then?"

"I think you just get extra smiles," I say pleasantly, feeling Holcum's eyes on me.

At the end of banking hours, when the tellers count out their drawers, I ease into a chair behind the counter, pretending to keep a watchful eye but mostly trying to get away from Holcum. Thai counts her drawer quickly, her fingers tapping the calculator and spitting off bills and receipts like a machine. She finishes and notices Manuel struggling.

"Manuel, honey, is this your first time closing?" Thai hands me her drawer for verification, then joins him.

"I think I'm getting the hang of it," he says. "I've got the deposits and withdrawals totaled separately."

"Good, good!" Thai chimes. "Then you stack your bills and

put receipts on top—always blue deposit slip on top, then pink withdrawal ticket next."

He nods, quickly adjusts the paperwork.

"No, no . . . Yes! That's it. And here's how you remember blue on top, pink on bottom: Blue go on top because blue is boy, and boy always go on top," Thai says with a wink.

I feel my throat go dry and suddenly notice Holcum listening intently. Manuel chuckles and thanks Thai for her help, but I imagine red flags pinging up in Holcum's brain. EEOC Charges! Sexual harassment complaints! Inappropriate innuendo in the workplace!

"That's a great way to remember," Manuel says, slightly red.

"Ms. Dombrowski?" Holcum hisses like a snake as he holds one finger in the air. "Have you something to say?"

I know he wants me to correct Thai, make an example of her, remind her of appropriate images in the workplace, but I cannot bear to harm the person who breathes life and humor and humanity into this bank. Thai does a damned good job; she would probably be branch manager if it weren't for the language barrier. I refuse to take her down.

I stand and face the glass wall of Holcum. "Yes, sir," I say, "if I don't see you before the holidays, have a good one." And I turn my back on him and bow my head over the cashiers' drawers and lose myself in the calculations until I don't care whether or not Holcum is there anymore. I just want to cash out and know that everything adds up correctly in the world of numbers. The rest of life never adds up properly, but numbers do not fail you.

31

That night on the way home I realize there is no delaying the difficult conversation I need to have with myself. I exit the bus before my stop and walk for a while, wondering when the white sky will let loose with snow. I pass a tree stand with evergreens stacked on the sidewalk like tired soldiers, their scent a visit to dark woods and neighbors' berms and Christmas mornings of my childhood.

Bundled in my scarf against the cold, I walk on and imagine terminating the pregnancy. It seems like the simplest solution—a trip to a clinic and then a chance to start over the right way. If I'd had my wits about me, if I'd realized just how close I was to ovulation the night Jonathan and I had sex, I would have gone to a clinic for those morning-after pills.

I turn down a side street, a quaint block of brownstones, where two toddlers are climbing down the stairs from the cheerful red door of a little day care center, a flag covered with apples flapping in the wind over their heads. Dad follows, but the children are far ahead, running into the arms of their mother who greets them with hugs and kisses beside a double stroller. As Mom lifts a child into the stroller I feel a swell of maternal instinct; I have always wanted a baby. Why not this baby? Would I resent the little thing because its seed came from Jonathan? I can't imagine resenting a baby. Somehow, I think I would love my baby, no matter who the father is; but how would I know for sure?

As the first flakes of snow begin to fall, I realize I cannot reason this out on my own. I call Jane on her cell, and she says she will meet me at Bellini's.

"The demon seed of Jonathan Thompson?" Jane pauses, holds her martini midair. "Thank God for Roe v. Wade."

"I don't know." I flounder, taking a chunk of cheese from the complimentary appetizers to look purposeful. Jane brings clients here all the time, and the waiters can't do enough for her. Richard seemed disappointed that I wouldn't accept a glass of champagne, but I stuck to my cranberry juice. "I'm thinking of keeping it."

"And why would you do that?" Jane asks.

I roll my shoulders back, searching for the answer. "Because it needs me?" Another question. "Okay, it probably sounds insane since I'm just a few weeks pregnant, but I think I can feel this baby begging for help inside me. Subtle changes in the past few weeks, like being tired all the time? The baby wants me to sleep more. It doesn't like oatmeal for breakfast. It made me switch from coffee to tea in the morning."

Jane tucks a strand of black hair behind one ear, her eyes intent on me. "When it tells you to start drinking formula, I'll start to worry."

"Seriously, I want this baby. It may not be the right choice for my life or for Randy, but that's how I feel."

"So keep the little drooler," Jane says casually, as if helping me decide which Pradas to purchase. She sips her martini, mulls it over, then breaks into a smile. "Shit, Emma! Are you really going to do this?"

"I guess. Yes." Suddenly I'm feeling wobbly about the issue of the baby's father. "And I'm not telling Jonathan. I've read a lot about a father's right to know, and I think it's a load of crap."

Jane lifts her hands, pretends to applaud. "Bravo, my dear. You need to avoid anything that might tie you to a man like Jonathan Thompson."

"But what do I tell Randy? I mean, if I don't say anything I'm sure he'll take total responsibility, and he'll be a good father. But is that right? Is it fair to him? Or is it immoral?"

"Emma Dee, no one can answer that question but you." Jane pops an olive in her mouth, waiting for my answer.

"I've always been totally honest in my life. You know I'm a terrible liar. But somehow, honesty doesn't *feel* right in this situation. It would hurt Randy. Do I have to hurt him?"

"Honesty is overrated," Jane says. "And our ride on this planet is short. Look at that nineteen-year-old rap star who was just gunned down. Nineteen. Christ. But you, Emma, have to decide what you want to do while you're here."

"Make the world a better place," I blurt out, then realize how corny it sounds.

Fortunately, Jane doesn't jump on me today. "And does having a child further that mission?"

"I think it does," I say. "Yes, a new life must be a good thing. Not that I can make that child into a model human being, but I can do my best to help him or her evolve into a decent, kind person." I pinch the bridge of my nose, shake my head. "Who am I kidding? Raising kids is a crapshoot. But isn't that why we're here on this spinning planet? To roll the dice and celebrate the lucky seven?"

Jane smiles. "Sounds like you're on the right track."

"I've never been a gambler. I like to play it safe. How did my life get so out of control?"

"Out of control is the reality," Jane says. "When you think it's in control, that's the illusion."

32

The producers of Randy's show have given him a tight deadline—sets must be ready by January second—so he must spend long days and nights at work the week before Christmas.

I miss him, but he stays in touch by cell, and I feel close to him. I am able to trust him, which is surprising after my experience with Jonathan, who had actually brought his other girlfriend's clothes home and tossed them into the laundry hamper. A strange T-shirt here, an oddly small sweatshirt there. The day I found strange panties, I knew it was over.

But not so with Randy, who calls for no reason to ask what I'm up to, how my day is going. He is on a later schedule, and yet he gets up early each morning to make my tea and toast. He brings me fresh produce from the greengrocer—hothouse berries and exotic looking orchids because he cannot resist their beauty. Jane finds his aesthetic sensibilities highly suspect—loves flowers, attended art school—until I shut her down, reminding her that Randy endured a childhood of teasing from his Republican family and his football-playing classmates. I am glad he fought their disapproval and continued to see the beauty in a flower.

Most nights I stop at the Japanese restaurant on our block for

an order of white rice and edamame—steamed soybeans.
Cooking for one is a bitch, and I don't have much of an appetite,
but I do enjoy popping open the pods of edamame, amazed at
the way the plump green beans nestle into their pods. I think of
the little one nestled inside me, so tiny now. I can't help but love
my baby.

In the quiet evening hours I go over the books for Ricki's
shop, The Christmas Elf. Although I have never visited North
Carolina I have seen splendid photos of the shop's well-trimmed
hearth and glorious trees on her website, and it pleases me to
know my friend has created such a wondrous place on earth.
Images of Ricki's glittery handmade pinecone ornaments dance
in my head as I tabulate, add columns, and subtract expenses.
Ricki worries that the swell of profits from this busy Christmas
season has knocked her ledger out of control, but I assure her
it's only numbers. We manage to straighten things out; compose
profit and loss sheets for tax purposes. Then I begin an inventory analysis for her, estimating profit per item.

"You are a lifesaver!" Ricki tells me on the phone. "Tell me
what I can do to thank you."

"I've enjoyed it," I say. "Really. This is the kind of satisfaction I
used to feel at work when I could make everything balance out. I
miss that."

"I'm just going to have to fly you down in the summer to fix
things up after I make a mess of them again."

"I'd like that." Where will I be in the summer? Very pregnant.
I realize I'm probably due sometime in September, that I should
see an ob/gyn and get pregnancy vitamins, that my life will
change inexorably in the next year. "But if you're ever in a jam
you can e-mail me your records. All the info I would need is your
computer files."

Ricki thanks me again, and I sign off, realizing that I need to
get to bed if I'm going to make my six-thirty alarm. Damn that
bank. If they'd only let me get back to numbers instead of tip-
toeing around bossy bank managers and chastising tellers for
taking too long on their breaks. My review from Holcum has not
come down the pike yet, but I am not hopeful. Next time the

bank downsizes, I will look for a buyout. Bookkeeping or accounting would be a nice change. Maybe freelance? I know tax season is a bear, but it's just a few months out of the year.

I bring a cup of decaf tea to the sofa, snuggle under the ivory fleece, and gaze up at the stars on the ceiling. The Christmas sky continues to delight and inspire me, and I marvel that I could have found a man who would create something like this for me. The tea is warm and sweet, and I place it on the end table as my eyelids droop.

I am on a flat desert plane, an arid land of pale sands and turquoise skies. I think I hear my baby cry, but it is the strange mew of the camel I am riding. My baby is a round ball in my tummy, a sweet little being who already fills my heart with joy. Randy leads the camel, tries to hurry it along, as we both know it's time for this baby to be born. The hospital was supposed to be in this direction, but there are no buildings in sight, just cacti and tawny warm sands and blue sky riddled with stars—a Christmas sky.

I wake up feeling light (minus the large baby-belly) and hungry. As I dip a butter cookie into my reheated tea, Randy returns from work.

"You're still up?" He kisses me, then rubs my back affectionately. "Great. I'm dying to show you these sketches of the new set." He takes boards from his worn leather satchel, lays them on the clean counter. "Milo and Robert just approved them. This is the first view of heaven."

My eyes feast on a landscape of flowers and spun gold topped by a starry sky that jettisons out over the audience. I gasp in delight. "You used our sky!"

He filches a cookie. "I hope you don't mind. I struggled with ways for the scene to encompass the audience, and the sky really accomplishes that."

"I love it. The producers are happy?"

"Thrilled. Still worried about our deadline, but I told them this crew can handle it. They're skilled artisans. The underworld set is already complete, and Kerry came up with a quick-drying laminate that makes the street look like it just rained." As he talks on about his colleagues I feel a rush of love for him. Confident in his own talents, yet appreciative of the creative gifts other people bring to the project, Randy maintains a beautiful balance.

Balance, it sustains me.

My job review arrives at the bank via cantankerously slow office mail. Oliver Pluckett twitches with curiosity, his eyes trained on the pages as he makes an excuse to pass by. I slide the review back into its envelope and take it into the ladies' room, where I stand before the mirrored wall and read.

To my surprise, Holcum was decent, checking "Shows Improvement" in almost every category. So he did not penalize me for allowing Thai's colorful humor in the workplace. The executioner was merciful, kinder than last time, but pish! It's a dinky review for someone who has worked as hard as I have. Really. Try your damndest and this is as good as it gets?

I am wasting my time here at this bank. Not a revelation, and yet it stings. I am tempted to leave the branch and take the bus over to headquarters, to resign on the spot. I clasp the envelope between my knees and lean over a sink to splash water on my face.

The door squeaks open, Thai pauses. "You okay, Emma?"

"Fine." I press a paper towel to my face, wondering what Oliver Pluckett will think now that I've washed off most of my makeup. That I've been crying? I don't have time to care.

"It's good that you wash up," Thai says. "I see Astrid in here. She don't wash hands. I give her hell, tell her, you piddle, you wash. Don't want piddle on bills I handle. Money dirty enough."

"You're right." I smile at her, petite Thai with her hand waving furiously in the air, her dark hair pulled back in tiny butterfly combs. She has made my time on this rotation bearable.

I tuck the envelope under my arm, deciding to sign the review and plan my departure after the holidays. If I wait until the end of January I can do Thai's end-of-year review, maybe even get her a promotion. In the meantime, I can put out feelers for a job as a bookkeeper—something with insurance benefits. Besides, if

I stay until the end of year, I collect my annual bonus, which will come in handy. Soon I'll be paying for two in this world.

Two. Like the edamame I crave. Two perfect green beans in a soy pod. Room for three if Randy wants to stay. And he probably will, as I have decided to withhold the ugly truth from him.

It feels like the right thing to do. God help me, I hope it is.

33

On Christmas Eve, Randy sets the table while I finish up in Marty's country kitchen in Easthampton. The salad and the pumpkin cheesecake are chilling in the fridge. I shred pepper-jack cheese on top of the individual lobster corn puddings and slide them back into the oven. Jane and Marty are walking down on the beach, having left the salmon to roast on a slab over the grill out back, and Ricki and Ben are in town stocking up on champagne and wine.

"I spiked the eggnog," Randy calls from the dining room. "I figured I might as well, since we're all drinkers."

"Good idea," I say, reminding myself to abstain. I set the timer for the pudding, then discover some white Lenox dessert plates and bring them out to the dining room buffet.

Randy stands at the French doors, eggnog in hand. I join him and he slips his free arm over my shoulders, closes the door behind us, and lifts his glass to the sky. "Look at the stars! You never get to see much of them with all the lights of Manhattan, but this . . . This is exceptional."

We stare up at the diamonds against black, pinpoints of light so vivid and close it seems the earth has spun out of orbit and plunged into a star field. Pockets of glitter fill every corner.

"A Christmas sky," I say.

"You were so right about it." Randy hugs me. "And here I thought it was Dombrowski family folklore."

"Uh-uh." I nestle into his chest, realizing that it's time. "There's something I need to tell you." The words hang in the air, and I wonder if he can hear my heart beating with unusual volume.

"I already know," he says. "I've known for a while. And I'm thrilled."

His lips press against mine in a kiss that takes my breath away, and I wonder at the possibility of making love here and now, on the cold wood of Marty's deck. I'm relieved that he's okay with this—of course he is!

"But how did you know?" I whisper.

"You're not the first pregnant woman I've lived with. My sister was staying with us when she was pregnant with my niece. My brother-in-law had shipped out overseas and Angie was trying to keep it a secret so he'd be the first to know, but I could tell. Something about the way your face is fuller, your eyes brighter. The cravings. She wanted cheeseburgers; you go for edamame. I saw it in Angie, and I noticed it in you before I left for Oregon last month. I was wondering when you were going to tell me."

"I . . . I just figured it out myself," I say quickly, trying to replay what he'd said for logic. *Before* Thanksgiving? But I wasn't pregnant then.

Or was I?

Me, with my high math aptitude . . . Had I screwed up the numbers? Miscalculated when I'd be ovulating? The science of it seems skewed, but then, miracles defy science, and this is one miracle I want to believe in.

"I'm so happy." Randy's eyes shine against the dark night as he rubs my arms.

"Me, too." I kiss him, then steal a taste of his spiked eggnog. "Mmm. 'Shows Improvement,' " I tease.

He shakes his head. "We both know it's better than that."

"Don't worry." I hold up one finger, thinking of Mr. Holcum. "You'll have time to earn a better rating." I press a hand against his chest, letting it slide under the fleece of his vest. "Lots and lots of time."

Epilogue

December, 2005

Jane

"**P**romise me you won't get married until you're at least thirty. Like me," I said quietly to the purring lamb in my arms. I had taken great contentment in holding Carolina in my arms since she was an infant, and now that she was more than four months old I was finding it difficult to kick the habit and break that connection.

It was Christmas Eve and Marty and I had just finished dinner with Emma, Randy and Carolina in the apartment I had grown up in. With the installment of the nursery in the second bedroom and a brand new granite counter kitchen, the place was barely recognizable as the home of my childhood, but I was happy that no ghosts lingered here, glad that these walls would shelter a new family, a family I adored. We were waiting for the bell to announce the arrival of Ricki and Ben, who were taking a cab from the airport. I was nervous about seeing Ricki, surprisingly nervous about breaking my news to her, so I closed my eyes and focused on the warm baby in my arms, trying to soak up her courage and downy peace.

"Aren't your arms tired?" Emma asked as I leaned back in the rocker and savored Carolina's baby scent, her buttery nose, her wild tuft of red hair.

"Never," I admitted. "I'm sorry. Am I being greedy?"

Emma and Randy exchanged a look of relief. "Enjoy," Randy said. "We get our fair share of her."

"More than our share at three A.M.," Emma added.

"Can't blame us for being night owls, right, Carolina?" I smiled into her shiny eyes, which stared back curiously. "We party girls have to stick together."

"Don't let her kid you," Marty told the baby as he leaned over my shoulder and tapped her booties. "She hung up her cosmo glass when she met me."

"He's right," I whispered to the baby girl. "Now I'm asleep by eleven-thirty."

"Way before Carolina's bedtime," Emma said as the intercom buzzed.

Ricki and Ben were on their way up, and Carolina and I made eyes at each other as the others rushed around, reheating chili for the travelers, setting desserts out on the buffet, lining up cups for eggnog.

"I'm nervous," I told the baby, speaking quietly while the others were in the kitchen. "I feel like I'm abandoning her, but I'm not. Not at all."

Carolina's steely eyes understood. The side of her rosy mouth twitched, as if to say: "What can I tell ya?"

"I'll always be here for her. But now, she'll have two people in her family."

Carolina yawned.

"Okay, you're honorary family, too."

She scooted a hand out and tugged a button on my sweater. Her hands were exquisite: pearly nails, gentle creases, doughy skin. Everything about Carolina fascinated me, mostly because I had long ago abandoned any notion of having my own child and realized this little person was my window to the world of tiny, innocent people. Emma had told me that I possessed strong baby mojo, but most babies did not interest me. Smart, attentive

Carolina was the rare exception, and from the first time I saw her wailing in the hospital nursery, I knew we were going to be friends.

Ricki and Ben burst in swinging three fat shopping bags of beautifully wrapped Christmas gifts, their cheeks pink from the cold. My sister's brown eyes seemed impossibly round and waifish, as if her laid-back lifestyle had allowed her to open wide and view the world around her for the first time in her life. With red highlights warming her dark, straight hair and a new pair of jeans hugging her hips, she looked stunning. Likewise, Ben seemed to glow in the light of her laughter.

After a flurry of hugs they settled in and we talked about their flight and made plans for the next week. When we discussed the agenda for Christmas Day Marty kept shifting his attention to me with leading statements such as: "We've got a Christmas surprise," and "They say Christmas is a time for miracles. Right, Jane?" It was my cue, but my lines were stuck in my throat, along with a pulse that beat rapidly.

Fortunately Ricki and Ben didn't seem to pick up on my stall, but just went on talking about a new addition to The Christmas Elf. I glanced down at Carolina for support. She seemed more concerned with the little bubble forming at her cherry lips.

Marty came over and pressed the back of one hand to my cheek. "You okay?"

I nodded, swallowing hard.

He slid his fingers behind my ear, to the nape of my neck, my weakness. I closed my eyes and pressed against his hand, secure in the knowledge that we were doing the right thing. I wanted to marry this man. But somehow, it was difficult to spill to Ricki. I felt like a ten year-old asking Dad's permission.

"I have some news," I said, surprised at the tears stinging my throat. This was happy news; why was I choking up?

"Oh?" Warily Ricki reached for Ben's shoulder. "Is everything okay?"

"Don't worry, I'm fine." I stood up and paced with the baby, wishing I could control this flood of emotion. I turned to Randy and handed Carolina over. "Anyway, I'm finished with surgery and radioactive pills, at least for now. My thyrogen levels are checking out just fine. Looks like they got everything."

"Great!" Ben said. "Some doc friends of mine were telling me about that treatment. They call it a magic bullet, the way thyroid tissue sucks up iodine."

I nodded. I had been through the magic bullet treatment, getting a strong dose of radioactive iodine intended to burn out remaining thyroid tissue. Marty had been supportive throughout the strange treatment, which mostly entailed me staying away from other people until the radiation died down. Marty had enjoyed singing, "She's radioactive . . ."

"The thyroid situation is looking good for me," I said. "Thank God. But I've got some other news." I shot a look at Marty— warm, kind Marty. So damned smart at work, so tender and sincere in the bedroom, so amusing when he wanted to make me laugh. I wanted to cry over having reached this surprising juncture, a place where I felt mature and vulnerable and yet sure, so sure of this decision. "Marty and I, we're . . ." My voice went hoarse as I turned toward my little sister.

"We're getting married. Tomorrow," Marty said as he stood behind me and placed his hands on my shoulders.

Ricki squealed in delight and Carolina let out a peep and there was some laughter but I couldn't track it all with the tears that blurred my vision.

"Janey! That's great news." Ricki was suddenly leaning over me, hugging me. "Why are you crying?"

I shook my head, not sure how to express it, though Marty seemed to understand. He handed me his handkerchief, then moved up to the arm of my chair and rubbed my back while I wiped my eyes.

"A Christmas wedding!" Ricki broke into a quick happy dance. "This is going to be awesome."

While the others talked plans I turned to Marty, who seemed content to sit by my side while I sorted things out. "I feel so . . . so overwhelmed," I told him quietly. Maybe I was crying over the rite of passage, no more detachment from relationships, no more pressing late into the night in search of the wildest party. It was a huge shift for me: investing my emotions in someone else, learning to live one day at a time.

Marty nodded, his beautiful eyes studying me. I thought of his extensive knowledge of politics in the middle east, his passion for foreign films and pistachios, the lyrical, sing-songy way he sang Hebrew at the Passover meal I had attended with his extended family. I had scratched the surface of a precious stone and found a mesmerizing gem with untold properties.

My Marty.

Ricki

I have to admit, I was a little jealous.

Oh, I was grateful that my sister had found Marty, that she'd found a man who could soothe her soul, make her laugh, cut through her cynicism and surround her with love. Janey deserved all that.

But I was needled by the fact that she was getting married before me. Granted, she'd been married before, but I was a kid back then, out of touch with her relationship with Philip, not really tuned in until it was over and Jane was meeting with a lawyer to argue over who would keep the Mikasa and the cappuccino maker.

Now as Ben and I rode the elevator up to our room in the Waldorf, I tried to work through the jealousy that clamped over my heart. I shouldn't feel this way. She was my sister and my best friend and I loved her. I should be celebrating her happiness. I should be looking forward to kicking off my shoes and opening the little miniature brandy from the plane and snuggling up under crisp sheets with Ben in the early hours of Christmas. Here it was Christmas, and I was in a funk.

Maybe the real issue was that Ben and I hadn't even discussed marriage yet. Over the past year we'd fallen into an easy lifestyle: we shared his big wicker bed overlooking the bay, we jogged on the beach most mornings, we sampled wines and tried new recipes. Don't think I'm complaining, because I'm not. We have something wonderful going, and I appreciate that every morning as we sip coffee and watched the sun rise over the bay.

But my good life back home wasn't doing much to vanquish the twist of jealousy in my stomach. Try as I might to rationalize away my bad feelings, they still gripped me like a determined shark. I wanted to pry its jaws open and fling it away, but as the bellman unloaded our luggage in the room I realized I was stuck with this evil thing clamped on my heart, at least, for the time being.

"Where's the brandy?" I flung off my jacket and shoes, then fished through my carry-on bag.

"Not wasting any time," Ben teased, opening the paper bag he'd brought from Emma's apartment and removing a thermos. "You might want to add a shot of this."

"I thought you were filching Christmas cookies. What's that?" I asked.

He smiled, that grin that deepened the creases beside his eyes. "Eggnog."

"That'll work." I mixed myself a drink in the hotel glass, then sat back on the bed with a sigh.

"Something wrong?"

"It's just . . . nothing. Everything."

"Did you ever hate yourself for feeling something, and then you try like crazy not to feel it but the harder you try to resist the stronger the feeling gets?"

He arched an eyebrow. "Sort of like falling in love."

"Sort of. Only this is a bad feeling." I cupped my glass and sank against the pillows of the king-sized bed. "Wicked, nasty jealousy. Because I am such a rotten person."

"Oh, that." He sipped his eggnog, as if considering the situation. "That is a problem, your wickedness."

"Very funny." It wasn't like me to be snappish, but I wanted to be alone to wallow in self-pity. I didn't want it to be a momentous Christmas Day, didn't want to face this gorgeous man sitting across from me, his long legs slung casually over the side of the bed, his knowing eyes peering into my soul.

Ben scratched his head, leaving his silver hair wild and kind of sexy. "Aah, stop feeling sorry for yourself and tell me what's really bothering you."

I crossed my legs demurely, not sure where to start.

"Clammed up? Then let me guess. Is it Jane's engagement, or Emma's baby?"

Was I so transparent? I squirmed back on the bed, reminding myself that Ben had lived with me for the past year. He knew me well. "It's Jane." I rolled my eyes. "Not that I mean to pressure you or anything, but do you ever think about getting married?"

"Sure, I do. But remember how we hooked up? You were fresh from a dysfunctional relationship."

"Was not!" I defended. His eyes narrowed, the stern Ben, and I grinned. "Okay, slightly dysfunctional."

"Semantics. And I was married before. Didn't want to fall into the same trap twice."

"Marriage is a trap?" I squeaked, suddenly concerned that we hadn't discussed this before.

"A bad marriage is. But I don't see that happening with us." He stared down at his eggnog, swirled it, then put the glass aside. "Honestly? This past year with you has been pretty damned wonderful."

"It has?" A thread of hope caught in my throat. "It has," I agreed.

Our eyes met. A moment later, we were on our feet, in each other's arms, locked in one of the bear hugs we enjoyed. Ben leaned back slightly, tipped me off my feet, and growled.

"So you want to get hitched?" he asked.

"Definitely. But let's wait at least a few months. I wouldn't want to cut in on Jane's glory."

He squeezed me tighter, then placed me back on my feet. "You'll need that much time to plan. I figure you and Georgia will be making up hair-bobs and doodads for all of us to wear. Weaving ribbons with pine cones or something."

I grinned. "Ooh! I like it. You'd wear a hair-bob for me?"

"Don't push your luck."

Emma

It is just after midnight on Christmas and I am addicted to my new book, neatly filling in the blanks with information for my daughter.

Her name, Carolina, which means feminine.

*Named After*_____

I pause, recalling the inspiration for our daughter's name. The summer of my pregnancy Randy and I traveled south to visit Ricki and Ben in Nag's Head, and time and again I caught Randy singing to himself, "Goin' to Carolina in my mind."

"What's that?" I had asked.

"A James Taylor song. Don't you know it?"

I didn't, but when we arrived in Nag's Head he picked up the CD, and it became the anthem of our summer, the song that inspired our forays in the shallow bay, our evening strolls for ice cream, our long walks along the beach beside a sky on fire with the setting sun. Our hearts latched onto that song, those memories. When the time came to name our daughter, we both smiled over the possibility of Carolina. Jane pointed out that it was old-fashioned, but any reservations fled when I saw Randy holding our bundled daughter in the hospital, crooning like James Taylor over her shiny face, his eyes wide as she twitched a smile in her sleep. "I thinks she likes it," he said.

Now Randy's footsteps whisper down the hall, and I finish a sentence and look up from my treasured new book. "She's asleep," he announces.

I smile. "You have the magic touch."

"Either that or I bore her to tears."

"No, you make her feel safe. Safe and secure," I say, tucking my feet up under my soft terry robe. We are tired but fighting sleep, reluctant to surrender a single minute of our Christmas. Ricki, Ben, Jane and Marty left after our midnight toast, and now it's just Randy and me and baby Carolina, the light of our lives.

Randy goes over to the Christmas tree, touching the new ornament at the top, a sparkling creation of blown glass and beads. "You hung Ricki's gift. It looks good, though I still can't imagine how she does it." The glass is shaped like a madonna with child, two figures cuddling under a cluster of tiny pearlized beads that appear to be the moon. She told me she wanted something to help us remember Cara's first Christmas.

"Do you want some more eggnog?" Randy asks.

"Just a little, please?" I return to my new book, a gift from Jane entitled *Memories for My Daughter.* While I shunned the overly sentimental mementoes and pelican-covered wrapping papers at my baby shower, I find myself sucked in by this book, pages and pages of sentimental questions for me to answer for my daughter, romantic questions about how my parents met, how Randy and I met, the first boy I kissed, as well as pages where I am supposed to write about my feelings for Cara—the moment she was born, her first steps, her first teeth, her first Christmas. I have never considered myself much of a writer, yet I feel compelled to put these records on paper for my daughter, driven to record her legacy lest it be forgotten.

Two years ago my great-great aunt Mary Jane passed away at the age of ninety-two, and I'm happy to say she passed on many a family memory before she left. She told me of secret passages in my great-grandparents Michigan home, of the terrible flu that swept through one winter taking the lives of her twin baby sisters Viola and Geraldine. And there were colorful tales of distant relatives—a great uncle on ice skates who ran barrels of rum from Canada to Detroit across the frozen Detroit River. The forlorn wife who disparaged cleaning and left her husband in Ohio for the life of a party girl in gay Paree in the Roaring Twenties. "How she cried when the family lost their fortune in the Depression," Aunt Mary Jane said. "I don't think she ever got over it. Kept telling town shopkeepers to put it on the her husband's tab. Spent her last years drinking martinis dressed in a fancy peignoir. She never realized she was in an old folks' home."

I smile over my family's checkered history, glad that Aunt Mary Jane kept up the family storytelling. With our families scattered from Miami to Oregon, I worry that my Carolina will lack a sense of connection. I want her to know where she belongs in the world, that she has a full, colorful family.

"You're writing furiously," Randy says. "At this rate, you'll have that thing filled out by New Year's."

I keep writing. "I just want Cara to know about her family. I mean, New Jersey is close enough but Maryland is a hike, and my mom's in Miami now, and your family is in Oregon and your sister is over in Germany. We're so scattered. Don't you worry about that?"

"Well . . . no, not really. Sometimes friends are all the family you need. Besides, the world is shrinking. By the time Cara is ten she'll probably be doing video e-mails to her cousins."

I sift through the watercolors on the pages, the old American homes with fat-pillared porches and climbing Ivy. Paintings of girls in Victorian lace serving tea to their dolls. A silver-haired granny shelling peas in the garden.

These nostalgic illustrations are a stark contrast to my childhood memories of suburban Jersey—strip malls and swim meets at the Y and traveling soccer.

I pull the pen to my chest and glance toward the bedrooms. "I just want her to have it all. Everything. The world at her fingertips."

Randy shakes his head, his blue eyes thoughtful, amused. "Never gonna happen, Emma." He puts the eggnog down and squeezes beside me on the love seat. "We can't give her everything. We can't protect her from disappointments and heartbreaks. It kills me, too, but kids are going to be mean to her. Boys will break her heart. Some things are inevitable."

I feel a mixture of exhilaration and exhaustion, a surge of maternal adrenaline to champion my daughter's cause. "It's our job to take care of her."

He nods. "And we will. She won't have everything she wants. But we'll make sure she gets everything she needs."

He tries to close the book, but I still have one finger marking the page. "There's a section about your family, you know. How your parents met, your childhood memories . . ."

"Mm-hmm." His face is close, his eyes closing lazily as he kisses me.

"Will you help me fill it out?" I ask.

"Sure. But can we leave it for a few weeks? I don't think she's going to be doing extensive reading anytime soon."

I laugh and his lips sink into my neck. "You think I'm neurotic."

"You're a wonderful mother," he says. "But it's Christmas Eve and I figure we'd better make good use of our time before Santa comes down the chimney and wakes up the baby."

I unbutton his shirt, still thrilled at the feel of his warm, bare skin under my fingers. Can I stave off tomorrow? Close the doors on my worries over Cara's childhood, the soaring rents in the city, our scattered families, my daughter's delicate developing psyche?

"Close your eyes, Emma. Close your eyes and remember our Christmas sky."

And I do. I turn off the cry of maternal responsibility, the song of mothers through generations, and listen for the sounds of the moment. They thread gently through the old apartment—the sweet wisps of baby breath over the monitor, the buzz of street traffic, the low murmur of Christmas carols from the apartment next door. Under the Christmas sky I press my lips against his and fall into the moment, tasting only my man, smelling the sweetness of baby and the lingering scent of nutmeg.

And I realize I have it all—momentary bliss—and I must scramble to soak it up and revel in my happiness before the sun rises, before Carolina wakes up, before the Christmas sky fades away until next year. So much to celebrate, so little time.

If you enjoyed Carly Alexander's

THE EGGNOG CHRONICLES

here's a sneak peek of

Roz Bailey's

GIRLS' NIGHT OUT

currently available in trade paperback

and coming in mass-market in January 2005!

PROLOGUE

Tell the world that you were giving away a million bucks, and the weirdos came out in droves. Or maybe it was the lure of television: the chance to have your image broadcast from coast to coast, your personality analyzed in workplaces across the country, your face stretched across the big-screen TVs at sports bars, your love life the topic of Internet chat rooms.

As far as Executive Producer Max Donner could discern, the biggest problem with reality programming was that it attracted the exhibitionists of the world. Viewers didn't want to watch weirdos, but it was difficult to get normal people to apply for a chance to expose their emotions and share the details of their sex lives with the viewing audience.

Max tossed another application into the rejection stack; then he skimmed the next one until it became clear that the applicant was an advocate of sex with domestic animals. "We'll just rename the show 'Lassie Is a Big Tease,' " Max grumbled as he pushed the application aside.

In one season of producing the show, Max had encountered all sorts of sexual behavior. There were the "straight sex" types, as Max had come to label them. Those ordinary Jane and John

Does who offered to let the cameras come into their bedrooms, under the sheets, up their orifices—whatever it would take to show the world that they "had it goin' on." Then there were the "dysfunctional sex" types, many of them totally whacked, some creative, who were willing to turn bisexual for the day, pop out of Russell Crowe's birthday cake, have sex standing in the skyroof of a limo cruising down Sunset Strip or strip in the window of Macy's at Herald Square.

Not that Max was surprised by any of it . . . just tired of the freaks and geeks his show attracted. So many people were willing to sell their sexual secrets for a million dollars. Unfortunately, most applicants failed to understand that *Big Tease* was not really about sex. What captured and held audiences, at least in the first season, were the emotional relationships plotted out before the viewers' eyes: the roller-coaster ride, the thrill of falling in love, the crushing blow of rejection, the negotiation required to keep it all together. People didn't want to see the physical mating; they wanted the mating dance, fully choreographed and edited with a rock 'n' roll soundtrack. Not to mention that the three women they featured last season lived in Los Angeles, Boston and San Francisco. Film it in Frisco and you've got a hit; that was one of Max's rules of television and film.

The top Nielsen-rated television show *Big Tease* had been conceived as a joke, a spoof of reality shows and soap operas, a stupid idea born of the haze of Dewars and the sting of unemployment. At the time, he'd still been reeling from the cancellation of the daytime drama he had directed for eight years. He'd even relocated from Los Angeles to take the job here, working in the Kaufman Astoria Studios. And then, faster than a thirty-second commercial break, Max and the rest of the cast and crew had learned that it was all over. Canceled. He was godfather to the AD's child. His sister had married one of the cameramen. Those people were family, and they'd been forced to say goodbye with less than twenty-four hours' notice.

Bringing the crew back together had been the most satisfying aspect of producing *Big Tease*. That day in the bar, a network executive for CBN had overheard Max's slightly inebriated "concept." In a nutshell: catfights via satellite. Three lovely, single women were chosen, and guerrilla camera crews followed them around in their private lives and well-publicized dates. Then, while on camera, each woman watched the others' dates via satellite and ranked them. After eight weeks, the audience voted for the woman who turned out to be the most worthy date, and that woman won a million dollars. Since CBN had been looking for a show to rival *Survivor*, the executive, Paul Eberheart, had asked Max to come in and pitch it to the development team, and the rest, as they said in the trades, was "broadcasting history."

Max pushed another application into the rejection stack and took a hit from his coffee. Would there *be* a second season of the show? From the looks of these applications, if he proceeded, the concept of the show would be totally skewed. He'd have to rename it "Sex Freaks." Or he could bring on the sadomasochistic couple who favor a poker iron and call it "Some Like it Hot." Or he could document the romantic strikes and gutter balls of a big-haired, fortyish Alabama bowling league and name it "Alley of the Dolls."

"Hey, boss," Lucy Ng said, breezing in on a cloud of billowing scarves. Today it was red, orange and black, sort of a flame motif. Sixty-something Lucy always dressed in black, with lots of scarf action. She'd worked with Max since the beginning of his career, when he'd been an assistant director for ABC, and Lucy had been working in Standards and Practices. "Hold onto your hat, boss," she said. "I'm about to make your day."

"Oh, really?" Max sat back and swiped a hand over his bristly dark hair. "I'd say that's a pretty tall order, but go ahead."

She waved a folder in front of his nose. "I hold in my hand three perfect applications for the second season. Three beautiful girls, none of whom escaped from mental institutions or have outstanding warrants for their arrest. I already started the background checks."

"No way." He stood and snatched up the folder from her hand. "Are you sure they're not aspiring actresses looking for exposure?"

She shook her head. "Already checked with the Guild. They

seem to be legit. A photographer, a magazine editor, and a corporate type. And even better, the three women are friends.
Applied together. How do you like that angle?"

"I like." He nodded, glancing at the photographs on their applications. Sad eyes bordered by a tangle of wild red hair. A
buttoned-down African-American beauty in a business suit. A smart-
looking brunette with a cute Irish nose. Hell, he was looking at
Charlie's Angels.

"Down, boy." Lucy wagged a finger at him. "You wouldn't want
to violate the no fraternization rule. This is a contest we're running, and we've got to follow the rules."

"A contest?" Max leafed through the file. "I thought it was a
network TV show."

"And I've got paperwork out my ears! Network forms and
policies. *Sheesh!*" Lucy was already turning to go. "Next time,
please, pitch the show to cable. And let me know when you want
me to call these girls in, boss."

"You're that confident?"

"Please . . ." She waved off his question. "I've already bud-
geted in my bonus."

Pushing back his coffee, he dropped the folder onto his desk
and spread out the three applications.

The redhead was a photographer, mostly portraits and weddings, but she aspired to have a show of her own eventually. Max
didn't know anything about art photography, but the woman
looked the part of an artist. A downtown girl, loaded with class
and angst. When he saw that her name was Apple Sommers, he
began to suspect a setup. A chick named after a fruit? Get out!
But her personal statement offered some explanation.

*A weird choice of name, I know, but my parents did it to
me. We've got this family tradition of fruit names—my
mother is Cherry, and my grandmother was Clementine.
At least it's distinctive, which is an advantage in the art
world. People remember my name, even if they do forget
my work.*

Max turned to the statement from the corporate type, Chandra Hammel. Born in a poor section of Philadelphia, she lost her parents at a young age and was raised by her grandmother in Queens. She had an MBA from New York University's Stern School, was planning to marry a man who was tragically killed two years ago. Hadn't dated since, but felt ready to move on now. A workaholic who'd made a swift, steady climb up the rungs of the corporate ladder. "A rags-to-riches story," he said aloud, tasting the ratings shares.

The third friend, Maggie the magazine editor, was not as classically beautiful as the other two; however, her personality came through loud and clear.

I know definitely if I am going to sleep with a guy in the first ten minutes, Maggie McGee claimed. Max nodded. Right. And does the guy have any say in this?

He read on . . .

And it's not just about looks. We're talking chemistry. If it's not there, the guy could be Matt Damon and he's not going to get anywhere. Which is the reason I'm still looking. I could fill the dance floor of Au Bar with all the guys I've met who are perfect on paper: gorgeous, successful, social, funny, wealthy or rising stars. But if there's no sizzle when he smiles, I've learned that he's meant to be with some other fearless female. Big sigh. And that's just a qualifier for getting into bed with me. For a proposal of marriage . . . well, I don't know what it will take because I've never met a guy who comes close to being Mr. Maggie McGee. But I'd certainly like to explore those options on Big Tease. And hey, I don't mind at all if the cameraman comes along. One of my boyfriends once accused me of being an exhibitionist—like it's a crime to play in public! How about the drink called SEX ON THE BEACH? Anyway, don't worry; I'll behave. So when do we start? Just so I can run out to Victoria's Secret and update my lingerie.

Max rubbed his chin. An interesting trio—photogenic, witty, smart.

He sprang from his desk and called down the hall. "Lucy! You are a genius."

"Compliments get you nowhere," she called back.

He handed her the folder. "Call the network and get the ball rolling. Tell them we've got a killer season lined up, with a new twist." He paused, scratching the bristled growth at his chin. "I never thought the same city thing would work, but since they're friends, it'll be juicy. Lots of conflict and angst . . . betrayal." He grinned. "Great stuff. And since they're all in New York, we won't need a satellite hookup. And we'll save on travel expenses for the crew. I'm liking this more and more."

Lucy tapped the file, tossing a red silk scarf over one tiny shoulder. "Do I make your job easy, or what?"

"Are you kidding? I could kiss you!"

"Sexual harassment," she said. "But I'll take that raise."

"You got it," he said. "Raises all around," he called, as if he were buying a round for the guys down at Darcy's.

One of the production assistants leaned out of a cubicle with a curious stare, but Lucy waved at him dismissively. "He's joking," she said pointedly. "Kidding." She slapped Max's shoulder. "Big mouth. Don't tease the children."

Part One

Three Ways to Wrangle
Your Romeo

1

"Never in a million years," Chandra Hammel said emphatically. She emptied her Perrier bottle into a stemmed glass and took a demure sip. "My answer is no, for various reasons. One"—she held up her hand, enumerating her points with firm resolve—"I have no interest in that low-concept reality trash they're putting on TV right now. Two, my appearance on such a program would not be in keeping with the profile I need to project in the corporate sector."

"I'd say your image is secure in the corporate sector," Maggie said, folding her arms to evaluate her friend. An African-American woman in her early thirties, Chandra wore her black hair short and stylish with flame highlights, her suits crisp and sleek. The woman was stunning and didn't really have a clue, sort of like Halle Berry when she stretched for *Monster Ball*. Maggie thought Chandra acted way too straight, and never hesitated to tell her so. "You don't fish off the office pier," Maggie went on. "You don't complain to your boss. You don't even show toe-cleavage. If I ever start covering cleavage of any kind, promise you'll shoot me."

"I'm sure that could be arranged." Sipping her Diet Coke from a straw, Apple turned to Chandra. "You are the most conservative dresser I know, Chandra. You should have renamed yourself Prudence."

"This is not about me or my sense of style," Chandra said defensively. "It's about the way people perceive television and reality shows and . . ."

As Chandra rattled on, Maggie McGee smelled defeat. Damn! Ten years in the magazine business had given her the sense to recognize a failing pitch. She needed to turn this conversation around as soon as Chandra took a breath. Which might take a while, since Chandra herself was a supreme negotiator. The girl could filibuster for hours.

"Three," Chandra went on, "it would be an embarrassment to Grayrock Corporation, and—"

"No one has to know you work for Grayrock," Maggie interrupted her friend as the waiter brought three Caesar salads, two with grilled chicken, one with tiger shrimp. The three friends were doing lunch at Saloon Le Funk, a favorite spot of theirs midway between Chandra's Rockefeller Center office and Maggie's 57th Street hub at *Metropolitan* magazine. "You know, Chandra, you're getting way too devoted to that job. How long have you been at Grayrock as . . . what's your title? M&M?"

"M&A . . . Mergers and Acquisitions, and I do it because I love it. That job is the only thing that's gotten me through these last two years."

"Well," Maggie went on, "before you continue the boardroom presentation, let me remind you that we're your friends. It'll be fun if we do it together."

"Oh, right," Chandra said, "catfight with your friends."

"Like we never argue!" Maggie felt herself straining to keep her composure. "Might as well get the heat on video and make some money on it!"

"Not worth it," Chandra said. "Not worth spending time on the application."

"I'll take care of the application, the photos . . . everything."

"I can do photos," Apple volunteered. "Hell, I think I have a roll of the three of us at Christine's wedding. Granted, those celery-silk bridesmaid gowns were deadly, but I can crop."

"Right, great!" Maggie nodded vigorously, her dark hair bouncing into her face. "You can be in charge of photos."

Chandra stabbed a square of chicken, a determined gleam in her brown eyes. "Not interested."

"Come on!" Maggie couldn't believe Chandra was squashing her idea so quickly. Time to bring out the big guns. "Look, I have a friend who works for the network. He doesn't work on *Big Tease,* but he thinks my idea is fabulous. The guy is in development meetings all the time, and he says the concept of three friends is irresistible. The producers will jump on it in a minute."

"I have to admit, I sort of liked that show last season." Apple swallowed a mouthful of salad and tilted her head thoughtfully. The gesture always reminded Maggie of a slender swan basking in the sun. Apple's thick hair was piled atop her head, gleaming orange whorls held in place by half a dozen clamps, a hairstyle that would have looked messy on anyone else, but somehow, Apple wore it with elegance. "It was sort of like a bad car accident. Once I started watching, I couldn't look away. Before I knew it, I was tuning in every Wednesday night, routing for the schoolteacher to get her man."

Both Chandra and Maggie swiveled their heads around to gape at Apple.

"You watched *Big Tease?*" Chandra said.

"You wanted the schoolteacher to win?" Maggie rolled her eyes. "I thought she was a total fraud with that damsel-in-distress crap."

"Oh, please!" Apple's eyes narrowed as she scowled at Maggie. "That woman was so real, I could feel her pain. Besides, she reminded me of my eighth-grade science teacher."

Chandra dabbed at her mouth with a napkin, still staring at Apple. "You, the WASP girl, the Bennington graduate from upperclass, upper-crust Westchester?"

"What's with the Westchester crap? I grew up in Queens with you guys."

Chandra was shaking her head. "I can't believe you watch that mind candy."

"Okay, consider me duly embarrassed, but the show is addictive." Apple popped a crouton in her mouth and crunched for a moment before focusing on Maggie. "But Maggie watched it, too. Why aren't you disgraced by her?"

"Maggie works for *Metro*," Chandra said. "It's her job to keep her finger on the pulse of the lowest common denominators in pop culture."

"Well, thank you, Margaret Meade," Maggie told Chandra. Sometimes it was hard to believe that her buttoned-down best friend had grown up in Queens. Was this the girl who'd led the charge sledding down the hill next to P.S. 203? The bikini-clad teenager who'd done cannonballs from the lifeguard stand at the Bay Terrace Pool Club? But then, Chandra was definitely a chameleon. She'd gone from being little Sharon Humphrey in the projects of South Philly to a middle-class teen in suburban Queens to a shareholder in a doorman building on the Upper West Side, and all along the way she had managed to fit in. Looking at her now in her silk suit and Prada heels, Maggie was dying to soften things up with a glittery pin or jangly bracelets . . . or a shiny nose ring. Ha!

Apple shifted in her chair, absently running her fingertips over the camera strap that dangled from the ladder-back chair. "Are they still giving a million dollars to the winner?"

"Absolutely." Maggie nodded eagerly. "A million, can you imagine? That kind of money would definitely bail me out." She flipped a lettuce leaf with her fork, imagining what she would do first. Quit her job? No, she would throw an awesome party at the magazine for all the good people who constantly got trounced by management. *Then* she would quit her job. Then, a day of beauty at Elizabeth Arden on Fifth Avenue, where women in cheery pink uniforms would trim and exfoliate and condition and soothe her body from head to toe. She could even afford a hot-stone massage to open up meridian channels and get in touch with the energy from the cosmos.

"A million dollars could definitely buy me a chunk of happiness," Apple said.

"Ladies, would you listen to what you're saying?" Chandra's eyebrows shot up as she cast a critical eye on her friends. "Money isn't everything. And contrary to popular belief, you can't buy happiness."

"I'm not too sure about that," Apple replied. "It does give you freedom, the freedom to make so many more choices. And certainly freedom from the stress of wondering how you're going to make next month's Visa payment."

"Amen, sister," Maggie said, reaching across the table for a crusty onion roll.

"Wealth has its advantages, yes," Chandra admitted, "but let's not fool ourselves into thinking the wealthy are problem-free. And material goods do not bring happiness."

"You sound like my father," Apple said. "And it's easy to disparage the worth of money when you have it. You're doing okay, but Maggie and I are perpetually broke."

"Really!" Maggie held a forked shrimp in the air. "I can't even afford this. I'm eating on borrowed money. Why do we come here, anyway?"

"You love it," Apple answered.

"It's close to the office," Chandra added.

"Oh . . . right. Anyway, there's nothing like an influx of cash to lift your spirits."

"Money is not a long-term motivator for employees," Chandra insisted. "Countless studies have proven that."

"Ah, but do they consider the tingle in your fingertips at the moment of purchase?" Maggie asked, wiggling her fingers. "The last time I was depressed I bought a leather bag—a buttery soft duffel in the warmest shade of toffee—and I'll be damned if that thing didn't cheer me up. It improved my mood by seventy percent. Countless studies have proven that shopping eases depression."

"I'm sure you were euphoric," said Chandra. "Until the bill came."

"Right! And if I had the money to cover the bill, maybe the euphoria would have lasted." Maggie tore off a piece of roll and popped it into her mouth, trying to think of a way to get her pitch back on track. Since it looked like Apple was her ally here, she turned to the willowy redhead, trying not to come on too strong.

"So you're interested?" Maggie asked. "I'm sure we can find someone else to be the third."

"If you're trying to make me jealous, it's not working," Chandra said.

Apple was already shaking her head. "I don't think so. You know how I freak in front of the camera." It was one of the many ironies of Apple; the woman who lived behind the lense always felt incredibly awkward when she was photographed.

"They're not looking for models," Maggie argued. "Oh, come on, Apple. Just think what you could do with that money! You could probably buy your own studio. And no more fights with Coop about who pays for what."

"Oh, please. With a million dollars I'd buy my own place and charge Coop rent. Not that he'd be there that often. Do you know, he hasn't made it home before midnight once this week?"

"Still entertaining clients?" Chandra asked sympathetically.

Apple frowned. "Only the drinking ones."

The stench of "guy trouble" hung in the air. Maggie knew that the honeymoon period had been over between Apple and her boyfriend, Brandon Cooper, for quite some time, but Apple usually spared the details about her relationships with men.

In fact, Apple's romantic life had always been a source of wonder for Maggie, who considered herself an expert in the area of relationships and sex. Or, at least, an expert practitioner. But then, when it came to relationships, Apple was on a different planet. A few years ago, Apple had left a group-share apartment to move in with her boyfriend—boyfriend #1, was all that Maggie could remember of him—and now here she was living with Coop, boyfriend #6. With few tears and very little counseling, Apple simply moved from one guy's apartment to the next, feeling that her life was very Zen and streamlined, not bogged down by furniture. How did she do it? How did she survive without her own bed, a favorite hutch, a room full of prized possessions? Maggie wasn't sure, but she was beginning to sense that it was time for Apple to move away from boyfriend #6.

"So Coop is drinking again." Maggie tugged a strand of dark hair behind one ear. When Apple nodded, Maggie went on, "See? See how this show could change your life?" She raised one small but well-manicured hand toward some fictitious path in the ceiling. "Go on the show with me and take your shot at a million dollars."

Apple lowered her head shyly, poking her salad with a fork. "I could never go on TV and talk about personal stuff . . . seductions and turn-ons and orgasms." She reminded Maggie of an adolescent who'd slapped open a *Playboy* centerfold for the first time. Curious but horrified.

"Apple, on a normal day I've edited pieces about striptease studs and erotic butt massages before I've even had my second cup of coffee," Maggie answered. "Surely you can make up a story or two about playing hide the salami under the covers."

Chandra waved a breadstick at Maggie. "Young lady, we've got to do something about your manners."

"Excuse me?" Maggie grinned. "I'm not the one menacing with a breadstick."

"Well, lookee there." Apple's gray eyes were alert and focused on the street activity beyond the restaurant's plate-glass window. She reached for her camera and stepped away from the table. "Look at the size of that entourage. God, is that Michael Jackson?" She squinted. "Is he supposed to be in town this week?"

It proved to be a rhetorical question, as Apple was already far from the table, sprinting through the restaurant lobby and out the door in pursuit of a pop idol. Although most of her income came from shooting portraits and weddings, she made a nice amount from selling the occasional celebrity photo to a tabloid.

Maggie turned back to Chandra, who seemed to be waiting for a cue. "Did I mention that the show is a venue for meeting guys? And not just any guy. They help you set up at least one high-profile date."

"Like I have time to date. Yesterday, I didn't even have time to breathe until I got home from work. At nine."

"Come on!" Maggie jabbed at the shoulder of Chandra's silk suit. "Loosen up, girl. A date doesn't have to be dinner or a movie. Today's woman is on the lookout for relationships around the clock. Riding in the elevator at work. Chatting at the coffee bar. Competing for a cab. I know two people who agreed to share a taxi to the Upper East Side and ended up getting married."

"Maybe in *Metro* magazine. Not in real life."

Maggie was about to argue when she noticed a young waiter eyeing their table. He sauntered over and cocked his head to the side, as if he were afraid to interrupt. In one look, Maggie knew she wanted him.

His brown skin was dark against the white uniform, his chocolate cheeks gleaming with a soft sheen. She longed to reach up and touch his beautiful face—broad mouth, high cheekbones, shiny shaved head. A perfect head.

He was an African-American god.

"Is everything okay?" he asked, gesturing to the empty place at their table.

"Everything's just fine," Maggie answered, hoping that lettuce wasn't stuck in her teeth as she flashed an enormous smile. She pulled her shoulders back, the better to show off the boobs.

Chandra gestured to Apple's empty chair. "She'll be back. We're used to having her disappear." She lowered her voice, adding, "She's paparazzo."

The waiter nodded politely.

"I think that would be paparazza," Maggie corrected. "Singular, feminine. But you say that as if it's a religious cult or something." She turned to the waiter, trying to engage him. "The first time we ate here, DeNiro was having lunch. Right over in that booth. Apple nearly fell out of her chair, but we restrained her. She doesn't take photos inside restaurants, anyway. Too tacky. But once he got outside—*ka-blam.* Not one of his best hair days, but with that jawline, who cares?"

"That's very interesting." The waiter lowered his chin.

Maggie licked her upper lip. Did he not get it, or was he being coy? *Oh, big man, give it to me!* she wanted to shout. How she longed to run her hands over that smooth, shaved head. Shiver her fingers down his chest. Down, down, down . . .

"After that, this became our favorite restaurant," Chandra went on, oblivious to Maggie. "You're close to the office, and good for Apple's celebrity photo stock."

The waiter smiled. "I'm glad you keep coming back."

"Oh, we'll just keep on coming," Maggie said suggestively.

His eyes met Maggie's. *Click. Kah-ching!* Contact!

She was in.

And then, the moment seemed to scatter as Chandra prattled on about something Maggie couldn't follow. She was too distracted by the feeling of ants in her pants. If only she could swipe the china off the table and clear out the hungry patrons. He could ravish her right here on the green linens.

Maggie started to send him a hot vibe, but he was listening to Chandra. No . . . no! The connection was fading!

On second thought, maybe she could slip him her business card?

He gestured to their food, backing away. "Enjoy."

Chandra dug into her salad as he retreated. Maggie watched him with her smokiest, sexiest leer. Chandra was chewing when her eyes met Maggie's.

"Don't say it," Chandra told Maggie.

"I'd love to get under his apron," Maggie said.

"Oh, please. You can't be in love with every guy you meet."

"Who said anything about love?" Maggie knew that her moral scruples were quite different from Chandra's. Her friend claimed that she hadn't had sex since her boyfriend's death two years ago, and Maggie believed her. Of course, she couldn't imagine abstaining that long, but for Chandra sex was an extracurricular activity. Sort of like the occasional dessert or a weekend hobby. For Maggie, sex was a daily essential, like breathing and drinking.

Across the table Chandra's face was a study in restraint. "What?" Maggie asked. "What? What!"

"Where is Apple when I need her? We've been wanting to talk to you about this, but—"

"About sex?" Maggie rubbed her hands together. "Oh, do tell. After all, I am the *Metro* sexpert."

"That may be so, but you seem to be missing one important point." Chandra's eyes softened as she let down her guard. "Oh, Maggie, it's not just about sex. I thought you were going to focus on finding a meaningful relationship."

"I am, I am! But in the meantime, you can't expect a sexually actualized girl like myself to sit at home watching MTV." When Chandra shook her head with a look of disappointment, Maggie groaned. "Yeeps! Don't pull the guilt trip, because it doesn't work on me."

"So don't feel guilty. But do try to pull yourself out of this slump. Really. There's got to be someone out there with whom you can share your life."

Maggie toyed with a spoon. "Yeah, yeah . . . now you're sounding like *Metro* magazine." Maggie wanted to stop the Maggie-bashing, but suddenly she realized that she could make this work for her. "You know, Chan, maybe you're right. And the best way for me to find a guy worth dating is to go on *Big Tease.*"

"Not that again." Chandra stabbed at her salad. "Have you talked to your parents about Thanksgiving? I think it would be fun for the three of us to go up to Westchester together."

"Don't change the subject," Maggie said firmly. "I'm still determined to get you to give in and sign up for *Big Tease.*"

Chandra groaned.

"No complaints. Just say yes."

"What is with you and this TV show? I know you're bull-headed, but I've never seen you quite so stuck on something so frivolous."

"A million dollars is frivolous?" Maggie quipped. "Not to mention a chance to meet Mr. Right?"

"And you think a decent guy is going to appear just because I reveal my personal life on television?" Chandra cocked an eyebrow. "That show is an invitation to every money-grubbing loser in America. And the way those women behave on camera." Her deep-timbered voice took on a whiney tone: " 'Love me! Protect me! Validate me!' " She rolled her eyes. "No, thank you. I prefer to earn my money with hard work, and you know upper management would disapprove of a Grayrock employee on that show."

"Since when did your life become all about Grayrock Corporation?" Maggie persisted.

"It's not." Chandra folded her arms defensively. "Grayrock isn't the only reason I can't do the show. There's always . . ." She stabbed her fork into a piece of chicken with a vengeance. "You know . . . *her.* The last thing I need is for her to spot me on television. And it's exactly the sort of show people like her watch."

People like her. Maggie knew Chandra was referring to her estranged mother who had passed Chandra on to relatives when she was a baby. It was part of Chandra's distant past; a piece that Maggie could barely conceptualize, knowing her friend as she was today: confident and low-key—"a gorgeous genius," as Jeff used to call her. "But you've changed your name," Maggie said. "And she hasn't seen you for years so there's no reason to think she'd recognize you."

"Why chance it?" Chandra placed her fork neatly across her salad plate and pressed her napkin to her mouth. "Look, Mags, it was a fun idea, this show thing. Ingenious. But lots of great ideas just don't pan out. Don't take it personally."

"Easy for you to say," Maggie muttered, stabbing a few leaves of lettuce with a vehemence. "You're slated for a promotion and a whopping end-of-year bonus. Me? I'm constantly in trouble with Candy these days, at least on days when she makes it into the office. I've been working for *Metro* for seven years, and my reward is to have outgrown my usefulness in a market that considers women 'ridden hard and put away wet' once they reach thirty."

"Oooh," Chandra said gently. "I didn't know we had career issues at stake here."

Maggie took a bite of salad, then chewed vigorously. "I ate ma nyob."

Chandra winced. "In English, please."

Maggie swallowed, lifting her chin. "I hate my job," she said with a British accent.

"No, you don't," Chandra insisted. "You just hate what they've done to you."

Maggie stabbed the last piece of shrimp in her salad, realizing Chandra was right. "I am so depressed."

Chandra nodded. "Aren't we all?"

Just then Apple tramped back into the restaurant looking beautifully unkempt and a little breathless. Orange strands of hair dangled over her pink cheeks.

"I take it that's the blush of success?" Maggie asked.

Nodding, Apple reached into the pocket of her khaki safari pants and dumped two rolls of film onto the table. "It wasn't Michael Jackson, but I think I got some great shots of the Artist Formerly Known as Prince."

"Really?" Chandra seemed impressed. "How does he look these days?"

Apple slung her camera over her chair and picked up her fork. "Petite but cute."

"I've always admired the way he does his eyes," Maggie said. "That smokey, mysterious look. Maybe I should use more eyeliner."

"Now, see that?" Chandra wagged a finger at Maggie. "That's the pat *Metro* response. You belong at that place. You are the magazine."

Maggie made a show of gagging. "That's a sad statement."

"But I mean it in the best possible way. If they're failing to use your talents, they need to rethink their management system."

"You go, girl," Apple said, digging into her salad again.

Chandra checked her watch. "We need to get back to work," she told Maggie.

Apple pointed to her salad. "Should I take it to go?"

"No, I'll stay with you," Maggie said, wishing she could sit here at Saloon Le Funk for the rest of the afternoon and into evening. "I have a phone interview at two, but I can do that on the cell while I'm walking back. No one will miss me."

"I don't understand that," Chandra said, taking a twenty out of her black Coach wallet and leaving it on the table. "In my line of work, you need to be there twenty-four-seven. With markets open all over the world, it just never stops and everyone has to push to stay on top of it." Maggie saw that familiar glint in Chandra's dark eyes: the look of a player anxious to get back into the game.

"You love it," Maggie said.

Chandra smiled. "I do. I really do."